THE BIG INTERVIEW

BOOK 2 IN THE STELLA REYNOLDS MYSTERY SERIES

LIBBY KIRSCH

Sunnyside Press
PO Box 2476
Ann Arbor, MI. 48106
www.LibbyKirschBooks.com

Publisher's Note: This is a work of fiction. Names, characters, places, and incidents are a product of the author's imagination. Locales and public names are sometimes used for atmospheric purposes. Any resemblance to actual people, living or dead, or to businesses, companies, events, institutions, or locales is completely coincidental.

The Big Interview/ Libby Kirsch -- 1st ed.

ISBN 978-0-9969350-2-9

❀ Created with Vellum

To my dear family. I love you. Thanks for being so supportive. And for not minding that it's breakfast for dinner. Again.

1

NEW GIRL

"Stella Reynolds. Hmm. You know, it's weird—I thought we were replacing our ugly reporter, but you're actually kind of pretty. Let's see... where's your tape? I know it's here somewhere..." The young, fit, oddly smiley man shuffled things around on his messy, mahogany desk.

Stella looked around the office for the hidden camera; surely this was some kind of joke. Her new boss couldn't be serious. Her earnest search for her imminent *Punk'd* moment, however, was interrupted when Keith Howard, the general manager of NBC2 in Bristol, Virginia, said, "Ah ha! Here it is."

He pulled her résumé tape out from under a stack of papers. Flashing a gleaming grin, he tossed the white case behind him and put the tape into the VHS player at his desk. "Old school. I like it."

She didn't explain that her old station was as old school as you could find. Instead, Stella's green eyes were drawn to her own image on the screen. Her long, auburn hair looked slightly tangled where it lay next to her face, and she noted with a grimace that she appeared slightly sweaty. You couldn't tell she was 5'9", and as she looked at herself with a critical eye, she thought her button-down shirt looked a bit sloppy. Keith pressed play and sat back with a confused look on his face.

"Right, I remember you now. It's remarkable sitting here, looking at her," he pointed to the Stella on screen, "and then you," he pointed to her in real life. "You look like shit on camera. Has no one ever taught you how to wear makeup, do your hair, or dress? Jesus, how do you people get hired?"

Her face flooded with heat. "Everything was, uh, pretty last minute at my old station in Montana. I mean, it was a really small market, and I guess doing hair and makeup for my live shot often took a backseat to shooting, writing, and, um, you know, editing the story." Keith grinned and she shifted from embarrassed to angry. She'd been driving for four days and this was her welcome?

In her first job as a news reporter, Stella had worked in the tiny town of Bozeman, Montana, as a multimedia journalist. That meant she had done *everything* to get her story on air—including lugging around the heavy, old, cumbersome equipment she used to shoot video. A few weeks ago, after just six months on the job there, the FOX affiliate had unexpectedly shut down, sending the four on-air employees scrambling for jobs.

Last week, she accepted a reporting job in this much larger TV market and left her friends and boyfriend, a fellow on-air journalist, behind. She'd driven more than 2,000 miles straight to the NBC affiliate in Bristol, Virginia, where she now found herself in front of an idiot.

Keith grinned. "Small markets are pretty crappy, aren't they?" He didn't wait for her to respond. "Listen, you're supposed to be filling my brainy/ugly slot, so I don't know what to do with you now that you're here. Are you at least smart? I guess you'll need to get settled in and meet with Marty—he'll know what to do with you."

He bounced up and walked Stella to the door. He was slightly shorter than her with dusty blond hair, and his light blue eyes scanned the room. "Cam! Take her to Marty. Tell him good luck."

Stella's lips puckered. She opened her mouth to set Keith straight on just exactly how smart she was—smart enough to not take crap from him—but once again, he spoke first.

"Yes! That's what I'm talking about. Ugly face. Work on that." He walked back into his office and slammed the door.

Keith's secretary took her gently by the elbow and said soothingly, in the thickest southern drawl Stella had ever heard in real life, "Don't you mind him, darlin', he's a hot mess just like his daddy. He runs this station like a frat house, but somehow we've got the best ratings we've ever had." Cam steered Stella to a seat by the door and practically pushed her down onto the comfy cushion. "Can you sit right here for just a minute? I need to get something out of the copy room, and then I'll take you to the newsroom. Be right back," she said brightly before disappearing.

Stella looked darkly around the office. She was tempted to walk out and never look back, but she'd signed a two-year employment contract from Montana. The terms were very clear: if she left the station before the end of the contract, she couldn't work for any other station until six months *after* the original contract was up! She was locked in, no matter what. Before she could spend too much time debating the legality of a contract like that, she heard the jingle of a cell phone out in the hallway.

Expletives rumbled out of a man's mouth like the engine of a semi-truck before he answered the call with a terse, "Hello?"

She smiled, loving that the F-word sounded much the same *with* a Southern accent as without. She also felt better knowing she wasn't the only one having a bad day.

The man on the phone stopped just outside the door to Keith's office, muttering more swear words and commands to whomever he was speaking. Her smile faded, however, when she actually listened to his end of the conversation.

"You can't kill someone over—no. No, you listen to me," he

sounded frustrated, "you can't do it—you'll never get away with it. You're both too high profile." Her mouth dropped open. "I don't care how good you are. You know who you need to talk to? Yes, I'm hearing there's been a rift. The right situation could push him over the edge, and he might just be angry enough to do it himself."

What the hell? Now she was convinced she was on some kind of *Candid Camera* show. She twisted her head around so she could look into the hallway, curious as to who was so cavalierly discussing death at her new job, but all she could see was the shadow of the stranger. She leaned forward to get a better view when the sound of Cam's voice echoed toward her. The stranger to her was obviously no stranger to Cam.

"Hi again, darlin'—oh, didn't see you were on the phone there. Sorry." Cam's heels clicked down the hallway, past the man, until she came to a stop by Keith's door. She blocked Stella's view of the hallway entirely when she turned halfway back to him. She made an exaggerated show of locking her lips and throwing away the key, and then backed into the office and smiled brightly at Stella.

"Ready?"

Yes, Stella was ready—ready to go and never come back. Despite her misgivings, she followed Cam out of the office and scanned the hallway, but it was empty.

She considered what she'd overheard. At first, the stranger tried to talk someone out of murder, but then he seemed to pass along a tip to help get the job done. A dull ache built behind her right eye.

She should have never left Montana.

CAM LED her down a hallway lined with framed poster prints of all the popular shows that aired on the network that year. Her bleach-blond hair stood in stark contrast to her ultra-tan, slightly wrinkled face, and her light brown eyes were trained on Stella. "Marty is great—he knew what news was before he knew how to talk. He'll get you set right up, sweetie."

Stella vowed then and there to never take another job without first seeing the office and meeting the boss.

Her new station was part of a much larger TV market made up of three small cities in the far northeast corner of Tennessee. Locals called it the Tri-cities—Johnson City, Kingsport, and the border town of Bristol, half of which bled over onto the Virginia side of the state line.

"The Book just came in, and we beat the competition hands down," Cam said, referring to the February Sweeps period that had ended a couple weeks before.

If Stella was grudgingly impressed there were pictures hanging in the hall, it was nothing compared to how she felt when they turned a corner and walked into the newsroom. It was so different from the dirty carpet and decrepit equipment she'd grown accustomed to in her old office that she forgot for a moment she didn't want the job, anymore.

The open, rectangular newsroom had at least thirty desks separated by half-height, cubical pin-cushion walls. The tile floor was clean and neat. Opposite Stella, daylight shined through a wall of windows, and a view of a beautiful park below expanded as the motorized blinds rose halfway up the glass panes. On the short wall closest to Stella, a huge station logo glowed brightly against a dark blue background. Across the space, TV monitors covered the other shorter wall, with news from the main cable stations flickering brightly.

Desks lined the fourth wall, which had an entrance at either end, and two dozen people moved across the room. It was four times the space of her old office with four times the staff. She felt giddy.

Cam tapped her shoulder. "It's impressive, isn't it? I think you'll like it here, even with Keith to contend with."

The wording wasn't lost on Stella, but by then people had noticed them standing in the doorway and she didn't have a chance to ask what Cam meant. A dozen people scrutinized the newcomer, and she subconsciously sucked in her gut as they made their way across the newsroom toward a man sitting at L-shaped desk.

He spun around to greet them. "Cam, who you got?" His drawl was less pronounced than Keith's secretary's, but still impressive. When he said "got," it stretched to two syllables.

"Stella Reynolds here just drove in from Bozeman, Montana, to fill *Sonya's* spot." Marty's eyebrows shot up and met his hairline. "I know," Cam said. "Keith couldn't believe it, either. Apparently she looks quite different on camera."

Stella shot an accusing look at Cam. She'd seemed so nice, but now she was singing the party line that Stella looked like crap on TV.

If Cam noticed the glare, she wasn't concerned. "I've got to get back to work. Keith has dinner plans tonight, and I've got to pick up his dry cleaning before five."

She walked out of the newsroom, and Stella turned her attention back to Marty. He was older—maybe her dad's age—and deep wrinkles lined his eyes and mouth. Wire-rimmed glasses settled into the crevices below his eyes and grey mixed liberally into his brown hair.

"Welcome to town, Stella. Thank God we got a redhead! We're about overrun with blondes ever since Keith came on board two years ago." Marty leaned close and stage whispered, "He thinks a woman without blond hair is smarter. No offense to you, but I don't believe hair color has anything to do with IQ. You'd have to prove yourself to me even if you had a pink mohawk, got it?"

She nodded, hoping Marty was one of the good guys in a sea of questionable colleagues.

"You're in luck." He looked over her head, "Our chief photographer just got in. I'll have him show you around town today. Billy Joe," he called, "come meet the new Sonya."

Stella turned and froze, her mouth stuck between a grimace and a smile.

The man walking toward her was someone she would actively avoid on the street. He stood around six feet tall, and his light brown hair was cut into a mullet, the front short and the back longer than Stella's own elbow-length hair. He wore a black canvas duster split down the back for maximum mobility, dark sunglasses, and a scowl. He grunted hello and muttered something else Stella didn't catch.

"Great idea, Billy Joe—take as long as you like." Marty turned back to her, "When you get back, we should have your computer all set up."

Billy Joe grunted again and stalked out of the newsroom. Stella scurried to keep up. She followed him down the hall to the elevator and stood in silence until the doors pinged open. He got in, and with a last, desperate look over her shoulder for a reason —any excuse, really—to not follow him into the tiny, enclosed space, she walked in after him.

2

TAKING LAPS

"Y ou been to the speedway?" Billy Joe asked in the same thick, southern drawl as Marty and Cam as the doors closed.

Stella looked at him from the corner of her eye. A gas station? "Uhh... I think I drove by it on my way into town this morning."

He snorted. "You'd know it if you'd seen it. We'll start there."

Stella wrinkled her nose. "Okay. Am I supposed to fuel up the news cars or something? Is that going to be one of my jobs?"

He grunted out a painful sound, and her head whipped toward him. A smile barely turned up the corners of his mouth, and after another weird grunt, she realized he was laughing.

She smiled, too. "What?"

"The speedway is the NASCAR track, darlin', not a gas station." He chortled some more and Stella shrugged. She was so used to making a fool of herself, it no longer concerned her—unless there was an audience to worry about.

They got off the elevator, and Stella attempted to hide her elation at not having to load up the gear. Billy Joe handed her the microphone and nothing else. After six months of breaking into a full-body sweat by the time she'd carried all of the heavy, clunky gear to the car at her old station, she was delighted to let someone else be in charge of the camera.

In the parking lot, they climbed into a blue GMC Jimmy SUV emblazoned with the NBC2 logo and the anchor team's faces on each side.

"Open the glove box," Billy Joe commanded as he pulled out of the parking lot. Stella looked at him sideways again; his lips didn't move at all when he spoke. She pushed the latch, and the small door fell open. "See that two-by-four?" She squinted around the mess of ketchup packets, hot sauce, napkins, and the car manual, and barely made out a piece of wood in the back corner of the compartment. When she nodded, he said, "Don't touch it. It's wedged up against the engine block, and if you move it even an inch, the engine'll drop right out of the truck."

She smiled at him uncertainly, looking for the joke, but he glared straight ahead. "Okay, don't touch the block. Got it."

As they drove, Stella tried to get a sense for where she was. The TV station was located on the Virginia side of the state line, but they were heading south into Tennessee. Although far from the impressive mountain chains in Montana—so tall that they were snow-capped even in the middle of summer—she was happy to see the rolling Blue Ridge Mountains in the distance.

The car jolted to the left as Billy Joe turned abruptly onto a wide, long, paved driveway. "We're here," he said a minute before the sign came into view.

"Bristol Motor Speedway," Stella read aloud. A huge arena rose out of the ground. "Whoa!" She ducked to see the top of the grandstands. She'd certainly heard of NASCAR before taking the job in Bristol but had never watched a race and didn't know much about the sport.

As they drove closer to the towering, metal seats, she remembered a friend from Montana who had once tried to explain why the sport was so popular. Janet had talked passionately about the fast, powerful cars with friendly, crowd-accessible drivers, but it just didn't interest Stella enough to ever watch a race.

Now that she was in the middle of NASCAR country, however, she racked her brain to try to remember what else Janet had said about racing. Most of the drivers were from the south and hired former college football players to be part of the team on race day. There was something else she couldn't quite remember—something about how the drivers always hoped their cars would run smoothly, like a jack-in-the-box... no, that wasn't right. Maybe it was a different toy? She screwed her face up in thought but then gave up. She had the next two years to become an expert if she needed to.

"How many people does it hold?"

"A hundred thousand."

They drove past row after row of empty, lined spaces in a never-ending parking lot. Billy Joe finally slowed the SUV and Stella thought they would turn back. Instead, he nodded to someone inside a guard shack and the gate swung up, granting them entrance to the outer ring of the speedway. They drove up to the grandstands and took a paved path under the metal seats onto the actual track.

Billy Joe slowed to a stop. The turns on the track were laid at steep angles, with the spectator seats only feet from the concrete racetrack. A chain link fence, like something you'd use to keep your mischievous two-year-old in your yard, was all that separated the fans from the cars during a race.

The paved infield was ready for pit crews, trailers, and team and track officials. It seemed to stretch on for miles, although she'd read a sign hanging over the entrance that said *World's Fastest Half Mile.*

She turned to thank Billy Joe for the behind-the-scenes tour, but he unexpectedly gunned the engine, and they rumbled across the track toward the first steep embankment.

She checked her seatbelt and searched in vain for the handle above the window. If she thought the banks looked steep from their earlier vantage point, she had a new appreciation for the angle as they whipped around the track. What kept all four tires on the ground seemed like a magical force, because she was sure they would tip at any moment.

They skidded to a stop outside the office. "We're here." Billy Joe threw the car into park and hopped out of the car.

Stella exited on unsteady legs and then bent in half outside the car and put her hands on her knees, breathing in the cool March air. When she caught her breath, she called out, "Billy Joe! If you ever do that to me again, I'm going to pull that two-by-four out of the glove box and beat you with it!"

He stared stonily at Stella for a beat, and then the edges of his lips turned up. She thought it might be another smile. "Let's go."

She stared up at the building. "We're going in?"

"You might as well meet everybody—we do stories at the track all the time." He led the way through the doors and nodded to several people in the front office; his smile for *them* seemed perfectly friendly. A man named Daniel escorted them to an elevator and up to the top floor.

"The general manager, Ryan Wexler, is up here, along with our whole communications team." A wall of windows on the far side of the room showed off the parking lot outside, while windows on the side closer to Stella revealed an amazing view of the racetrack below.

Their guide tapped on a door. "Oh, uh... hey, boss. I didn't realize you already had a visitor."

3

FEELING LUCKY

S tella might not have known much about racing, but you'd have to live under a rock to not know NASCAR's biggest star. Lucky Haskins was tall and lean with tousled, blond hair and dark chocolate-brown eyes. His hundred-watt smile showed up regularly in gossip and sports magazines in every supermarket in the country.

He and the other man in the room had been arguing—their faces were red—but when Daniel pushed the door open, Lucky uncrossed his arms and his sullen face broke into a smile.

As she stared at the national heartthrob, Stella didn't realize Daniel had stopped walking until she almost bumped into him. She pulled up short and recovered, but Billy Joe plowed into her hard. She stumbled into Daniel, and then all three went down like Dominoes.

"Oof," she grunted when Billy Joe landed on her, forcing all the air out of her lungs. He bounced up, but she lay on the floor; Billy Joe had to weigh around two-hundred pounds, and he'd landed with the grace of a hippo. After she caught her breath, she still didn't move, embarrassment now holding her down.

"Is she okay?"

"Someone call 911!"

The thought of being carried out of the office on a stretcher finally moved her to action, and she pushed herself up to a sitting position, her face red and her mind racing. She felt several pairs of eyes staring at her. "Did anyone get that on camera? That Three Stooges impression went off like Jack the Bear!"

The room was silent for a beat, and then Lucky burst out laughing. Even Billy Joe chuckled before he remembered to scowl. She'd thought of Janet's silly NASCAR phrase at the last minute and blurted it out. She was relieved to find she might have even used the term correctly.

She stood and brushed off the seat of her skirt as a man at the conference table spoke. "Jack the Bear? I haven't heard that expression in ages. Daniel, what kind of racing junkie have you brought us?"

Billy Joe looked at Stella suspiciously as introductions were made. Ryan Wexler, the general manager, stood from the table. His lean face looked aristocratic with high cheekbones and thin lips, and he smiled faintly and reached across the table. A huge ring glittered at his fingers, and she felt the cool metal against her palm when they shook.

When Lucky Haskins walked over, he brushed her outstretched hand aside and pulled her into a side hug. "Stella the Bear—that's what I'm going to call you. Maybe it'll be good luck for me on the circuit this year." Stella blushed when he squeezed her shoulder and made to step back, but his grip tightened and he leaned in conspiratorially. "You got here just in time, Stella. You were just the shot of humor this room needed."

Ryan stared at her, unconcerned, and she wondered what they'd been fighting about.

Billy Joe squinted at her sideways. "Stella was just telling me at the station this morning how much she loves NASCAR. Girl, tell them all about the speedway."

She cleared her throat as every eye turned to her. "Oh, uh, I just... love that it's a... uh... a circle." She shot a glare at her photographer and again tried, successfully this time, to disentangle herself from Lucky's grasp.

"Mr. Haskins, I don't suppose you have time for a quick interview? I'm sure our viewers would love an update on your... racing." She had no idea what she'd interview him about, but surely finding the sport's most popular driver in Bristol was newsworthy.

Lucky led the way out of Ryan's office, and back outside, Billy Joe set the shot up so the track was in the background. Stella turned the microphone on and looked up with a friendly smile. "Why don't you tell me how you're preparing for the season, Lucky." The driver grinned back, and after a moment of silence, she said, "What?"

"Sweetheart, the season started a month ago." He tilted his head to the side, giving her his best endearing smile. Billy Joe guffawed.

Blood rushed to her cheeks *again*, and she had to wonder how many times she could embarrass herself in front of this particular celebrity. When she saw Billy Joe's shoulders shake with laughter, however, she chuckled, too. "I guess I don't need to tell you I know absolutely nothing about NASCAR, huh?"

"Jack the Bear?"

"I heard it from a friend," she lifted one shoulder, "but I hope to learn all about NASCAR now that I live in Bristol."

Billy Joe snickered and quickly related the story from that morning when Stella had mistaken the speedway with a gas station. Soon, both men were laughing.

After a minute, she cleared her throat, ready to take control of the interview again. "All right, Lucky Haskins, what can you tell me about how the season is going for you *so far*?"

They were off and running, with Lucky giving her funny, off-the-cuff answers to even the most general questions. She was used to pulling answers out of unhappy cops or tongue-tied witnesses, but this guy was the polar opposite. He was obviously a pro, and it was the most fun Stella had ever had during an interview.

She thanked Lucky for his time, and as she and Billy Joe walked back to the news car, his phone rang.

"What's up?" she asked when the phone was back in his pocket.

"Breaking news in Johnson City."

"What do we know?" They walked around the car and Billy Joe opened the hatch to load up his equipment.

"No," he shook his head, "I'm supposed to drop you off at the station and then head over."

Her brow wrinkled. Why wouldn't they send the reporter to breaking news? Before she could ask, a voice came from behind her.

"Well, that'll put you even more behind." Lucky, his bag slung over his shoulder and keys in hand, came to a stop by the front bumper. "You want me to drop her off, so you can get on with it?" Both men had southern accents, but while Billy Joe's was twangy, Lucky's was just plain sexy.

"Shoot, if you don't mind," Billy Joe smiled, "that'd save me thirty minutes."

"Does she know where she's headed?"

"Naw—first day. You'll want to take the highway into town and then head south on State Street. The station's on the left—can't miss it."

"Excuse me," Stella looked between both men, "I am standing right here. You don't have to talk about me *in front* of me."

Billy Joe slammed the back hatch and handed a tape to Stella. "Give that to Marty. Thanks, Lucky."

He got in the SUV and drove away, and Stella stared after him with her hands on her hips. She felt like they'd gotten friendly, with an inside joke already between them, but Billy Joe was still just as gruff as he'd been first thing that morning.

"So," Lucky smiled at her, "*do* you know where you're going?"

Stella crossed her arms. "Of course. Take the highway into town, and then head south on State Street," she said.

"Which highway was that?"

"*The* highway." He broke out into a hearty laugh, and it was one too many people critiquing or laughing at her for one day. "Lucky Haskins, don't think that, because you're some kind of famous race car driver, you can mess with me! I've had people like you for *breakfast.*" She turned away and fought the urge to drop to her knees in defeat. *I've had people like you for breakfast? What does that even mean?*

"You want me for breakfast?" Lucky's eyes bored into her. "I think we can arrange that." He closed the gap between them and stopped when they were just inches apart.

Stella had felt off her game since getting into town, but with his corny line and even cornier stare, a huge grin stretched across her face. "Get outta here!" She slapped a hand on his chest and pushed him back. "Has that deep-eyed nonsense *ever* worked for you?"

Lucky grinned, unconcerned. "You bet."

She snorted. "Let's go, Haskins. Which car is yours?"

He led the way to a midnight blue Chevy Camaro and used the key fob to unlock the doors. He hurried in front of Stella and opened her door. As she sank down into the bucket seat, she wondered how she was going to turn her Lucky Haskins interview into a story for the news that night.

"Lucky, what are you doing here in Bristol, anyway? Didn't I read somewhere that you and your fiancée live in Chattanooga?"

"Hmm. Can we talk off the record here?" He eased the car out of the lot and drove slowly through the winding parking lot lanes. "She's my ex-fiancée, and we *did* live Chattanooga."

Her eyes flicked to his face, but he stared straight ahead. "I'm sorry. I didn't know, Lucky."

"I'm glad you didn't. We've managed to keep it hush-hush, just for our own sanity. We'd been growing apart for a while, and... well, you know how it goes. I live in Knoxville now, but that's off the record. Officially speaking, I have business here in Bristol. I came in to check on things before I head to Talladega for the weekend."

"For the race?"

"Right."

Lucky's blond hair was long enough to tuck behind his ears, and he put on a ball cap when the wind from the open windows whipped his hair into a frenzy. He spent the rest of the drive regaling her with racing stories that always seemed to end with him outmaneuvering the competition at the last minute and winning "the cup," whatever that was.

When they got to the station, he reached out and touched Stella's arm. "Darlin', I promise I'm not getting fresh here, but I just wondered—you're new to town, and I'm guessing you don't have a place to live yet. I own a few buildings here—rental properties—and happen to have a couple spots open. It's four-twenty-five a month, and that includes utilities and cable. Let me know if you're interested." He pulled a business card out of his wallet and scribbled on the back of it before handing it to Stella. The card listed a phone number and email address for Haskins Property Management. "My cell phone number's on the back, in case you need anything after-hours." He said it nonchalantly, but Stella heard the double meaning behind the words.

She rolled her eyes. "You're too much, Lucky."

"I'm just looking to have some fun, Stella—nothing serious."

"Well, I'm not really a 'fun' kind of a girl," she replied tartly.

Lucky laughed. "You're no fun?"

"That's not what I meant!" she groaned, but he looked so unabashedly adorable that she felt her grumble turn into a laugh.

She pushed open the car door. "I'm going to look around town for a bit before I rent anything, but thanks."

"All right. See ya around, Bear."

~

"REYNOLDS!" Stella swung around to see Marty waving her over. She clutched the interview tape in her hand and crossed the office. "I hear you have an interview with Lucky Haskins."

"Yes, he was at the track when Billy Joe took me by this morning."

"Did you ask him about switching from Ford to Chevy this year?"

"Uh... no."

"Did you ask him about his pit crew chief resigning before the season started and then changing his mind?"

"No, I—"

"What about—"

"Marty, I don't know much about NASCAR... yet, so, um, I just asked him about how he thinks the season is going—uh, you know, and other pretty general things like that."

He made a face. "Go ahead and give that tape to sports; we'll have them pick out a sound bite. Now that your tour is over, you're officially in training this week. I want you to spend time with the producers today, and then watch the newscasts from the booth." A scanner tone rang out from one of the speakers behind him. "Dismissed!" He spun in his chair and picked up his phone in the same second.

She winced. A week of training sounded painfully boring.

An hour later, she scanned the classifieds online. It turned out *watching* wasn't really a full-time job—the producers had left for lunch and the newsroom was deserted. She decided to use the downtime to start looking for places to rent and found apartments in town ran from six- to eight-hundred dollars a month.

She wrinkled her nose; she was making more money here than at her last station but still hardly cleared minimum wage.

She drummed her fingers on the desktop. Lucky's offer of an apartment for under five-hundred dollars a month seemed pretty tempting. No doubt, it was a bad idea. Her fingers reached out and dialed his number, anyway. He answered on the first ring.

"When can I move in?"

4

GETTING TO KNOW YOU

"Stella? The girls and I are headed out to dinner. Can you join us?"

It was Wednesday night, and Stella was just packing up her desk to go home. Kate Werner was one of the many blond reporters at the station. Over the last few days, she'd found herself distinguishing them by the *kind* of blond hair they had. Kate had soft, wavy curls, and reminded Stella of a figure skater —she wasn't just slim but tiny. She did a consistently good job with her stories and managed to stay out of anyone's line of fire.

Stella smiled, glad to be included.

She got the details and caravanned a couple of miles down the road. When they walked into the restaurant, Stella surveyed her coworkers from a distance. Candice (short with bangs) was already there, along with Amy (long and straight), Jen (bob), and Joan (bottle-blond). When she and Kate joined the small group, many people stopped to stare.

"It must be so strange for viewers to see all of us together outside of the newscast," Kate said with a wink. "We always make kind of a splash."

Stella thought back to the one time she'd seen a Cleveland

news anchor in the grocery store when she was growing up and remembered her excitement. Imagine seeing the whole news team cruising down the pasta aisle! She tried to ignore the stares and sat on a bench next to Candice. "Nice job with the trash story today."

"They can't all be Emmy winners, all right?" Candice snapped.

Stella's eyes widened. "I was being serious. You had great natural sound incorporated throughout—I thought it was a great piece."

The woman's face flushed. "I'm sorry, I'm sorry. It's been a day. Larry Howard just makes me so..." She scoffed, unable to put her frustration into words.

"What happened?" Stella asked. Larry was the station's main anchor, news director, and general manager's father. Apparently he'd been the main anchor at the station for more than twenty years and had taken over the news director job by default after the last person was fired shortly after Keith came onboard.

Joan leaned forward. "He calls her Candy Cane on air. It's so inappropriate."

"Have you ever talked to him about it?"

Candice rolled her eyes. "Of course! The first time it happened, I thought the old guy just couldn't hear my real name. It happens every night, though, and no one's around to make him say *Candice Cayne*. It's just so frustrating. Even my mom calls me Candy now!"

"Have you ever corrected him on air? I mean, if every time he tossed the live shot over to you—you immediately corrected him, maybe he'd stop."

"Correct Larry Howard on live TV?" Candice looked appalled. "You have no idea how that would go over. I'd be public enemy number one—especially with Keith." She shuddered just thinking about it.

The hostess called them over and Stella slid into a comfort

zone she hadn't experienced since leaving Montana: a night out with friends, or at least people who might become friends. It was nice to feel included socially again.

"So, Stella," Joan leaned forward so she could see Stella diagonally across the long, rectangular table, "give us the scoop on you and Lucky." Joan was the bottle-blond, her dark brown eyebrows, which currently wiggled up and down suggestively, the big giveaway.

Amy laughed at Joan's tone but turned to see Stella's reaction, along with the rest of the table.

Stella shook her head incredulously. "Lucky Haskins? I promise, there's nothing to tell!"

"All the sports guys are talking about that interview you did with him on Monday. Big Bob says he's never seen Lucky laugh so much."

She smiled at that unexpected news but shook her head again. "I promise it was just an interview. I have a great boyfriend back in Montana and we're very happy."

Joan frowned. "Well, that's no fun at all," she said to a chorus of laughter.

Stella looked thoughtfully at Joan. She could be imagining things, but it sounded like the woman had a little twang in her voice. "I know Kate is from Wisconsin," Kate nodded in agreement, "and Candice is from Florida," Candice nodded, "but what about the rest of you?"

"Why do you ask, Stella?" Amy said with a grin, her eyes on Joan. Amy was tall and slim with long, stick straight hair that gleamed under the lights. She always looked polished, and tonight was no different with a colorful scarf tied in a sophisticated knot at her neck, perfectly bringing a spot of color to an otherwise dark outfit.

Joan groaned. "Did I—"

"Yes!" The other four girls called back.

She groaned. "Oh, that accent. I don't even hear it! How did y'all—oh. Yup, there it was. I heard it that time."

Joan ducked her head. "Yes, I'm from here, but I've been working with a voice coach to get rid of my accent. It just sneaks back in from time to time when I'm not payin' attention."

"Or when she drinks," Amy called from across the table.

"Yup, that *shore* does it, too," Joan purposefully made her twang as thick as possible. Laughter rang out across the table.

"Stella," Kate spoke in a low voice, looking down at her lap, "I'd seriously consider ending it with your boyfriend now." The other reporter's eyes shifted sideways to her face. "He works in TV, too?" When Stella nodded, she continued, "It never works. You think he's going to get a job here when his contract is up, but there are too many balls in the air: his contract, which stations are hiring, and your contract. Save yourself some heartache and end it now. Next time, end it before you leave."

"Don't listen to her, Stella," Candice said from across the table. "Her long-distance relationship burned up in a flaming ball of sh—"

"They all do!" Kate interrupted hotly. "Also, if you're going to date someone *not* in the TV business, make sure they'll move if you get a new job, otherwise you'll get stuck in this small town, just like Alexa did. Is that what you want?"

Stella didn't know Alexa, the main anchor at the station who worked opposite Larry, very well, but Kate's news certainly explained why she was still in Bristol. She was really good at the job, and Stella had already found herself wondering why she hadn't moved up to a bigger market yet. Now she knew.

Amy piped up from two seats down. "Girls, what a way to welcome Stella to town! Lighten up down there. She and her boyfriend will make it work or they won't, but it won't have anything to do with you and your ex, Kate!"

Stella smiled gratefully at Amy and was glad when the conversation moved on to happier subjects.

~

"BYE GIRLS! BYE—SEE YOU TOMORROW!" she called as they all walked to their cars after dinner. She looked down into her bag and dug around for her cell phone, unaware she was walking toward someone until they collided in front of her car.

"Oof," she said, hastily looking up and rubbing her knee. "I'm so sorry!"

She smiled apologetically and made to move past him when he stepped in front of her. "No problem. Stella, right?" Surprised, she looked suspiciously at the man now standing between her and her car in the dimly-lit parking lot. He held his hands out and laughed. "Sorry, that sounded creepy, right? I'm Scott Lyon, a photographer for the ABC affiliate in town. I saw you in there with all the NBC2 ladies and figured you were the new girl."

Satisfied that he wasn't dangerous, she smiled and they talked about the TV market for a few minutes. He was chatty, and she soon learned he made extra money by working at the speedway —the track, not the gas station—and that he lived in Kingsport and worked the weekend shift, making Wednesdays and Thursdays his days off. After a few more minutes of talking, Stella realized why they seemed to get along so well: Scott was from Cleveland, Ohio, just like her.

"Where did you grow up?" she asked.

"Bruxville," he said. "What about you?"

"Avon Lake!"

They went through the do-you-knows and have-you-beens that anyone from the same city goes through, until Stella looked at the time on her cell phone. "Well, it's getting late."

"Sure. Nice talking to you, Stella! Welcome to the Tri."

She watched him walk away and then slipped behind the wheel of her trusty, old Plymouth Reliant. While the engine warmed up, she took out her phone to find she'd missed one call from her boyfriend and two from Lucky. She looked at the clock on the dashboard and decided to start with Lucky, since it was getting late in their time zone.

"Hello, Lucky Haskins's phone," a woman's high, twangy voice answered on the fourth ring.

"Oh, umm... can I speak to him?" Stella grimaced. Maybe she should have waited until the next day to call back.

She heard a flirtatious giggle and then a man's annoyed voice in the background. There were muffled sounds before Lucky's hard voice finally came on the line. "What?"

"I-I'm sorry, Lucky—I'll call another time." She cringed at catching him with another woman. More power to him, but she didn't want to interrupt.

"Stella? No, wait—hold on, please." She heard stern words and then a shrill voice complaining. Finally, there was some muddled arguing. "I didn't ask you to come here, Star, but now I *am* asking you to leave." Next there was stomping, and finally a door slammed in the background. After a moment of silence, Lucky came back on the line. "Stella."

He didn't say anything else, so after a minute, she said, "Yes?"

"I can't tell you how nice it is to talk to a woman without any drama."

"That's me: drama-free." She navigated her car through the parking lot and turned onto the main road. "Is everything all right with the apartment?"

"Yes, yes, everything's fine. We'll get you the key tomorrow, and you can move in Friday, just like we planned."

"Do you know the other people on my floor?" Stella asked, curious about her new digs.

"There are only three other apartments on your floor. One unit is being renovated, the second is owned by a long-haul truck driver who's on the road most of the time, and a little old lady, Mrs. Lanster, lives in the last one. It should be a nice, quiet place for you, Stella."

"Okay, great."

"We can take care of the paperwork when I get back. I, uh... I leave tomorrow for Talladega, and you know, I just... I guess I just wanted to see if you were free tonight."

"Oh," she said, startled. "That's so... um. Wow." Tongue-tied by the question, she coughed and cleared her throat. "I went out with some work friends. Sorry." She then snorted, remembering who'd answered his phone a few minutes ago. "I guess you filled the slot pretty quickly."

"That wasn't—well, it was my ex—but I didn't invite her here and she just left. There's just so much drama in my life; drama with Star and drama at the track. I guess it was nice to talk to you the other day and just be, I don't know... normal."

She smiled. "In the few days since we met, you've called me no fun and now normal. I don't want to give you dating advice, but I'd recommend picking out some more flattering words for your next target." Lucky guffawed on the other end of the line. "What's going on at the track? Is NASCAR like WWE wrestling, where you have to make up fights with other drivers?"

He gave another snort of laughter. "No, darlin' we don't have *pretend* fights on the track. They're already there, honest to goodness."

"So, who are *you* fighting with?"

"That's just it: I don't know. It's just been a weird vibe around the garage lately—"

"Oh, crap!" Stella exclaimed when she drove over a giant pothole.

"What?"

"I think I just broke my car! What the hell? That was like a crater in the middle of the road!"

"Are you on Lane Avenue?"

"Yes! I think I left my bumper back there." She looked in the rearview mirror to make sure that wasn't the case; the road was clear, and she relaxed her grip on the steering wheel. "Sorry, what were you saying?"

"Nothing, Stella. It's just nice to hear your voice. It's late—you probably have a boyfriend to call." He used a funny voice when he said *boyfriend* that made her laugh.

"Yes, you're right," she agreed. "Thanks for fast-tracking the apartment, Lucky."

"Goodnight, Stella."

"Goodnight." She disconnected and smiled in the dark of her car. After a moment, she blinked. He was too easy to like.

Back at the hotel, she dialed another number. John's voice-mail picked up, and she sighed at having yet another conversation with his answering service.

"Hey, John, it's me. You're probably getting ready for the news. I'm getting ready for bed. I guess I'll talk to you tomorrow. Goodnight." She walked around her room feeling oddly unsettled. She'd lied to the girls at dinner that night: she and John weren't very happy. In fact, they hadn't talked in days.

He had tried to be supportive when she took the job in Bristol, but things had been strained between them ever since she signed the contract a few weeks ago. Now she wondered what was keeping him so busy. Should she and John have made a clean break before she left Montana? She fell asleep thinking about Kate's advice at the restaurant and wondering what would become of her long-distance relationship.

5

EXPLOSIVE NEWS

By Friday, Stella was ready for a break. She'd spent the week learning the ins and outs of her new station by day and trying to furnish her new apartment by night. The week-long training program crawled by as she learned the computer programs, became familiar with the equipment, and wrote practice stories. It was dead boring, and she hadn't written anything for air or done a single live shot since arriving.

Her cell phone rang, and it was the most exciting thing to happen to her that day. She turned away from her computer and dove into her bag, hoping it was John.

To her surprise, Lucky's name flashed across the screen. "Hello?" She didn't expect an answer, assuming he'd butt dialed her.

"Hey, Bear." She could hear the smile in his voice.

"Lucky? What's up? Aren't you in Alabama?"

"Yep, I'm here at the track, but I know you're moving into the apartment today and just wanted to say I'm glad we're doing this. I'm glad for a reason to get to know you, Stella." She took the phone away from her ear and looked at the screen. What was going on? "I've been talking to Jim about it for the last three days. I can't *stop* talking about you, actually. I know we just met, but I think you're the kind of person I need in my life right now. You're smart, funny, don't take any shit from me, and in the three times we've talked, you've called me out on my BS without hesitation. You're the total package, Stella, and gorgeous to boot."

Who was Jim and why was Lucky talking to him about her? "Lucky, I—"

"Those were more flattering words, weren't they?" He laughed softly. "See, I even took your advice already. I know, I know: I don't know anything about you and you don't know anything about me, but there's time for that."

"Listen, I think you've got the wrong—"

"Can I call you after the race? Let me take you to dinner Monday night. Tuesday?"

"Lucky, you're coming on stronger than my nephew's Axe Body Spray and that is *not* a good thing! I'm sorry if I gave you the wrong impression, but I already *have* a boyfriend!"

"See? I love that you don't hold anything back. I'll call you Sunday—no, Saturday night, after the race."

"Did you hear me? *I have a boyfriend!* You can't just steamroll over that fact because *you've* made some kind of decision."

He paused. "Where is he?"

"Montana."

"If you left him and moved across the country, you can't be that serious about him."

"Lucky—"

"I have to go. I'll call you Saturday night. Bye, Stella."

He disconnected and she stared at her phone. Had that really just happened? Was Lucky Haskins seriously announcing his intentions with her, like her opinion didn't matter? She chuckled. He really didn't know her at all.

"Stella, you working on a funny script today?" Marty peered over his wire-rimmed glasses; the assignment editor didn't look amused.

"Oh, uh, nope. Just heading out for my lunch break."

He nodded and watched her pack up her bag and walk out of the newsroom.

Her hour-long break was crammed full of move-in day activities. She let in the deliverymen from the secondhand shop in town. Earlier in the week, she'd bought a bed frame and some furniture, and now she was looking forward to sleeping in her apartment and finally enjoying some privacy. Her hotel had paper-thin walls and her neighbors were noisy night owls—sleep had been hard to come by.

By four-thirty that afternoon, Stella was chomping at the bit to clock out for the day. She looked up from her practice story at a group of coworkers gathered around the monitors at the far end of the newsroom. The Race Network played on two of the six screens, and cars zoomed around the track. She assumed it was Talladega and wondered if Lucky was on the track.

"I just don't get it," she muttered, watching the race. "It's not even really a *sport*."

Big Bob Buchanan, the sports guy, along with Barry, the six o'clock producer, Marty, Billy Joe, Candice, and a photographer named Elbee crowded around the screen.

She bumped Candice's shoulder with her own. "What's going on?"

"Qualifying for tomorrow's race." Her eyes never left the screen. "Lucky Haskins is in a pissing match with Jenkins Jones. It's like they're going to run each other off the track!"

Lucky's number thirteen car came awfully close to another car on the track. A number in the lower right corner of the screen showed the drivers' speeds: one-hundred-eighty-seven miles per hour! She sucked in a breath and bit her lip.

"That looks kind of…"

"Dangerous?" Big Bob asked. "It sure is. He's just getting Jones back for the last race." He let out a belly laugh and said, "Jones spun him out at Daytona with just two laps to go and cost Lucky the checkered flag. He almost beat him in the points, too."

Stella's brow wrinkled as she tried to follow the terminology.

"One lap left!" Elbee said, rubbing his hands together, as more people crowded in to watch.

The two lead cars headed up a bank into the final turn when Lucky's car wavered, losing speed. He fell back, and Stella exhaled a sigh, glad—it wasn't even the real race, for heaven's sake!

His car continued to lose ground as others passed him, and then sparks spewed from under the tires. Flames shot out, and soon the entire car was engulfed before it spun out of control and flipped, tumbling over a half-dozen times before skidding to a stop upside down. A collective gasp went up from the people gathered around the monitors when a small explosion produced a fireball that rose into the sky. The whole newsroom stopped to stare.

"God *damn* it! Get him out, get him out!" Billy Joe said.

It took a moment for Stella to realize he was talking about getting *Lucky* out. Lucky was inside that fireball! Men in fire suits raced over to the car, white foam spewing from their extinguishers. Her mind buzzed louder than the monitors, and she could barely focus on the screen. Finally, the fire was out. The medics who approached the car, however, did nothing.

"Why are they just standing there?" she asked through the hand covering her mouth.

The voices coming from the monitor finally registered in her head, and the announcers at the track were obviously as stunned as everyone else.

"This is unprecedented for qualifying—"

"Unbelievably tragic situation unfolding here in Talladega—"

"No idea whether anyone could survive that kind of explosion and crash—"

"Certainly not a good sign that medics aren't moving in to save Haskins—"

In a flash, her mind traveled back to the day before, when she'd met Lucky at her new apartment to get the keys.

~

WHEN LUCKY OPENED THE DOOR, she gulped. He was casually dressed in dark jeans and a black, V-neck T-shirt, and he looked good.

She got a whiff of his aftershave and inhaled deeply. *Mmmm.* She might have closed her eyes.

He grinned devilishly. "Stella the Bear, how's it goin'?" He held the door open.

"Thanks for meeting me." She slid past him into the apartment. *Stay cool, Stella,* she admonished herself.

"Hey, I'm glad to have you. This is a great place; I think you'll love it here. The best thing about it, besides those windows, is that you're on the Tennessee side of Bristol."

She waited for the rest of his thought, but when he didn't add anything, she asked, "Why is that good?"

"Because I'm from Tennessee, of course!" He chortled at his own joke and then watched her walk through the apartment from one end to the other.

The floor plan was modern and open, with wide-plank, wooden floors, an entire wall of windows that overlooked the quaint downtown, and polished cement countertops in the kitchen.

Looking up, she said, "These ceilings are amazing. How tall are they?"

"The windows are about fifteen feet tall, and I think the ceiling is twenty-five." He folded his arms over his chest and leaned back against the wall. "I'm not going to lie: it's a pain to heat and cool this place, but the views more than make up for it."

"How many apartments do you own?" she asked, looking around her new place appreciatively.

"I have total ownership of ten buildings in town, plus partials, like in this building. I didn't get in early enough to buy the building outright, but I bought up a few of the units. I have both commercial and residential properties in Chattanooga and Knoxville, too. I'm hands-on with all the rentals. I know racing won't last forever, and I wanted a plan for after. You can't go wrong by investing carefully in good real estate, you know?"

Stella was impressed he had a plan. She hardly knew what she was doing next week, let alone after retiring.

"I have movers you can hire to help get your stuff in," he offered.

She laughed. "Nothing to move, yet." She'd driven across the country with only her clothes and a few mementos from Montana. "What do I do if something breaks? I assume you spend most of your time in Knoxville—is there a local property manager or anything?"

Lucky let out a low chuckle. "Girl, you've got to calm down. Knoxville's only a quick drive away. You call and I'll be here for *anything* you need."

Stella turned to look at him after those last words, her hands on her hips, and he chuckled again. "Sorry, Bear. You're just too fun to tease."

"Don't get cute with me, Lucky. I—"

"I know, you've had men like me for breakfast," he said, his eyes narrowing. "That's something I want to learn more about, Stella..."

He moved toward her with purpose now, and she had every impression that he was a lion heading toward his prey. She swallowed loudly and her breathing hitched. Lucky stopped just inches from her and pointed out the window. "Do you see that sign? The one that's lit up like a Christmas tree? It goes right over the state line, Stella. It always looks so good from up here."

Their faces were just inches apart, and if Stella moved even a fraction closer, their bodies would touch. She took another deep breath and then mentally shook herself. *Get a grip,* she chided before taking a step away and clearing her throat. "The place is great, Lucky. Thanks."

He chuckled. "All business, huh, Stella? How long you been a reporter, anyway?"

"Only about six or seven months."

"Well, you do a great job of staying focused," he grinned mischievously.

~

"FOCUS, PEOPLE!"

The smoldering wreck on the TV monitors burned holes into her eyelids. Even when she tore her eyes away from the screen, she saw the smoke, fire, and shell of a car. The whole newsroom had been still and silent until the overhead speakers came to life.

"We are show open in five minutes, everyone," the woman's voice echoed across the newsroom. "I need a director in the booth, a reporter at the newsroom camera, and someone writing updated copy about this accident *now*. Let's move, people!"

The newsroom burst into action. People crisscrossed the floor like spiders in a giant web, running to computers and from the printers, down the hall, and toward the stairs—no time to wait for the elevator.

Stella still hadn't moved, though. She felt glued to the floor, her mind refusing to move past the fact that Lucky might have been—

A tap on her shoulder interrupted her grim thoughts.

"Stella, I need you to do the newsroom updates on the crash. I'll write copy, but you'll have to read it live off the teleprompter. Can you do that?" The six o'clock producer's eyes bore into her own.

"Yes, Barry, of course." Every other reporter was already assigned a story for the day; only Stella was free. Her eyes started to water, but she shook herself. She couldn't allow herself to think about Lucky—she had to report on what happened.

She grabbed her IFB cords from her bag, hustled over to the newsroom camera, and clipped the microphone to her shirt. After she pushed the tiny earpiece into her ear, a woman spoke.

"Stella, this is Samantha. Larry and Alexa will toss to you right off the top. Barry is writing copy now and you'll read it live. Are you good?" The five o'clock producer was really asking if Stella was capable of doing a breaking news live shot.

She nodded at the camera, forcing her own emotions off to the side. There was no time to explore them now. "I'm ready, Samantha."

Barry jogged past and shoved papers into Stella's hands. "I'm headed to the booth. There's your first copy. Marty is calling Talladega now for updates."

A special report graphic flashed across the screen and Larry broke in, his official, deep voice a good mimic of one of the old network broadcasters. Even though he'd grown up in the south, he didn't have any trace of a southern accent.

Larry: Good evening, I'm Larry Howard.

Alexa: And I'm Alexa Robinson.
We begin with late-breaking news from the NASCAR track in Talladega, Alabama.

Larry: Lucky Haskins was involved in a fiery wreck just moments ago. Stella Reynolds joins us live in the news-room with what we know.

Stella: The crash happened just minutes ago during qual-ifying laps for the NEXTEL 500 at the Talladega Super-speedway in Alabama.

Take: Video

Haskins appeared to lose control of his car on turn four of
the last qualifying lap. The car spun out and flipped
multiple times before bursting into flames. Once again,
this happened just minutes ago on the track. We saw
emergency crews rush the scene with fire extinguishers,
but there was no effort to pull Haskins from his car. No
official word yet on the extent of his injuries.

Stella: On Cam

We'll be monitoring this situation all night, bringing you
the latest information as it becomes available. If you're
just tuning in, devastating news out of Talladega as
NASCAR's number one driver for three years running,
Lucky Haskins, is involved in a dangerous crash during
qualifying. I'm Stella Reynolds, back to you.

"Nicely done," Samantha said in her ear. "Stay there. You'll do
updates throughout the ninety."

She blew out a breath and rolled her shoulders to release the
tension. Keith stormed into the newsroom. "Great job, Stella. You
looked really *smart* up there." He nodded in satisfaction and
pivoted on the spot, heading for Marty's desk.

Stella glanced at her reflection in the camera lens. She hadn't
been prepared to go on camera that day and wasn't wearing any
makeup. She raced to her desk, grabbed her makeup kit, and was
back in front of the camera before anyone missed her.

"It's confirmed: he's dead!" Marty called from across the
newsroom.

Stella's nose tingled and her eyes welled up. She looked up at
the ceiling, refusing to let the tears spill over. Dead? It didn't seem
possible. Lucky was so full of life and charm—he'd had so many
plans for his future! It was hard to believe he was gone in the

blink of an eye. They'd just talked on the phone, for crying out loud!

"Coming back to you live in twenty seconds, Stella, for an update."

She cleared her throat and nodded at the camera, ready.

6

TEARS AT THE TRACK

Ninety minutes later, Stella was exhausted. She'd given updates in front of the newsroom camera as soon as new information came in from the track in Alabama. Sometimes she read scripts Barry or Samantha had written, but sometimes she had to ad lib information on the spot as Marty fed it to her from his desk. It was grueling work that required complete concentration, and she finally signed off for the last time and collapsed at her desk. She'd only been sitting for a moment when she felt a hand on her shoulder.

"Stella," Marty said, "if you can, we need you to go to the track tonight."

"You want me to go to Alabama?"

"No, to the *Bristol* Motor Speedway."

She must have looked as confused as she felt, because his face softened. "People will go to the nearest track to mourn, Stella— thousands will come. Keith wants you to be live there tonight at eleven. Our regular nightside crew will cover the press conference by satellite. Larry's trying to get in touch with Lucky's pit crew chief, Jim Cruisner. We need additional crews on the ground tonight, and we're calling everyone in. You and Billy Joe, live at the track at eleven, okay?"

Lucky had just mentioned Jim to her on the phone a few hours ago. At the time, she'd been curious about who he was, but now the information couldn't have seemed less important.

She couldn't imagine going to her cold, empty apartment to sit and watch the news by herself. Being surrounded by people, with first access to any new information—of course that's where she wanted to be!

She looked up at Marty and nodded. "I'll do it."

A STUNNING NUMBER of people already crowded the track parking lot when they arrived. The accident was only two hours old, but hundreds were already in the parking lot, desperate to remember their favorite driver.

Candles flickered in the slight breeze that blew through the open space, and Stella pushed her hair back over her shoulders so she could button her wool coat as they got out of the live truck.

It was dark, the sun had set hours ago, and the air felt heavy with emotion. She turned to look at Billy Joe uncertainly. "I don't get it. Most of these people never even met Lucky, but they're crying." A giant of a man, at least three-hundred pounds, leaned over the flatbed of his pickup truck, his shoulders shaking. "They're not just crying but sobbing? This is..."

"They've been watching him for almost thirteen years, just like me. They know him as well as I do and they're just as sorry as anyone to see him go," he drawled.

She blinked up at him, her eyes slowly focusing on his long, brown hair, the stubble on his chin, and finally on his sad eyes looking back at her. "I'm sorry, Billy Joe. I know this is hard for you, too."

He nodded, and she felt her nose start to tingle again. She'd never known anyone who died. Even her grandparents had been gone long before she was born. She didn't feel equipped to handle the feeling of loss.

"Been watching him race from the beginning," he said, a frown on his face. "Never saw him let up on a turn like that before." After a small sniff, she felt a laugh fight to escape. Leave it to Billy Joe to talk racing tactics at a time like this. He put a tape in the camera and handed her the microphone. "Let's go."

She composed herself and followed him through the parking lot to a makeshift memorial forming near the main gates. Candles, flowers, and hand-lettered signs swelled from a section of the fence, and the number of offerings grew by the minute as more people added items to the pile.

While Billy Joe got video, Stella scanned the crowd for someone to interview.

Her phone rang, then, and she glanced at the screen and hit a button to silence the ringer. It was her mom; they could talk later.

"Over there, by the number thirteen car." A couple sat in a black pick-up truck painted identically to Lucky's race car. Stella cleared her throat and tapped the woman on the shoulder. "I'm sorry to interrupt. Can we talk to you for a moment?" The woman nodded, and the man slipped his arm around her shoulders. "Why did you come out here to the track tonight?"

The woman wiped at her tears with a tissue and said, "We been watchin' Lucky since before we were married—"

Her husband took over, "We had a NASCAR theme at our wedding," he held up his wedding ring, which featured checkered flags on the sides and a prominently displayed number thirteen in the middle of the gold band. "Lucky's been lucky for us since day one."

"Our first date was here at the speedway," his wife said, "and we've been back here every year for our anniversary."

Stella and Billy Joe moved through the crowd, listening to

many similar stories from people who'd grown up watching Lucky race and were stunned by the accident.

"We just thought he'd stop racing someday and become a team owner. Never thought we'd see a day without Lucky," a man with ghost-white hair said as he wiped his eyes with the back of his hand. "It just don't make sense, like something went wrong with his car. He's steered out of worse spins before, no problem."

After a half dozen interviews, Stella and Billy Joe went back to the live truck to start writing their story. While Stella picked out sound bites, Billy Joe turned on the Race Network.

Half an hour later, she handed her script over. "Hey. A few people, including you, talked about how Lucky wasn't racing like usual just before the crash. Why do you think that was?"

Billy Joe scratched his chin. "I been wonderin' the same thing, Stella. He must have known something was wrong with his car before that final turn and that's why he slowed down. He'd usually try to edge Jones right up into the wall, but I don't know... might could be he didn't want to wreck his car in qualifying. I guess we'll never know."

Stella shook her head. *Might could be?* That was a new one. As she sat back in her seat, her mind tried to pick out something Billy Joe had said as important, but she couldn't latch onto the idea quite yet.

"I'm going to get some air," she said after she'd voiced her package. She hopped out of the live truck and scanned the crowd, now surely twice the size it was when they'd first arrived an hour ago. After a few minutes, she spotted him.

She wove her way through the mourners, finally locating the man with ghost-white hair she'd interviewed earlier. "Sir, you mentioned that you think something went wrong with Lucky's car just before the crash?"

He pulled the gate of his pickup truck down and sat on the edge and motioned for Stella to do the same.

"I'm a mechanic, but I used to race myself—cart racing—until one too many crashes had my wife on my tail about findin' a safer hobby. Now I fish," he added with a wry smile.

Stella smiled. "Can you talk to me a bit more about your impressions of the accident? Professionally speaking."

"Well, it's like we've all been sayin': something didn't seem right about the last turn. I swear I saw sparks flying before he slowed down, and there's no reason his car should be sparkin' hot like 'at—not when they weren't even going full racin' speeds."

"What do you think happened?"

The man shrugged. "No idea, but it didn't seem like Lucky's usual style, is all. He's more take-no-prisoners than no-no-after-you, you know what I mean?"

On the way back to the live truck, she saw Scott, the photographer from Ohio she'd met earlier in the week. They waved but didn't stop, too busy to chat on a night like this.

She climbed in the front seat just as the press conference started in Alabama, and Billy Joe stopped editing and turned up the sound on the monitor. "There's Kevin Nalor. He's the general manager at the track. First year on the job—what a way to start." He shook his head.

"It is with heavy hearts that we, along with NASCAR officials, have decided to cancel the Saturday and Sunday races here at Talladega and instead devote the weekend to investigating the accident that took the life of our fellow driver and friend, Lucky Haskins." The press conference echoed through the parking lot, many cars tuned in by radio. Nalor's face was somber and his tone grave. "Our NASCAR family is devastated, and we promise you a full investigation into what went wrong is already underway. Goodnight, and God bless."

Flash bulbs created a strobe-light effect as Nalor deflected questions from reporters. Security guards ushered all the speakers out of the room.

Just before the station went back to Alexa and Larry at the

anchor desk to wrap up the special report, she caught a glimpse of Ryan Wexler as he left the room at the Superspeedway. An odd smile flashed across his face, and Stella squinted at the screen. Maybe she'd imagined it; there was certainly nothing to smile about that night.

7

STARS COME OUT

Back at the station, Stella ran into Larry Howard in the lobby.

"Great job tonight, Stella."

"Thanks, Larry. Sorry your interview with Jim didn't pan out. I'm sure he's just too devastated to talk yet."

"I've known Jim since high school, believe it or not. We grew up together. Haven't talked in years and years, but I gave it a try."

"What a small world!"

"Very small, Stella, especially when it comes to NASCAR. We're all interconnected. Can't find a stranger, especially when you're as high-ranking as I am."

"High-ranking? What do you mean? Like here, at the station?"

Larry laughed, bemused. "Not only that, but it's true I'd be a great resource for the drivers on media relations. I'm talking about my twenty years on the NASCAR board. It's quite a responsibility, especially at a time like this."

The buzz of working a twelve-hour shift had worn off hours ago, and combined with the draining sorrow over Lucky's death that was finally seeping into her mind, she didn't think she'd last much longer. Larry, however, wasn't done sharing his résumé.

"These young drivers could really benefit from my knowledge, experience, and connections, but they just don't take the time. Lucky should have been at our board meetings, learning about what we do, but he was too busy being famous—and now look at him. He's dead with no legacy!"

She wrinkled her nose; it seemed a strange time to attack Lucky. "Well, goodnight, Larry," Stella said as she pushed through the lobby door.

"I'm gonna kill you!"

She froze. Was that the same voice she'd heard on her first day, still talking about some kind of murder? There was nowhere to go but forward, and the other person was heading toward her at a fast clip.

"You stupid, dang—" Elbee rounded the corner. She'd met the photographer earlier in the week, and he'd seemed friendly enough. He stared at a small screen in his hands, his face red and his mouth drawn down in a grimace. He looked up at Stella and ducked his head. "Excuse my language. This dag gone game drives me crazy! Why do I keep playing it?" His eyes flashed down and he tapped the screen. "Die, you m—" He bit his lip and sheepishly stuffed the game console into his pocket. "I got it from my son a few weeks ago and I'm certified addicted... or just certifiable!" He chortled as he disappeared.

Had she mistaken a video game for a murder plan outside Keith's office on her first day? It was hard to tell if it was the same voice, but it had a similar slow, soft drawl. It certainly made more sense that it had been Elbee threatening a video game than someone else planning a murder. By the time the elevator doors closed to bring her up to the newsroom, she resolved to ask Elbee about it the next time they worked together. She would put it out of her mind until then.

∽

SHE PRESSED her cell phone against her ear and wiggled the key into the sticky lock at her apartment. "Mom, there's nothing to worry about—everything is fine. It's just a real shock that he's dead. No, I... uh, I *didn't* know him well," she jiggled the key harder, "but he seemed really nice." She felt a pang in her stomach. She'd had no intention of dating Lucky Haskins, but she knew after their phone call that afternoon that he would have been a fun person to call a friend.

The key wiggled uselessly in her hand. She glared at the lock, blew out a breath, and then finally cranked the key sideways and pushed open her door. Her mom hadn't stopped talking and was now back to her initial rant about how worried she was for Stella.

"Mom, I'm serious. There's nothing to worry—" The door across the hall opened. It was close to midnight, but Mrs. Lanster was dressed for high tea.

"Stella, what news tonight. What terrible news." The older woman patted her tightly curled hair. She'd met her neighbor earlier that day when her furniture was delivered. At the time, Mrs. Lanster had spent thirty minutes filling her in on all the neighbors in the building. "I just never in a million years expected Lucky to go out in a fireball like that. His brother, Hap, now that's a different story, but Lucky was always so strong and reliable. Well, not with the ladies, but you know what I mean, bless his heart."

"It was a shocking day, Mrs. Lanster." She pointed to her phone, still held tight to her face, but the older woman didn't take the hint.

"I am *beside* myself, dear, just beside myself. I can't believe I'll never see him loping down the hallway again. It breaks my heart, yes it does." She clicked her tongue and looked at Stella through narrowed eyes. "You never did sign any rental papers, did you, dear? Oh my—that really will complicate things, I'm afraid. It's hard to settle an estate with a squatter on site." She looked down her nose at Stella, as if Lucky's death had somehow turned *her* into a criminal.

"Goodnight, Mrs. Lanster," she kept her tone light and friendly. When she got into the room, however, she grimaced. "Mom, are you still there?" She dropped her bags and ran a hand through her hair, trying to stay calm. A squatter! What was she going to do?

"What did that woman say?" her mom asked. "Stella, are you homeless?"

"No, Mom, everything's fine. Don't worry."

"Well, who's going to take care of you now that your landlord is dead?"

"Mom," Stella said through gritted teeth, "I am a grown woman! I can take care of myself."

"How's John?"

Stella bit back a groan. She and John had been playing phone tag since she arrived Monday. "He's fine, Mom. Just busy, you know? We're all really busy."

Her mom sighed, her worry audible though the receiver. "Okay, dear, I get it: you're *too busy* to talk to your mother."

"That's not what I meant. I'm just tired. It's been a long day."

"I know, sweetie."

"Listen, the apartment is great. Things here are great." The lie passed easily off her lips. After they hung up, she got ready for bed, taking particular interest in brushing her teeth, flossing thoroughly, and then tidying up her bathroom. Finally out of tasks, she perched on the edge of her mattress.

Lucky Haskins is dead.

Even though she'd said the words a dozen times that night while reporting on the story, she hadn't really allowed them to penetrate her mind. Now, however, with no distractions inside her quiet apartment, she couldn't stop thinking about it and replaying the fire exploding around his car.

This was her first brush with death; she supposed she'd had a very lucky life so far.

Her lip trembled. *Lucky* life.

She took a shaky breath and thought over everything she'd learned about Lucky at the track that night from his legions of adoring and devastated fans. Her main takeaway was that she didn't really know Lucky at all. She didn't know he had two Great Danes, that his father was a legendary Brickyard driver, or that he once shaved his head to show support for a young fan who'd lost her hair during chemotherapy. She envisioned his slightly shaggy mane and wondered what he'd looked like bald.

Somehow, the knowledge of all she *didn't* know changed her sadness. She felt the pain of missing out—of not knowing—and of regrets and what-ifs. A hollow feeling with no cure bloomed inside her. Death was too final and somehow too emotional and emotionless at the same time.

Exhausted, she climbed under the covers and hoped she could stop thinking about Lucky, the explosion, and her apartment long enough to fall asleep.

THE SOUND WAS like a squirrel chomping on a nut. It woke Stella from a dreamless sleep not because it was noisy but because it went on for so long. It came from the hallway, and the clock over the oven said it was 9:35 in the morning. She threw on her robe and then turned the lock and opened the door.

The scream in the hallway startled her so much that she screamed back.

Mrs. Lanster's door opened in a flash, and the older woman stood at the threshold, a commanding vision in overalls and a striped, red shirt. Flour dusted her cheek, and she smacked a rolling pin against her hands.

"Sakes alive, Stella, you startled me!" Her eyes swept over the hallway. "I see you have a visitor."

The woman in the hallway had dark, brown hair pulled back into a sleek bun and was almost as tall as Stella. She was probably twenty pounds lighter, though, and she looked long and lean in tight, designer jeans and a boxy, black sweater. She held a key between her fingers.

"*Stella*, did you say Mrs. Lanster?" Her eyes narrowed as she took in Stella's rumpled pajamas and sleep-weary eyes. "Your name is *Stella*?" Recognition flickered in her eyes, but Stella didn't know why. They'd never met.

"Who are you? Is that a key to my apartment?"

"Your apartment?"

They both looked down at her hand, and she dropped her arm and the keys jangled at her side. "I wasn't breaking in. I didn't know Lucky had rented it out again."

"Who *are* you?" Stella asked, thoroughly confused.

"I'm his fiancée, Star Coleman."

Ex-fiancée, she thought, remembering what Lucky had said on Monday, but she looked at Star and felt bad for the woman. "He did. I just moved in this week, actually. Can I help you with something?"

Star seemed to shake herself before rearranging her expression into something calmer. "I'm so sorry—how rude of me. I didn't mean to startle you. I was just looking to be close to somewhere Lucky had been lately and found myself driving clear across Tennessee to be here, at his old apartment. You must think I'm crazy."

Stella shook her head. "I'm so sorry for your loss." Star continued to look at her expectantly, so she added self-consciously, "I hope Lucky's in a better place." She wasn't sure what Star was waiting for, but Stella felt compelled to fill the silence. "'Tis better to have loved and lost—"

"Star, come on in, dear. I've just baked up some apple fritters, and it sure looks like you could use one," Mrs. Lanster glared across the hall at Stella's complete lack of tact.

She cringed at her less-than-stellar platitudes and then noticed Star seemed to be cataloguing the inside of her apartment for a long moment before she reluctantly turned and walked across the hall.

"Oh, um, Star? Uh, this is awkward, but can I have your key? I'd feel unsafe knowing someone else could get in. You understand."

Mrs. Lanster cleared her throat, and Stella steeled herself, expecting her neighbor to tell Star she didn't have an official lease. Instead, she said, "Of course, dear; Star knows she can't keep the keys. Lord knows why you have them to begin with— surely an oversight on Lucky's part. Now, dear, you hand those over to Stella like a good girl. I've got some sweet tea I brewed up fresh this morning, and we can reminisce about our favorite driver."

Star had no choice under Mrs. Lanster's watchful eye than to hand over the key.

"I'm so sorry for your loss," Stella said again as Star moved inside Mrs. Lanster's apartment and turned back. Stella felt more words come burbling out of her mouth. "'Any mind that is capable of real sorrow is capable of good,'" she called. She backed into her apartment and locked eyes with Mrs. Lanster as they both closed their doors. A grin flashed across the older woman's face.

"Harriet Beecher Stowe at a time like this?" she muttered, slapping a hand on her forehead and groaning.

She wondered why Star Coleman had really come. She didn't drive seven hours overnight from Chattanooga after watching Lucky Haskins explode on the track for the memories.

She looked around her apartment—an apartment Lucky had apparently lived in at one point—and tried to spot anything unusual. She opened every closet and cabinet door but didn't see anything suspicious. No red envelopes shouted "I'm what Star is looking for," and after about twenty minutes, she gave up.

She threw herself into getting her apartment fit to live in and spent hours at Goodwill and the secondhand shop she'd found earlier that week. She didn't want to have time to think about Lucky's horrific death—she couldn't stand it.

Later that day, she was in the lobby waiting for the elevator, her arms laden with bags from the nearby grocery store. When the doors opened, Mrs. Lanster stepped out. "I'd watch out for Star, dear. She's a slippery one. I never understood why she and Lucky stayed together for as long as they did, and it didn't surprise me one bit when they broke up a couple of months ago. It only surprised me that it took that long. Enjoy the day, dear."

Stella stared after her retreating figure, bemused.

The grocery bags cut into her arm, and she climbed into the elevator and rode up to the fifth floor. She dumped her bags on the counter and then walked to the windows, admiring the view.

Exposed brick walls and steel ventilation tubes ran the length of the apartment, and its warm, wooden floors were polished to a high shine. Floor-to-ceiling windows filled the whole far wall and bathed the room in bright white light. She crossed the room and heaved out a resigned sighed. She'd better enjoy this apartment because it wouldn't be hers for long. Two things kept circling in her mind: one, Mrs. Lanster was right that she'd better watch out for Star, and two, she needed to watch what she said around Mrs. Lanster, because that woman picked up news and information like an award-winning reporter.

8

SAY WHAT?

On Monday, Stella graduated out of training and was officially cleared to work on air. She hunched over the conference table when Marty picked Candice to follow up on the explosion at Talladega. Instead, Stella would cover an afternoon budget meeting at Bristol City Hall with Elbee. She spent the morning making beat calls—boring work that involved calling every police department and firehouse in the area and asking if anything was going on. No matter what was going on, the dispatchers always said nothing was going on, and she wondered why anyone ever made beat calls in the first place.

The mindless work allowed her far too much time to think about the sad state of her life. John hadn't called her back all weekend, Lucky was dead, and she would likely be homeless in a matter of weeks.

Around noon, an older blond woman (short and wiry hair) pulled her aside.

"I'm Corey Adams, IT director for the station. I was on vacation last week but hear you need a press badge."

"I do?"

"Yup. If you're new, you need one, mostly for official press conferences, but more and more we're finding regular people want to make sure you reporters are who you say you are." Stella nodded; she guessed that made sense. "Follow me."

They walked out of the newsroom and down the hall, past Keith's office into an airless room with two utilitarian chairs and no windows. Corey gestured to the seat across the desk and Stella sunk into it.

The other woman picked up a camera, pushed a button behind her desk that turned on some spotlights, and said, "Okay, here we go in three, two, one."

Stella smiled winningly, she hoped, and Corey snapped the picture. The IT expert looked at the digital screen and grimaced. "Ock, no. Let's do that again—my frame was off. Wow, lots of teeth, huh?"

Stella pursed her lips. Why did people at this station feel the need to critique her looks every other day? Lots of teeth? Yes, she had them all. Before Stella could morph her expression into another, less-toothy smile, Corey clicked the camera again, looked at the screen, and said, "Perfect. Framed just right."

Her mouth dropped open, and speechless, she watched Corey press a few buttons before a printer hummed to life. Within a minute, she held a warm, credit card-sized press badge with her name, employee number, and the worst picture of herself she had ever seen. Her glaring eyes were topped by what appeared to be a unibrow, and the way her lips were pushed together made a mustache-y shadow impossible to ignore.

She closed her eyes, but before she could ask Corey for a do-over, Elbee tapped on the door.

"Breaking news in Kingsport. Let's roll."

~

"STELLA REYNOLDS, NICE TO SEE YOU," Samantha said calmly

through her IFB earpiece. "Elbee says you have great video of the fire. Let's get a mic check, please."

"Hey, Samantha. Yes, it's been a crazy couple of hours out here at the fairgrounds. I've never seen flames shoot so high into the air!"

"Any luck on finding a witness?"

"Yes?" Stella said, a question in her voice. Elbee had scrounged up their eyewitness while she was working on her story, but it had apparently been slim pickings.

"We've got Terry Massey from Kingsport," she said. Elbee touched a button and the camera lens zoomed out to include the witness. "He saw the fire break out from his back porch—had his binoculars and everything." She stared into the lens expectantly.

"Oh, great, another nutjob," Samantha said in Stella's ear. "Elbee can talk anyone into doing anything, but sometimes I wish he could find more normal people."

"Yes, that's exactly right," she nodded. She'd only said, "Hello," to Terry so far, but even his twangy, "Hey, darlin'," sounded off. His sandy, blond hair was slicked back into place, his brown eyes were set a bit too close together for him to be called attractive, and he *still* wore the binoculars around his neck.

Samantha came back into her ear and said, "We've got Candice off the top with an update on the Lucky Haskins investigation and then we'll have a quick video intro to set up your story. Larry will toss to you. Standby, Stella. We're about a minute-thirty away from the show open."

Stella turned to Elbee. "Did you hear that? Probably two-and-a-half minutes away from us."

"I heard." He tapped his earpiece. "You know, these IFBs are really amazing. We run them through cell phones these days, which is somewhat less reliable than the old hard lines we used to use..."

Stella tuned him out. He could wax poetic about, well, earwax, and just then she needed to concentrate. A nervous feeling bloomed in the pit of her stomach; live shots were still new for her. Add to that the fact that she'd only done one other *live interview* in her short career—back in Montana—that hadn't exactly gone according to plan, and she was almost short of breath by the time the newscast started.

Music trumpeted and a graphic swooped across the monitor in front of Stella. An official voiceover promised exciting coverage of the fire, a school board meeting, and a murder trial update. After Larry and Alexa opened the newscast, they tossed to Candice with an update on Lucky's crash.

Candice stood in front of the green screen in the studio. "Alexa, officials are planning a memorial service for Haskins one week from today to give his fans time to get to Talladega."

"'Scuse may, Ms. Stella?"

Her nerves were forgotten as soon as Alexa said there was new information on Lucky's death. Instead of finding out what it was, however, she looked over at her eyewitness. "Is everything okay, Terry?"

"Whale, I's just wundrin' how lawng this is gunna take?"

She squinted up at him, certain he'd asked a question by the way his voice went up at the end, but she had no idea what it was. She sucked in a sharp breath—she couldn't understand her eyewitness! His southern accent was so strong that it was like listening to another language. How was she going to interview him on live TV?

She opened her mouth, ready to tell Elbee to bag the live shot —call the station and cancel—when Samantha came into her ear. "Standby, Stella." Alexa started the introduction to her story, and it was too late to back out. She wrung the microphone cord in her hand and stared straight ahead.

Alexa: Tonight, a fire is blazing just east of Kingsport at the County Fairgrounds.

Larry: Firefighters from four different districts were called in to fight the flames. Stella Reynolds has been out at the scene all afternoon. She joins us now live with new information. Stella?

She gripped her notebook a little tighter to steady her shaking hand. "Good evening, Larry. I just spoke to the fire chief here in Kingsport. He tells me crews finally have this blaze under control, but much of the eastern half of the fairgrounds was destroyed. Terry Massey saw the fire ignite from his front porch. He's joining us live now." Stella sucked in a big breath of air. "Terry, tell me when you first realized there was a problem." She held out the microphone and really concentrated. Maybe she could read his lips if she couldn't understand his words.

He swirled coffee around in his mug and looked up at sky with one eye squeezed closed. "Hmm. I guess when I heard Suzanne next doh-or yell, 'the far's on far, the far's on far,' I looked out tha winda, and shore enuff it was."

The last word she understood was "Suzanne." Rushing blood roared in her ears. She was about to make an ass of herself on live TV yet again, but there was no way to go but forward. She glanced at the camera. "I'm sorry, what did you say about how far away it was?"

"It wasn't far away a-tall. She just say-ed, 'the far's on far, the far's on far,' and I jus knew I had to call for hey-up."

She leaned a bit closer and something finally clicked in her brain. Stella shouted triumphantly, "She said the *fair* is on *fire!*"

Elbee guffawed, and heat flooded her cheeks. She cleared her throat and said in a calmer voice, "So you called 911. Describe what you saw when firefighters got here."

He looked at her, nose wrinkled, and said, "I seen them trucks pull up, sirens singin', and the hay was jus too much for 'em. It burned up like a dang matchstick and wasn't nothing left but the horses. Weren't long afore they burned up, too."

Stella's eyes darted down to her notes. Horses? She hadn't heard anything about any horses dying. "You saw horses die in the blaze?" she clarified.

Terry cocked his head to the side, a strange expression on his face. "I mean, I guess? They melted right into the ground. Broke ma heart to see it."

Elbee whistled to get her attention, and she glanced over to see him twirl his hand. Understanding dawned immediately.

"Right! The plastic horses on the carousel melted." Terry nodded vigorously and Stella continued, "Yes, very disappointing for sure. Terry, any idea how the fire ignited? The fire chief is asking for help from the community. Did *you* see anything suspicious?"

Terry took another sip from his mug just as a small gust of wind cleared the air. Instead of burned plastic and smoke, Stella's nose filled with the distinct, sharp scent of barrel-aged whiskey. She took another sniff and quickly connected the dots: Terry wasn't drinking coffee. No wonder she couldn't understand him —not only were his words camouflaged with a southern twang, but he was also three sheets to the wind!

"I was watching for my neighbor with these," he held up his binoculars. "She usually changes for the gym right around three, and that's when I seen Oliver Young sneaking around. That assho—"

"Whoa, my goodness," Stella moved the microphone away from Terry and stepped off to the side, but before she could figure out how to cover up the problem, a giggle escaped her lips. How did she wind up interviewing a drunk pervert on live TV? She swallowed another laugh. "Umm, my apologies for that language, folks; emotions are uh, obviously running hot over this dangerous fire," she cringed again at her word choice, "but um, if you have any information..."

Stella finished her live shot and got an all clear from Samantha. She hung her head in defeat and then turned accusingly to the man next to her. "Terry, that was unbelievable! You can't talk like that on TV—or drink! That was…" Before she could ponder *what* that was, her cell phone chirped.

"You just keep your mouth shut and you'll be fine," Elbee said.

She'd never heard him be so concise, and for the first time ever, she wanted him to explain, but he was already breaking down the gear.

She dug the phone out of an inside pocket of her coat. "Hello?"

"I just assumed you knew to pre-interview your people before you put them on MY air during a newscast," Keith snarled. "If you ever put a drunk person on TV again, I will personally see to it that you're stuck on the overnight-morning-weekend-holiday relief shift for the rest of your two-year contract…"

Stella opened her mouth to explain what happened, but Elbee whistled and shook his head. "Zip it, and it'll be done before you know it," he said in a low voice.

"If you ever laugh again *on air* when the shit is hitting the fan…" Stella clamped her lips and listened to Keith for another five minutes, but her lower lip trembled with his final words. "Another thing: you're supposed to be filling my *smart* reporter slot. If you can't do that, then at least comb your hair and add mascara, so you can be one of the pretty ones. I don't have any room for dumb and ugly on my staff!"

She tried to ignore the sinking feeling in her stomach. It was going to be a long two years in Bristol with this guy as her boss. She wondered if he'd wrap things up in time for her six o'clock live shot.

9

YOU AGAIN?

"**Y**ou caught a break." Keith glared at her like she'd done it on purpose. "The Kingsport arson investigator just called to thank you for shaking loose some information on that fairground fire."

She looked down at her notebook; she didn't think she could look at him without her anger coming through. He'd spent so long yelling at her between live shots that they'd almost missed officers arresting Oliver Young on arson charges at the fairgrounds. She'd finally hung up on her boss so they could get the video, and she and Elbee had even managed to send it back to the station in time for an update on the story at six. She'd already seen the station run a promo on air about her exclusive.

Stella meant to nod and walk away, but she couldn't stop herself from saying, "Well, it turns out police had wanted to question Young on several other fires in the area but didn't have any witnesses tying him to the crimes." She looked at Keith. "Terry Massey was the missing link."

"Well." He glared at Stella and then walked out of the newsroom.

"At least you didn't have a lurker," Candice said from the next desk over.

"A what?"

"A lurker—you know, the guy who stands in the background of your live shot, dancing or making obscene gestures? A lurker. They're so distracting!"

"Maybe Keith's right: maybe I *did* catch a break," Stella said dryly. They exchanged smiles. "I missed your story, Candice. What was the update from the track?"

"Billy Joe and I spent *all day* working the phones just to get the tiny bit of information we finally got." She rolled her eyes. "He's probably our best photographer, but oh my gosh, he hardly says two words in a row! He's not the person I would pick to help me cajole people on the other end of the line to give us information."

"And the only update was—what?" Stella asked.

Candice smiled wryly. "Just that they don't have much to investigate. I guess the fire burned pretty hot—most evidence was destroyed."

"Oh." What a horrible way for Lucky to die. She hoped he hadn't suffered.

"Yeah," Candice went on, oblivious to Stella's distress, "I guess the explosion burned everything to a crisp. There's really nothing to examine, so they're having trouble ruling on a cause of death or what caused the accident. They did, however, schedule the memorial for a week from today, so that's something."

STELLA'S PHONE chirped from the coffee table, and she groaned when she saw it still wasn't John. They'd been leaving each other messages for days but just couldn't seem to connect—which seemed par for the course, since they weren't connecting even when they did speak.

On the second ring, she set her sandwich down and wiped one hand on the napkin on her lap. She didn't want to talk to her sister, Blanche, but she tapped the phone, anyway.

"Stella? What's going on down there? Mom says you're homeless and you and John are already having trouble."

"Hi, Blanche." She settled back into the couch for what was sure to be a lengthy chat.

"Well? Was one week all you two could last long-distance?"

"No, Blanche, things are fine."

"Stella."

"Well, I mean, it's just a change is all, and it's going to take some getting used to. It's hard with the time difference, and our work schedules are opposite, you know. We've only had the chance to talk a couple of times. So, it's just an adjustment."

She could picture Blanche, sixteen years her senior, propped up, already in bed, even though it was only nine o'clock.

"How's your book?" she asked with a half-smile.

"Hmm, what? Oh, it's pretty good, Stella. I think you'd like the way the author—oh, no you don't. We're not talking about my latest book club find or Alex's alarm clock—although it's ridiculous to hit snooze six times, and I don't think anyone would disagree with that." Blanche took a loud breath, and then said simply, "We're all worried about you, Stella. Are you doing all right?"

Stella was the youngest of four in her family—the youngest by fifteen years. It was like having an extra set of parents at any given time. As a teenager, it had felt suffocating, but more recently, her perception was changing.

"I'm completely fine, Blanche—don't worry about me. Now put that book away and get to sleep. The kids'll be up in just a few hours."

Blanche chuckled. "You've got that right, but it's Alex's turn to get them ready for school, so I'm sleeping in!"

Stella said goodnight and set her phone back on the coffee

table in front of her. She frowned and wondered why she was telling everyone things were fine between her and John when the opposite was true. Things were very strained, and she worried they just weren't cut out to be 2,000 miles apart—it didn't work for them. Their heat, their passion—it had kindled from the start when they were *staring* at each other. Even across town had seemed too far away for them. They'd been naïve to think their new relationship could survive Stella's move. She stared up at the ceiling, wondering if they'd make it. Three weeks ago, she'd had no doubt. Now, she wasn't so sure.

The phone rang, interrupting her weary thoughts. Finally, John!

"I can't talk, Stella, just wanted to call and check in."

"You called to say you can't talk?"

"Right. I'm on my way to the park for a thing with a moose."

"Huh?"

"I know, only in Montana. A moose charged some campers at Yellowstone, and they've been stuck in a tree for an hour. One of them finally got a cell signal and called for help."

Stella smiled, missing Montana. She was about to say as much when she heard a woman's voice in the background. "Who's with you?"

"Our new intern is along for the ride today. Katie is going to work the map; her job is to not get us lost at night in the park."

Katie laughed, and jealousy flared up in Stella like angry ants. She tried her hardest to tamp it down—after all, she'd spent all day working with Elbee—and there was certainly nothing for *John* to be jealous about. Elbee, however, wasn't a college student named Katie who laughed with a breathy giggle.

They hung up after perfunctory goodbyes, and she frowned again. She didn't think she or John were enjoying their new relationships *with their phones*. It hadn't even been two weeks, though; maybe they'd fall into a pattern they could live with until

John's contract came up in six months. Hopefully he would move closer then. She sighed. Or maybe he wouldn't. Wasn't that the real problem neither of them seemed willing to broach? What if John couldn't get a job near her in six months? What if his next job was in Spokane, Washington; or San Diego, California; or Gainesville, Florida? There was no guarantee he could get a job in Bristol—it all depended on when jobs came open in each market and what kind of position they were looking to fill.

She flopped back against the couch, her sandwich forgotten, as a feeling of unease filled her empty stomach. It felt like they were heading toward an inevitable, slow, painful breakup, but then again, maybe these were just growing pains as they worked through an obviously difficult situation.

She stared at the ceiling for a long while, her mind going back and forth between the two scenarios, and she fell into a restless sleep there. When she woke up with a kink in her neck in the middle of the night, Stella moved to her bedroom, peeling her clothes off on the way.

Within minutes, she was asleep again.

In her unconscious mind, she heard creaking floorboards and wondered, in that unworried way you have while dreaming, what was going to happen. When the mattress moved, however, her mind burst into full awareness, realizing in the same moment that she wasn't dreaming and she wasn't alone.

She sucked in a deep breath, ready to scream, when a hand clamped down over her mouth. She struggled under the covers, trying to kick out at the intruder, when a man said, "Shh, Bear, quiet. It's okay."

Her eyes opened wide, and her body went limp. "Lucky?" In the near perfect darkness of her room, she could just make out his stubbled face. As her eyes adjusted, Lucky's big, brown, tired eyes stared at her intently. He moved his hand away from her mouth and she wondered whether she really was awake. Her alarm clock said it was 3:34 a.m., and she pinched her bicep and felt the pain radiate up through her arm.

Lucky's eyes crinkled at the corners. "Hey, Bear. Yes, you're awake, and let me tell you: you sure are a sight for sore eyes."

10

START TALKING

"What—how—what's going on?" Lucky stood and ran a hand through his already tousled, blond hair. "I don't know, Stella, I don't know. I don't know what's going on, but these have been the worst days of my life. I'm sorry to barge in, but I had to get out of Alabama and didn't know where else to go."

He hadn't shaved in days, and the stubble growing in gave him a rough look she wasn't used to.

"I saw you die! I-I watched your car explode into a fireball." Her hand flew to her neck and she stroked the skin there as she watched Lucky pace the small room. "Medics didn't even try to get you out—there was n-n-no hope." He stopped moving and turned to face her. "Lucky, *someone* died inside that car on Friday. If it wasn't you, who was it?"

He slouched down at the edge of the bed and hung his head into his hands. The mattress shook in time with his ragged breathing. "It was my brother. My brother, Hap, is dead."

Stella started to sit up in bed, but that's when she realized she was practically naked. She slid out from under the covers on the far side of the room with her back to Lucky and picked her robe up off the floor. Once it was secure, she sat on a chair opposite him. "You'd better start at the beginning."

After a few minutes, his breathing slowed. She handed him a tissue from the box on her nightstand and waited while he wiped his eyes.

"Hap is five years younger than me, and, well, he's been a hot dang mess since we were kids—never could hold down a job, in and out of rehab, a different woman every week. He tried racing and just couldn't ever get any traction in the rankings, so he left the sport and tried to start a reality show." His chin jerked up and he rubbed the back of his neck. "It was a disaster, just like everything else he tried to do. He's been married and divorced twice. I was ready to wash my hands of him long ago, but before our mom died, she asked me to watch after him.

"He sometimes traveled with our team, and sometimes I let him drive my car—usually just for the practice laps." He avoided Stella's eyes. "It's completely illegal, and I don't know how it even started. He just needed the exhilaration of being behind the wheel, and I guess I wanted to see him get his high in a completely drug-free way, you know?" She nodded. "We haven't done it in a long time, but he showed up at the track Friday and asked if he could drive. He'd missed the practice laps, but I thought, 'Why not? Let him do qualifying.' My head wasn't in the game, and I thought a night off would do me good." He sank back down onto the bed. "So, Hap was the one driving my car. Hap was killed in the explosion."

"Oh, Lucky. I'm so sorry."

He dropped his head into his hands and fell quiet. After a few minutes, Stella started tracing his steps around the space. "Who else knows you're alive? Why are you *here*?" He slumped forward even more and she backtracked. "I mean—obviously I'm glad you're here, and I'm really, I mean, I'm just... I can't believe you're here! Why not go right to track officials—to the police—and explain what happened, though?"

Lucky pulled his hands out of his hair and looked straight into Stella's eyes. "I was stunned in the trailer; I just couldn't move for a good ten minutes while watching my car burn on the track on TV. I finally came to—snapped out of it, I guess—and was just about to storm out there and pull Hap out of the car, no matter how pointless. I saw a playback of the last minute of the race, though, and I—I knew then, as sure as I know I'm talking to you right now, that someone tried to kill me and got Hap by mistake."

Stella fell back into the chair. "Murder? Everyone says it looked like some kind of mechanical failure. Maybe an engine overheating?" She fell silent after a quick glance at Lucky's face. "Oh, obviously I don't know the right terminology, but all the race experts are saying it looked like a terrible tragedy—an accident."

Lucky shook his head. "Despite all of his problems, Hap is a great driver, and he knows—" he took a shaky breath and started again, "he *knew* Talladega like the back of his hand. A simple engine overheating wouldn't result in an explosion like that. I'll need to hear the radio traffic to know for sure, but I'll bet my life he knew something was wrong before he spun out."

"How did you guys pull it off? I mean, surely someone would recognize that it wasn't *you* getting behind the wheel. What about your chief pit... person? Don't you two chat while you're getting buckled in?"

Even in his anguish, he looked at Stella incredulously. "Gawd, woman. No, we don't *chat* on the track!" He ran his hands roughly through his hair. "There are superstitions all over the dang place. I never talk to anyone once my helmet is on, and I put it on in my trailer before the race, so everyone knows not to bother me when I'm getting in the car. Jim Cruisner—my pit crew chief—" he enunciated the words clearly, "wouldn't know more than anyone else that it was Hap getting in the car and not me." His voice quivered and he swallowed hard. "I thought I was doing him a favor! I had no idea—no idea at all—that this would... that he would..."

Stella moved next to Lucky. "You couldn't have known the car would do that. You couldn't have stopped it from happening. This is not your fault." She rested a hand on his arm, and to her surprise, he covered it with his own. Despite the circumstances, heat zinged up her arm at the contact.

"It is *someone's* fault, though, Stella. Don't you see? Someone rigged my car. It wasn't an accident, it was murder."

"Who would want you dead, Lucky? Is someone angry with you?"

He gripped her hand tighter. "I don't know, Stella, but I need to find out."

She leaned away from him and readjusted her robe. Maybe it was the shock of seeing someone she thought was dead, but Stella felt flushed and out of breath.

She shot off the bed. "You need to go to the police! They need to know you're okay. They're the ones who can investigate. We should call them now!"

"Bear, it's been a goddamn long few days. Let's figure it out tomorrow, okay?"

She blushed when his eyes took in her flushed cheeks. "Of course. I'll make you up a bed on the couch."

He hesitated. "Thanks, Stella. I appreciate it."

To her relief, they walked out of her bedroom. The main part of the apartment was cooler, and the chilled air ran across her overheated face and legs.

"How did you get here?" she asked, pushing the futon couch into a bed.

"I took Hap's car. Couldn't get to mine."

She snapped a blanked over the mattress. "Why come here? I mean, no offense, but surely there's someone you know better than me who was closer to Alabama?"

"I need to figure out who might have done this and I can't rule out anyone from my team yet. I needed some distance to think it through," he smiled sardonically, "and I don't know you well enough for *you* to want me dead."

He took a pillow out of her hands and she became aware again that she was nearly naked under her robe. She moved into the kitchen to put some space between them. "Are you hungry?"

"Starving." He stared at her like she was a seven-course meal.

She leaned into the open the refrigerator and then felt Lucky move in close.

"How 'bout a beer? It's been a long damn day," he said again.

She set the food back down and reached for a bottle of beer. His hand closed over hers and they stood up at the same time, holding the smooth glass together. She licked her lips and his eyes widened slightly before they slid down her body. As he set the beer down on the counter and stepped toward her, Stella felt a stirring in her stomach that had nothing to do with food.

She cleared her throat. "Lucky, I—" she cut off, not sure what to say. He was on the verge of closing the distance between them when she finally blurted out, "I'm going to bed. We'll figure things out tomorrow." His lips slowly turned up and he stepped closer still. "Goodnight," she said, and practically ran to her room.

Behind the closed bedroom door, she heard him blow out a breath, and as she listened to the clinks and rattles of food being assembled in the kitchen, she finally allowed herself to think wicked thoughts. That man was hot, and he was in her apartment —and she was almost naked! She ripped off her robe and changed into actual pajamas.

Another thought pushed through her mind as she climbed back into bed: she was sitting on what could be the biggest exclusive of her career. Lucky Haskins was alive! The news would make headlines all over the world, and she could be the one to break the story. Her eyes grew large in the dark room, picturing her immediate rise to network news after a story like that.

A sound broke her out of her reverie. It was Lucky, quietly sobbing. She closed her eyes, disappointed that all she could think about was sex and fame when Lucky's brother was dead—

murdered. He had come to her for help. Could she sit on a major story like this to help someone she hardly knew?

Things were going to get interesting over the next few days, and she wondered how long she could resist the pull to get involved. Did she even want to?

11

THE PLAN

S he awoke in an instant, like an alarm went off in her head; her heart banged wildly against her chest as soon as she opened her eyes.

She was alone and convinced herself she'd dreamed everything when the shower cut off. She cracked the bedroom door open in time to see Lucky walk from the bathroom to a pile of clothes by the futon. One of her red and yellow, flowery towels hung off his hips, exposing the most captivating abdominal muscles she'd ever seen. She gulped and then jumped when her alarm clock went off.

"Mornin', Stella!" Lucky called across the apartment with a smirk. She ducked her head and then hurried to turn off the blaring noise coming from her nightstand.

She slipped her robe on before she walked out of her room and then hesitated when she saw Lucky buttoning up his pants. "Oh, sorry, I—I'm going to take a shower, and then we can um... talk about your plan?"

In the bathroom, she squeezed her eyes shut. *I have a boyfriend, I have a boyfriend,* she repeated to herself under the steady stream of water.

She got dressed in her room while Lucky banged around in the kitchen. After tying her wet hair back into a loose bun, she walked out to face the day and Lucky.

"Eggs?"

"Sure."

He divided a scramble in half as her coffee pot percolated in the background and then carried the plates over to the TV. "Pour yourself some coffee."

Had she entered an alternate reality? She took a mug off the shelf and poured herself a full cup before following Lucky to the couch.

"Where's the clicker?" He moved cushions around, searching, until she pointed to the remote. He pushed buttons and the screen lit up.

"So..." Stella pushed the eggs around on her plate, not hungry, "what *is* the plan, Lucky?"

"I'm going to figure out who killed Hap and why they wanted *me* dead." He shoved a forkful of eggs into his mouth. "I might need your help."

She took a sip of coffee and nodded. "You can stay here as long as you need to, Lucky, no problem. This is going to be a major story, but I'll sit on it for now."

He looked at her sideways. "For now?"

"Yes." She looked down at her breakfast. "It's going to get out that you're alive, Lucky, and let me remind you that you came to a TV reporter's house! You know this is going to make headlines around the world, but hopefully not until you're ready—or until you run out of time."

He shifted his gaze to the TV and slowly nodded. "Okay."

"Why *not* go to investigators right now?" Stella asked, still not sure why he hadn't done that straightaway on Friday.

"This is going to get swept under the rug as fast as the track owner can do it. The general manager over there is brand new—he's not going out on any limbs, investigating. Besides, whoever did this made damn sure it looked like an accident, and that's all they'll need to close the case. They'll call it a terrible tragedy and move on, and I can't let someone get away with killing Hap. I will find the killer."

"Lucky, if you go to the track, you'll be recognized in about two seconds." She took a sip of coffee, thinking. "In fact, how did you get out of Alabama without anyone seeing you?"

He finished his eggs and wiped his mouth with a napkin. "I put the deadbolt on and stayed in my trailer the whole time. Someone tried to get in once, but after that, all was quiet. I left at night—took Hap's car from the lot. Do you see what I mean? They're already treating it as an accident! They should have been dusting my trailer for prints, looking at my team and my life—but they're not doing any of that!"

She set her mug on the table. "You're not going to be able to ask questions around the track. You're Lucky Haskins! Plus, everything will be locked up tight, especially now!"

"I know. That's why I'm going to have to let Jim know I'm alive."

"Your pit man?"

His eyes cut to Stella. "My pit crew chief, yes."

She leaned forward. "Why haven't you talked to Jim already?"

"I can't get ahold of him." He gestured to the TV. "The news reports are saying no one can find him. I think he's pretty torn up about the whole accident. Poor Jim—he's been with me since the beginning. If I can go to him and let him know what happened, I can get started looking into who did it."

"Don't take this the wrong way," Stella bit her lip, "but what if Jim had something to do with the accident? I mean, if someone messed with your car, we can't rule out anybody who had regular access *to your car*. I'm assuming that would include Jim?"

He flicked her comment away like an annoying fly. "Jim would never."

"They said on the news yesterday that you've had a

contentious relationship." His shoulders tightened, but she continued, "In fact, my assignment editor said he resigned at the beginning of the season. What happened there?"

He shook his head. "That's not true; you know how the gossip magazines don't exactly get things right. Years and years ago, we had a fight over a woman. We cleared the air about it and things were fine again."

She picked her coffee up and blew across the surface. "Where is that woman now?"

"I don't know," Lucky scratched his head. "I haven't seen her —really since we fought. Maybe five or six years ago?"

"What happened recently? There was some kind of issue just a few weeks ago, right?"

Lucky waved her off again. "It was nothing—just a disagreement. The magazines made it out to be something more than it was."

Stella wasn't satisfied but decided to move on. "So, if Jim wouldn't mess with your car, who would? Who has an axe to grind with you, Lucky? Whoever it was, they went to a lot of trouble to make it seem like an accident, and that takes time and patience. So, let's go. In the last five years, who've you pissed off?"

Lucky, however, had tuned her out. He stared, mesmerized, at the TV screen. Stella shifted her gaze to a Lucky Haskins memorial piece that had just started playing on the Racing Network.

"Thirty-three-year-old Lucky Haskins entered the national racing stage already a star," the announcer read the lines while images of a younger Lucky filled the screen. "Although he rose to fourth in the rankings in his first year as a driver, his mother said he was a force to reckon with long before that."

An image of a well-dressed, plump woman with striking, silver-grey hair filled the screen. "He was born to do this, Lucky was. His father always said Lucky was his lucky charm when he had a race. Now he's working his magic on his own."

The announcer continued, "Sadly, Lucky's father, Indy cart

legend Goose Haskins, never had a chance to watch his son. He died of a heart attack when Lucky was just sixteen years old, and his mother passed just a few years later.

"Lucky in life and in love. Over the years, Haskins was linked to many gorgeous women, most recently fiancée Star Coleman."

A tearful Star came on screen. "We were meant to be together, me and Lucky. I guess I'll just have to wait to join him up in heaven."

Stella rolled her eyes.

"Investigators say Friday's fire burned so hot there's not enough left to test. The same is true for the coroner's office. Determining the cause of death won't be easy—officials say they might have answers by the weekend. Still no word from Lucky's pit crew chief or his only surviving family member, his brother Hap. If either man is out there listening, the world wants to pass on our condolences."

"What a way for Hap to go," Lucky said quietly.

After a few minutes of silence, she couldn't hold back any longer. "When I first met you out at the track here in Bristol, you said you'd been fighting with Ryan Wexler. About what?"

The sullen expression returned to Lucky's face and, instead of answering, he picked up their plates and brought them to the kitchen.

"Do you want my help or not?" She scowled at his retreating figure. "Obviously I'm not going to be the person who figures out someone took a pin out of an engine-block-timing belt thingy in your car to make it crash, but I am the person who can brainstorm who had motive to do what and when—but not if you don't talk to me, Lucky." He turned the disposal on and started scrubbing dishes. She threw her hands up and then turned off the TV and stalked into the kitchen. "You know, Star came by Saturday morning—tried to get in here with *her key.*"

He snapped the disposal off and his eyebrows shot up. "She did?"

"Uh huh. It seemed like she was looking for something."

"Did you—"

"I didn't let her in, and I took her key back. Why doesn't anyone know about your supposed breakup?"

"It's complicated."

"As complicated as murder? Does your *ex-fiancée* have a reason to want you dead, Lucky?"

Lucky barked out a humorless laugh. "Nothing would surprise me at this point, but I can't imagine why. Our breakup was kind of a mutual decision, to be honest."

Stella blew out a breath. "Well." She didn't know what she was doing, playing the part of detective, anyway. She started packing up her work bag. "I have to go." He looked up blankly. "I have to go to work! You need to get ahold of Jim, and you should go to police," she added grimly.

He sighed. "All right, Stella. I'll keep working on Jim, but I'm keeping the police out of it for now."

She shook her head and pulled the door open. He was exasperating, and she was glad to escape to the hallway, until she looked up and saw Star directly in her path.

"Oh!" Stella pulled the door quickly shut behind her, inserted her key, and flicked her wrist. For once, the lock worked without resistance. She glanced guiltily at Star's face, wondering if she'd seen anything, but was met by irritated disdain.

"Stella, right? I'm so sorry to ask, but I'm going to need to see a copy of your lease. Like I said over the weekend, Lucky didn't tell me he'd rented the place out, and now that he's gone, I just want to make sure everything's in order."

Stella headed for the elevator. "This isn't a good time, Star. I'm already late for work, sorry..." she climbed into the elevator. Star's expression morphed from irritated to angry within a few seconds. "Sorry!" she said again as the doors closed. She blew out another breath when she was alone. She had a feeling Star wasn't going to go away easily.

12

THE BETTER TO SEE YOU WITH

"**B**oss wants to see you, Stella." Marty surveyed her over his computer screen, and her heart dropped to her toes. Did they know she was harboring a supposedly dead, famous NASCAR driver? Before she could hyperventilate, Marty added, "Cam said it's about tonight's live shot."

She dumped her bags on the floor by her desk. Cam was waiting for her when she finally got to Keith's office.

"Darlin' did you get the glasses?"

Stella looked at the older woman blankly. "Huh?"

"Well, Keith asked me to, so I put them on your desk this morning."

"I didn't see them, but—glasses for what?"

Before Cam could explain, Keith's door opened and he stepped out of his office, already glaring. "Stella Reynolds! I do not want to be thinking about what a crappy job you're doing every single day!"

She battled the urge to look around the office for another Stella. "Keith, I already apologized for that interview last night, and to be honest, in the end it helped solve a crime, so..." What did this guy want from her?

Keith shook his head. "I'm talking about your glasses."

"I don't wear glasses!" she exclaimed. "Twenty-twenty vision, actually."

Keith looked up at the ceiling and sighed dramatically. "Cam, get the note."

Cam left and hurried back a minute later with a piece of paper and a pair of black glasses. Keith snatched them out of her hands. "We want you to wear these on air from now on."

Cam handed her the paper, and Stella's eyebrows drew together as she read it. *Look smart, be smart.* Keith grinned at her triumphantly.

"Are you kidding?"

Keith loosened his tie, and Cam jumped in. "It's just an idea the station consultant had to make you *look* smarter."

"I'm not going to—that's just the..." Stella spluttered, at a loss for words. "You want me to wear *fake* glasses so I *look* smart?" She looked from Cam to Keith and back again.

Keith threw his hands up in the air. "They're helping already: she finally gets it!" He stormed back into his office and slammed the door.

Cam jumped and then hurried over to her computer.

Stella watched her type for a moment, her mouth hanging open. She finally shook herself and turned to go.

"Just try it, Stella. You might like the look," Cam called after her.

~

"Show open in five... four... three..." the floor director finished the countdown silently with his fingers as Stella fidgeted in front of the green screen.

Her story was third on the rundown, but she couldn't pay attention to anything. All she could think about was that she felt like a fraud wearing the new, ugly glasses. She pushed them up on the bridge of her nose and wondered how people could stand to have these things on their faces. She had to force her eyes from looking sideways at the thick, plastic frames that blocked her peripheral vision. They felt heavy and cumbersome, and she'd only been wearing them for two minutes.

When the anchors got to her story, she had to force her eyes forward to the teleprompter.

Larry: Moving on, now, to a story on numbers.

Alexa: Numbers and letters, to be exact. Stella Reynolds joins us live with all the details.

She was annoyed, and her voice came out sounding wooden as she read her line.

Stella: Sodium Chloride, or NaCl, is commonly called salt. Besides putting it on your food, the city also uses it to de-ice slick roads in the winter. This year, officials with the Bristol planning commission tell me they have an NaCl surplus, which is good news for the numbers-crunching budget department.

Roll: PKG

Stella blinked, not sure what she'd just said. She had attempted to write a "smart" story but might have only succeeded at losing viewers with some scientific-sounding garbage.

One glance at Alexa confirmed her suspicions.

She pushed the glasses up the bridge of her nose again and sighed. At least the day was almost over.

"Standby, Stella. Back to you in ten," Barry said into her earpiece.

She cleared her throat and pushed her shoulders back. When the light on top of her camera turned red, she was ready.

Stella: The city says they plan on storing the extra NaCl for now. Taxpayers will see the savings in next winter's budget. Reporting live, I'm Stella Reynolds, back to you.

Keith waved from the control room and gave her an exaggerated thumbs-up. She read his lips, "Looking smart, Stella."

Ten minutes later, she cranked up the music in her car, needing the distraction. She'd had about enough of this new job at this new station and wanted a break—but, of course, she wouldn't get one. When she got home, she'd have to think about explosions, investigations, and Lucky Haskins.

When she unlocked the door and walked inside, however, the apartment was empty. Maybe Lucky had left to find someone else more qualified to help—or maybe he was talking to police? There was no way to know, since he hadn't left a note, but she was glad to be alone. It was 6:45, and she couldn't even muster up the energy to order dinner. She took out her phone and tried John, but the call went right to voicemail. She knew he'd be getting ready to go on air in Montana but had just hoped to hear a friendly voice.

She sank down to the floor. There *were* no friendly voices here in Bristol—she was surrounded by mean, rude people. Anger flared inside, and she took the black glasses out of her bag and threw them toward the far windows. "I hate those glasses!" she yelled to her empty apartment before dropping her head into her hands. After a moment's contemplation, she muttered, "I hate Keith." She leaned over sideways until she rested against the couch. "I hate drunk witnesses. I hate when people don't answer the phone." She sat in silence for a minute and felt her eyes grow wet. To distract herself from crying—because really, it was so clichéd—she thought about what else she didn't like. "I hate the speedway. I hate NASCA—"

A knock at the door interrupted her musings, and she sniffed loudly and sat up. "Damn it, I am trying to have a moment here!" She heaved herself up off the floor and saw her pink, chenille robe lying over a chair. "I hate when I forget to put my stuff away," she grumbled, shrugging out of her suit jacket and pulling the robe around herself. The big apartment was drafty with the last of winter's chill permeating the room, and the soft fabric was comforting.

There was another knock. "All right, already, hold your damn horses." She shuffled over to the door and pulled it open. "Lucky?" He stood on the threshold like the lead singer of a rock band: dark wash jeans hugged all the right places; an orange hoodie lent his skin a healthy glow; and even a worn, green ball cap pulled low over his face proved to be the perfect contrasting color to highlight his chocolate-brown eyes. She looked down at her grungy robe and felt misdirected anger building toward the unusually handsome man. "So, you're back?" she asked accusingly.

The smile slid off his face as he took in Stella's appearance. "What's the matter, Bear?"

"Ugh, don't call me Bear, and nothing's *wrong*." Even as she said the words, though, a giant tear rolled down her face. She flicked it away. "I'm fine. Stop *looking* at me like that," she grumbled at his sympathetic eyes and felt another tear streak down her cheek.

Lucky tilted his head to the side and said, "Stella, you're even beautiful when you're crying."

They were the first kind words she'd heard all day—maybe since leaving Montana, come to think of it—and they unleashed a sadness Stella didn't even know had been building up inside. Her face crumbled. Lucky made to move toward her, but she held out a hand in warning. She was going to keep it together, goddammit! When she heard him make a sympathetic sound, however, the dam burst.

"I ha-ha-hate it here," she stuttered, loud sobs punctuating her words. She turned away from Lucky and walked into the apartment. After a few steps, she stopped and wailed, "I don't even own any tis-tis-tissues yet. This place is te-te-terrible..." she trailed off as sobs overtook her.

After a minute, she felt a handkerchief against her arm, and took it, annoyed. "Who carries a dumb handkerchief a-a-anymore?" she looked accusingly at Lucky while she cried, and he returned a small smile.

After another few minutes, he cleared his throat. "I feel like you need a hug."

She sniffed and nodded, and he stepped forward and folded her into a strong, warm embrace. After a minute, her stiff body relaxed against him, and she rested her cheek against his chest. "Why is everyone so m-m-mean here? What happened to southern hospi-hospi... oh, never mind."

By the time her tears dried up, she felt silly for breaking down in the first place. She started to pull away, but he squeezed her tight and said, "Stella, I was wrong before." She looked up at him, confused. "You're not beautiful when you cry —that was a hot dang mess, and it makes me like you even more."

He grinned, his eyes twinkling, and Stella smiled. She rubbed her nose with the handkerchief again and sucked in a deep, shaky breath. "I feel so dumb for having a meltdown over stupid work stuff when you have an actual crisis happening. Where were you, anyway?"

"Nope, not yet. What has you so down in the dumps?"

"It's nothing."

"Bear."

She wrinkled her nose, not wanting to relive any of that day, but after another minute of Lucky's unwavering stare, she filled him in on the terrible live shot from the night before and then the glasses fiasco.

Lucky whistled low when she'd finished. "I'm the first to admit I don't know anything about TV news, but wearing fake glasses doesn't really sound like you, you know? Did you have to do that kind of stuff in Montana, too?" She shook her head. "Then what changed when you moved here to Bristol?"

Stella considered his question. "I don't know. Things have felt off from the minute I first got to town and met with Keith. I've never had anyone so blatantly critique my looks or performance before, and I guess he's in my head."

"Stella—"

"Wait. Oh my God. *He's in my freaking head!* I didn't even realize what was happening. Keith keeps telling me I'm less-than, and I'm letting it be true!" She sucked in a loud breath. "I can't believe I've turned into one of *those* girls, just like that. One jerk and I'm questioning my every skill? What is wrong with me?" Lucky let out a low chuckle. "I mean, he's just so infuriating, that man—and for a boss! I've just never dealt with such overt sexism!"

She felt like she'd taken off someone *else's* ugly, plastic glasses and could finally see clearly. She may not have always looked picture-perfect, but she was a great reporter and Keith couldn't change that with snippy comments and critiques.

After a few minutes of watching her think, Lucky finally stepped back and held up a file folder. "Okay, *now* me. When I heard Star out there, asking about your lease this morning, I knew we'd need to make you official. She's like a dog with a bone —we haven't seen the last of her, that's for sure."

"Lucky," she groaned, "you can't go traipsing around town and not expect everyone to know you're alive. I think you *should* tell everyone what happened, but if you want to keep it a secret, you can't go out."

"I kept my hood up the whole time."

"So... you looked like Lucky Haskins wearing a hood—not exactly a disguise."

He shrugged and rubbed his chin. "I couldn't shave in the trailer. Now I think this beard growing in is a pretty good disguise, don't you?"

She squinted and looked at his face from all angles. Even with only a few days of growth, his beard *was* actually coming in fast. "Maybe," she said, still assessing his look. "You're usually so clean cut. This makes you look like a grizzly bear." He growled and she laughed. "Why is everyone I meet here crazy?" She signed the lease with the pen Lucky offered.

He picked Stella's cell phone up off the counter and tapped in a number.

"Yes, ma'am," he looked at Stella through narrowed eyes, "I'd like two number sevens, two orders of hot and sour soup, double egg rolls, and a gallon of sweet tea."

He hung up the phone. "Did you have plans?"

"You mean besides crying my eyes out and going to bed early?" She shrugged, "Nope, that about covered it for tonight."

"Well, then, let's brainstorm. I think Star wants to find the prenup we'd signed before we broke up."

"But why? You never got married, right?"

He shrugged. "She's not the brightest bulb, ya know? It divides my estate between her and Hap if I die."

"Hmm. If there was a prenup, there must have been a will. Is she in your will?"

"Nope—no will. Just hadn't gotten around to it yet."

Stella nodded slowly and then took a deep breath and closed her eyes, thinking. "Would a prenup even work if you never got married?"

"I'm not sure what the precedent is, but it would at least give her an angle to try in court."

"That'd be quite a windfall for her. She might think she just has to find the prenup and she'll get half of everything. She said you used to live here, so maybe she thinks you kept some paperwork here, too. How long ago did you break up?" She finally opened her eyes and found Lucky staring at her unabashedly.

"It happened about two months ago, but it hasn't been picked up by the press yet," he answered.

"That's unusual. How'd you guys keep it so quiet?"

"Well, honestly, I think she's embarrassed the full story might get out, so she's keeping quiet. I didn't want to tell anyone, either."

Stella tilted her head to the side. "Wait a minute. You said the two of you were growing apart, but is there something more?"

Lucky raised his eyebrows and smirked. "It involved chocolate sauce, handcuffs, and a stranger."

13

STAR TROUBLE

Stella narrowed her eyes. "I don't think I believe you."

"Believe it." He leaned against the counter. "I'd just gotten back from a training session a day early. When I walked in the house, I heard Star *moaning*." He grimaced. "I thought she was hurt, so I hightailed it to our room. When I walked in, she was naked, handcuffed to the bed, and calling for somebody named Wes to hurry up and get out of the bathroom. There was a bowl of melted chocolate on the nightstand. It was a pretty unreal scene to walk in on."

"Did you throw him out?"

He shook his head. "I didn't even see the guy. I was so disgusted that I walked out of the house and never went back."

"I'm really sorry, Lucky. That couldn't have been easy."

"Well, like I said, we'd been growing apart. I was on the verge of breaking up with her a few weeks before that but just couldn't get the timing right. I guess it all worked out in the end." He gazed over Stella's head, lost in thought.

Her finger tapped against her lips. Love gone awry; a potential financial windfall... Star sure looked like a prime suspect to her.

Lucky didn't want to hear it, though, so she cleared her throat and said, "Any luck getting in touch with Jim?"

Lucky pushed up from the counter and crossed his arms. "No —it's the darnedest thing. His phone is disconnected. I'm at a loss, really. Without Jim's help, I'm not sure what we should do."

"Well, *you* should probably go to the police." Stella looked at Lucky expectantly, while he looked back at her with a challenge in his eyes. "Hey," she said, suddenly remembering something from a few days ago. "Why don't you call the main anchor at my station? Larry Howard was just telling me he knows everyone in NASCAR—maybe he could help connect you with... What?"

"That old bag doesn't know anything about anything," he said, irritated. "He's always trying to get a hand in NASCAR business, and I don't even know how he got on the board in the first place. He has no history with NASCAR—no racing background. I just mounted a campaign to replace him. This is the last year of his last term." He nodded with satisfaction, but Stella was surprised.

"Do you have something against Larry?"

"I've never even met the guy, but we need NASCAR people on the board, not friends of NASCAR people. Larry is essentially a huge fan with friends in high places. That shouldn't be enough to be on the board that votes on rule changes and race schedules."

She shrugged; at least he'd put some thought behind his reasoning. They stared at each other for a few moments, the silence broken only when Stella's stomach rumbled.

The door buzzed and she signed the credit card receipt in the hallway, not wanting to take any chances that someone might see Lucky.

Mrs. Lanster opened her door and eyed the bags of food with interest. "Hungry tonight, Stella?"

She looked at the six takeout containers. "They, uhhh... they were having a special—buy one, get one."

The delivery guy scratched his head, and she shoved the

receipt into his hand before he could weigh in. "Thanks so much; have a great night." She'd added a ten-dollar tip to the order, and he noticed and grinned on his way to the elevator.

She nodded politely to Mrs. Lanster and took the food into her apartment, closing and locking the door behind her.

"What'd that old busybody want?" Lucky asked from the couch.

"Information," she said with a smile, "on how one girl can eat so much food."

They unloaded the tiny takeout cartons onto the coffee table, and Stella sat on the floor and pulled an egg roll out of the bag. Lucky tried to fold himself between the couch and coffee table, but he was all arms and legs and angles, so he gave up and eased back on the couch.

"I thought race car drivers were supposed to be short?"

"Some are. It's probably easier to be shorter, but you work with what you've got."

"Hmm."

"You *look* short on TV," Lucky shot back, expertly using his chopsticks to move rice from the container to his mouth.

"Everyone looks the same height on TV, you know that." Stella jabbed her chopsticks into her rice, only managing to move a single grain into her mouth. Lucky grinned. "Oh, shut up," she said, throwing the useless pieces of wood at him. "You've probably *been* to China to practice with chopsticks. Do they run NASCAR over there?

Lucky's grin widened. "No, but one of my sponsors does events in Japan all the time. It's a fun place to visit."

She picked up a fork. It was nice to have a normal conversation with someone, and she felt relieved to have her work problems out in the open. A moment later, her fork clanked down onto the coffee table.

"Stella, what is it?"

"Oh my gosh, I'm having one of those—those things, where there's a lightbulb and a great idea—"

"An epiphany?"

"Yes! An epiphany!" She sat up on her knees. "I'm going to go to Alabama with you, Lucky. I'm going to help you figure out what happened, and when we do, I'm going to interview you about it on live TV." She needed to prove to Keith—and herself—that she was more-than, not less-than, and if that meant having a huge, live, exclusive TV interview about Lucky's murder, then that's exactly what she was going to do. She would conquer her fear of live interviews, and she'd do it on a major story like Lucky's supposed death.

"Well, all right, Stella. That's my girl."

"We need a plan, though. You've *got* to get in touch with Jim. I'll work on a contact with the speedway in Alabama. Maybe we can figure things out at the track, but we're gonna need some help."

After a few bites, Stella glanced at her cell phone to check the time. She thought she might hear from John soon and hoped she wouldn't have to explain why a man was in her apartment, never mind that it was actually a famous national heartthrob who was now basically living with her, even though the world thought he was dead.

"You got a hot date tonight?" he asked, noticing her diverted attention.

"Not a *hot* date, but a *phone* date. Maybe," she added. John hadn't called in days. He'd sent a quick e-mail and text but hadn't even tried to call. She hid a grimace—or thought she did.

"That's not going too well, huh?" Lucky gestured to her phone with his chin.

"I don't know. It's weird. It's only been two weeks since I was there, but it already seems like..." Her face screwed up. "It just makes you wonder how it's all going to work out, you know?"

He smiled. "Well, I hope things *do* work out for you, Bear."

"Thanks."

They stared at each other for a beat before Lucky cleared his throat. "You know, 'working out' doesn't necessarily mean *he'll* stay in the picture."

"Ugh, don't ruin it, Lucky!"

He grinned, but not before a flash of emotion crossed his face. It might have been sorrow or maybe regret, but before she could analyze it, someone knocked on the door.

"Stella? It's Star. Can we talk?"

She and Lucky jumped up and collided in front of the coffee table. He looked at her expectantly and she panicked. "Uhh... okay, um, hold on!"

His eyes bugged out. "Okay?" he whispered. "She *cannot* come in here."

She slapped a hand over her mouth, racking her mind. "I'll-uh, I'll be out in a minute!" she called.

Lucky's fingers slid under the ties to her robe and pulled. She watched the fabric fall away, surprised to find she was still fully dressed underneath. She looked up at Lucky in time to see a wicked gleam in his eye. "Too bad," he muttered before handing her the lease papers they'd signed just that evening. He walked back to the bedroom with her robe and shut the door, and then she opened the front door and slipped out into the hallway.

"Let's sit down and talk, Stella." Star reached for the door-knob. In a panic, Stella chopped her hand down and got to it first. Lucky's ex blinked in surprise at the aggressive move, and Stella smiled sheepishly.

"I'm sorry, Star, I'm just not ready for visitors today. I—I just moved in and the place is still a wreck. We'll have to talk out here." She held out the paper. "Here, I have the lease agreement, if it makes you feel better."

"Is this your only copy?" Star took the paper and scanned it from top to bottom.

"No, I can—uh, I can get another," Stella grinned at how true that was.

Star handed it back with a flourish. "Everything seems to be in order." She looked hungrily at the door but didn't move. "Well, I'm headed to Alabama tomorrow—I want to be there for the investigation. I'm sure you can understand how I'm feeling." Lucky's ex made a show of taking a tissue out of her purse and dabbing at her eyes.

"I can't even imagine." How *would* she feel if she got caught cheating on her fiancé who then died several weeks later? "Guilty, probably," she said aloud, "and sad."

Star's eyes narrowed, and Stella felt like smacking herself. No one was supposed to know about the breakup! Stella scrambled for the right words. "Guilty, you know, that you couldn't have saved him, somehow, and sad because he's gone."

The other woman's eyes took on a faraway look. "Yes, that's exactly right."

"Well, it's getting late. You have a safe trip, Star." Stella opened the door and Star gasped. She scanned the sliver of the main room that was visible, trying to see what she'd found so shocking. Her eyes finally landed on Lucky's worn, green ball cap sitting on the futon. "See, I'm a terrible slob," she said, thinking quickly. "My brother's hat, takeout cartons littering the table—it's hardly fit for *me* to be in there." Star's mouth hung open, and Stella backed into her apartment. "Well, goodnight."

The last thing she saw was Star's shocked expression turning to confusion as the door closed.

A few minutes later, she and Lucky watched Star leave building and look up at them. A protective coating on the windows made it impossible to see inside from the street, but they still jumped back when her head swiveled up. Stella giggled at their dramatic reaction. The sound made Lucky chuckle, and they both relaxed a bit. Star pressed her cell phone to her ear, and a minute later, a black SUV pulled up and she got into the passenger seat and rode away.

"It sounds like we'll get to see her again soon," she said, remembering she, too, was heading to the track in Alabama.

"We'll see," Lucky said, rubbing his face. "We'll see."

14

CHECKMATE

L ucky took Stella's advice and stayed inside her apartment over the next few days. He didn't have much to do, though, except call the few numbers he had for Jim, and he grew temperamental in his self-imposed isolation. Increasingly melancholy over Hap's death, frustrated at his inability to get in touch with Jim, and angry that he wasn't solving the crime in Alabama, he was also over-the-top flirty with the only person he *could* interact with. Stella spent half her time worried about him and the other half locked in her room, away from his distracting sex appeal.

In the meantime, she was unsettled at work. Twice on the job, she felt like something was off, but she couldn't figure out what. She tried to stay busy to keep her mind off of things, and after work she made a couple runs to Goodwill to beef up Lucky's wardrobe.

Through it all, Stella pitched mundane stories to Marty every morning and covered boring city hall meetings by day and "smart" live shots at night—as if the biggest story of the decade wasn't sitting in her living room!

By Thursday afternoon, she was spent. Sitting across from

Billy Joe in the live truck, she wrapped a scarf around her neck with a shiver. "Can we turn the heat on? I'm freezing."

Billy Joe shook his head. "The carbon monoxide detector keeps going off, so we need to keep the truck off as long as we can. Go do some jumping jacks or something."

A generator powered the editing equipment in the live truck, and occasionally, if they left the truck motor running too long, fumes seeped back into the truck. It wasn't usually a problem, but today, for whatever reason, the detector in the truck kept sounding an alarm.

Billy Joe had been cranky with Stella all afternoon, and she found herself pining for her days in Montana when she almost always worked alone. Back then, she'd thought working with a photographer would be amazing. It turned out having a group project every single day was exhausting.

The two-way radio mounted on the dash came to life. "Base to Live One—call into the station ASAP."

"You got any bars?" she asked.

He held up his phone. "None. You?"

She looked at her phone. "One bar. I'll try." She climbed out of the truck, pulled her hat down over her ears, and when she got about ten feet away, another bar appeared on her phone. She stood still and dialed the newsroom number.

"News," a man's voice barked.

"Hey, it's Stella. Someone asked us to call in."

"We've got snow in Bristol. Need you to hustle back and go live on the weather at the top of the five."

"But we've got our story on the budget meeting all ready to go!" She and Billy Joe had been in Johnson City all day working on the story.

"It's snow, Stella, snow! We're doing team coverage starting with you live in Bristol. The budget story will run later in the newscast."

He hung up and Stella turned back to the live truck. "Shut it down," she called. "We're heading to Bristol." She looked at the time; they had forty-two minutes to tear down, drive thirty miles to Bristol, and then set up and go live. It was going to be tight.

"What am I supposed to talk about?" she asked Billy Joe as they drove. "We won't have any time to get video of anything—no time to get sound from anyone." Go live about the fact that it was snowing? In Montana, where it snowed more than seven feet every winter, they mentioned snowfall in the ski report at the end of the weather block.

Now it was flurrying in Bristol and weather was going to lead the newscast.

She shot Billy Joe a dirty look as he took a turn too fast.

"What? You're buckled up."

"Just be careful," she grumbled, wiping the lipstick off the side of her face where it had smeared. She swiped some on her lips on the second attempt, and then applied mascara and blush.

They didn't see any snow until they got off the interstate near Bristol. There, the ground was covered by a light blanket of white. Grass and early spring flowers poked through in glorious, brightly colored contrast, and big, fat flakes drifted lazily through the air.

Stella picked up the two-way microphone and called in. "Live One to base. We're still about five away," she warned.

"Do your best," Samantha's voice replied through the radio.

She and Billy Joe exchanged looks. "That means get your ass live by five or don't come back," he quipped.

She snickered. Samantha was the picture of calm authority, but she didn't suffer excuses.

Billy Joe parked the live truck at his favorite spot that overlooked the valley below but which also had a nice view of a gas station, hardware store, and grocery store, depending on which way you turned the camera. As soon as he threw the van into park, he and Stella swung into action.

She jumped out of her seat and threw open the doors to the

passenger area. Billy Joe already had his cell phone pressed to his ear as he rounded the side of the truck toward her. "This is Live One. I need engineering now."

While he tuned in the shot, Stella flung open the back of the van and pulled out a coil of cable. She grabbed the end of the line and unspooled it to a spot that looked good for their live shot. The mast rose up from the vehicle, its giant antenna connecting them to the station via a microwave link. She then went back for the microphone cord and her IFB box, plugged in her IFB, and pressed the tiny earpiece into her ear.

"Mic check, please, Stella."

"How much time do you have me down for, Samantha?"

"Mic sounds good, Stella," Samantha replied. "Just fill thirty seconds. Standby, show open in ten. You're off the top."

If she looked past Billy Joe, she could just see what he was shooting through a monitor inside the live truck. The double doors to the van were wide open, and she watched him zoom in on her nose to focus the shot and then zoom back out to a wide shot that included the snow.

The newscast music played in her ear, and she cleared her throat, still not entirely sure what she was going to say.

Larry: Good evening, everyone. I'm Larry Howard.

Alexa: And I'm Alexa Robinson. Snow tonight across much of the Tri-Cities. If you don't see it out your widow yet, just wait a few minutes.

Larry: We'll check in with Brian Tilley in Storm Center 2 in just a moment, but first, a look outside with our very own Stella Reynolds. Stella, what have you seen out there tonight?

She ignored the fluttering of panic in her stomach. "Good

evening, Larry and Alexa. Most people here in the Tennessee Valley probably thought they were done with snow for the season, but tonight, a fluffy, white surprise."

She gestured to the store below. "Just in the last few minutes, we've seen cars lining up at this gas station, everyone wanting to fill up *just in case* the weather gets any worse." A line of cars wrapped around the pumps and into the street, brake lights making pretty colors in the snowfall.

She was off-camera now, and Billy Joe panned left to the hardware store.

"And if you don't have your snow shovel and didn't think you'd need one until next winter, you're in luck. It looks like this Ace Hardware store in Bristol is having a half-off sale on all winter supplies. Now might be the perfect time to stock up."

Samantha said, "Wrap," in her ear.

Without a break or bobble, Stella said, "So, the big question on everyone's mind is how much snow are we going to get? Will you need that shovel, or can you get by without it? For an answer to those questions, I'll send it back to the studio. Reporting live, I'm Stella Reynolds."

"You're clear, Stella. Great job," Samantha said through the IFB.

Stella and Billy Joe leaned into the truck to watch Brian's weather forecast in the playback monitor. When he said they'd only get a dusting of snow before the weather warmed significantly over the next few days, Stella groaned.

"Warmer tomorrow? That was worth a live shot about the snow?"

"Every damn time," Billy Joe said, "and you know the crazy thing? People want to watch it! If it's snowing, they absolutely want that to be the top news story of the day." He recoiled cables and then stowed away the tripod and camera.

Stella climbed in the passenger seat and rolled the tension out of her neck while fanning her face. It was cold outside, but the stress of that last-minute live shot had warmed her considerably. They were live several times throughout the evening newscasts, and then it took twice as long to repack the live truck as it had to set up the live shot. It was 6:32 by the time they were ready to go.

When Billy Joe started up the truck, Stella took her out her cell phone.

She had one missed call. John had finally made time in his schedule to talk.

IT WASN'T until she unlocked her apartment that she got him on the phone. "Hey, it's me," she said and then froze. Lucky's half-naked body pulsed down to the floor and then back up. Sweat glistened on his bare back, and all his muscles worked together for a set of pushups.

"Hello?" John's irritated voice finally broke through her mind.

"I'm sorry, John, I was distracted." She turned away from Lucky and set her bag down on the couch.

"No kidding," he said dryly.

She stared at the phone in disbelief. Really? He took five days to call her back and then acted irritated? A silence stretched between them that neither could seem to break.

Eventually, John blew out a loud breath. "Stella, this isn't working."

Her stomach dropped out of her body. "I know," she said, hating to agree but not wanting to lie.

"I know?" he repeated, upset. "That's all you have to say?"

Stella's irritation flared as quickly as John's. "Yes, *I know*! You've been acting strange since before I even left Montana, and I know that *this*," she emphasized the word angrily, "obviously isn't working. Half the time, you don't call me back, and when you do, we have nothing to talk about!"

"Nothing to talk about because you don't even pay attention to what I say! It's not worth saying anything!"

"John, I'm sorry I wasn't sitting on the couch, waiting for you to call, but that's proven to be a waste of my time, since you hardly ever care to pick up the phone. I've only been gone for two weeks, but it feels like we haven't seen each other for two *years*!"

"Between the time zone change, the different hours we work, and the physical distance between us, there's no time to call! When I get off work *here*, it's one in the morning *there*. When are we supposed to talk?"

Stella took a deep breath and lowered her voice. "I don't know, John." Her anger subsided and exhaustion took over. "I honestly don't know."

Another silence stretched between them, and Stella became acutely aware that Lucky had finished his workout and now leaned against the counter, watching her, while he drank water. She turned to face the wall, not wanting her relationship drama on display.

"Listen, John, I—"

"I can't, Stella. I can't dissect our relationship right now. They're calling for mic checks."

She sighed. Of course they were. "Okay, John, let's talk—"

"Let's have the we're-breaking-up conversation later," he interrupted hotly.

She took another deep, cleansing breath, and was ready to forgive his abrupt, rude tone so they could talk later after they'd both calmed down. In the background, however, she heard that dumb college intern, Katie, her voice breathy and sympathetic, "Oh, John, it's going to be all right." Something inside Stella snapped.

"Oh, I think there's enough time to say this," Stella's tone matched his. "We're done—it's over. Goodbye!"

"Goodbye!" he shouted back.

She pressed a button on her phone to disconnect the call and then stalked to her room and slammed the door, avoiding Lucky's stare as she went. There was no privacy anywhere in her life. She was under a microscope at work and had a hot, sweaty man taking up real estate in her apartment every minute she was at home—and her *ex*-boyfriend couldn't even clear five minutes of his schedule to properly end the relationship!

She ripped off her work clothes and pulled on her robe before rolling her shoulders to try to release the tension. It didn't work, but maybe a hot shower would. She tied her hair into a knot on top of her head and headed back out to the main room.

Lucky leaned against the counter in the kitchen, and when she saw him, inspiration struck.

"We're going to Alabama *tomorrow!*" He looked at her over his glass of water but remained silent. "Screw having a plan. I'll pitch it to my boss in the morning and we'll leave at nightfall."

He set the glass down on the counter and tilted his head, his eyes never leaving Stella's face. "Are you sure?" he asked. "Do you want to think about it at all?"

"No," she snapped, "I don't want to think about it. I want to leave Bristol and *do* something. Why not solve a murder and make sure a killer is held accountable?"

Lucky nodded slowly, resolve filling his face. "Yes," he said. "Tomorrow we'll get answers." He took another drink of water, grabbed a towel off the counter, and rubbed the sweat off his head.

Stella licked her lips. Her emotions were all jumbled up from the fight with John, and staring at a half-naked man had turned her passionate anger into something else entirely.

He noticed her stare and took a few slow, deliberate steps toward her. When she didn't back away, he closed the distance. "Bear, you're going to be all right."

"I know," she breathed, her anger dissipating as quickly as it had flared up.

He reached out and gave her arms a gentle squeeze. "Whoever that man is, he's crazy. I'd move mountains to be with you, and he's letting mountains get in the way."

She shrugged out of his hold. "I don't want to talk about it." After stepping around Lucky to the kitchen, she picked his shirt up off the counter and threw it at him. "Put some clothes on; you're driving me crazy."

"I think I like that," he said, but he pulled the fabric over his head before he cornered her in the kitchen. With one hand resting on either side of her against the counter, he leaned in close. "We're adults—we can have fun and not feel guilty at the end of the day, Stella." She gulped and he nuzzled her neck; his whiskery face left a trail of goosebumps across her skin. "Just think about it." His teeth raked across her earlobe, and she was surprised to hear herself moan. Their eyes locked and he leaned back. "Your move, Stella."

15

YOUR MOVE

Her stomach clenched and she took a shaky breath as a charge of electricity zapped through her body.

"My move?" Lucky nodded, his eyes burning through the pink, fluffy material of her robe. She bit her lip. "I think I'm going to *move* to the bathroom—alone." She turned slowly and walked into the bathroom, shut the door, and turned on the shower. As she fanned herself with one hand, she considered getting under the spray of water while it was still ice-cold.

"Ho-lee shit," she muttered, picturing Lucky's face as he watched her close the door. His look had been pure desire. She knew what she *wanted* to do, but she didn't want to get caught up in the moment. She'd just broken up with her boyfriend, after all —she should have taken a minute to process that.

Steam filled the bathroom, and under the steady stream of water, her shoulders relaxed and her face smoothed out. Yes, she and John had just broken up, but it wasn't *really* something that happened five minutes ago—it had been in the works since the week before she left Montana. Things had gotten awkward as soon as she'd accepted a job on the other side of the country, and she couldn't really blame John for that.

She lathered her hair and rinsed out the bubbles before rubbing in the conditioner. She kept her mind homed in on the task at hand; her fingers pressed firmly into her scalp, her mind focused only on the feeling of the water streaming down her body.

She rinsed out the conditioner. "Oh, screw it," she said softly, pulling the shower curtain aside. "Lucky!"

"Thank God." He must have been standing with his hand on the doorknob—that's how fast he was in the bathroom.

Stella laughed and watched him peel off his clothes and step into the shower, gloriously naked. He soaped up, rinsed off, and then turned off the water and wrapped Stella in a towel. "Not in the shower?" she asked.

He shook his head. "Too slippery. No traction."

His words, combined with his scorching hot look, sent a shiver of excitement down her spine. He scooped her up and carried her out of the bathroom, and then set her down on the bedroom floor. Rivers of water trickled down his shoulders and arms.

He looked her up and down. "Do you think—"

"I don't want to *think,* Lucky." He opened his mouth again, but she spoke first, "And I don't want to talk."

That was all he needed. He reached out and loosened the towel, and heat zinged through her body. He slowly pulled the flowery print apart and smiled a slow, sexy smile. As he let go of the fabric, she shivered when it dropped down her body and pooled around her feet.

He stared at her appreciatively and then shrugged off his own towel before closing the distance between them again. Stella wrapped her arms around him as he slowly lowered her onto the mattress, his mouth devouring hers. He moved down her body, his lips, teeth, and tongue grazing her sensitive skin.

She knew this was crazy—as reckless and unpredictable as she'd ever been—but at that moment, she needed him. She needed this. All of her stress and fear and anguish from the last week poured out of her with every touch, and she moaned as they moved together, perfectly in sync. She cried out moments before him, and afterward, they lay together, panting.

"So, did I just... get Lucky?" Stella asked with a smirk.

Lucky pried one eye open and studied her face. "No," he finally said, "I think I did." He pulled her close so she was wrapped completely in his arms.

Her mind slowly awoke to her new situation, and her body stiffened. What happened next? She felt guilty that she didn't feel guilty. Why—

"Stop," Lucky commanded, dancing his fingers up her arm and over her back. He lazily drew circles over her body. "No thinking tonight, remember? Or talking."

She nodded and tried to relax back into him; he helped with well-placed and distracting touches and kisses. They made love again, this time without the frantic pace from before; it was just slow, steady passion building between them.

Finally, sheer exhaustion, combined with Lucky's steady breathing and warm body, lulled her into a deep sleep.

HOURS LATER, she opened one eye and looked at the clock: 6:42 a.m. Lucky's arm rested heavily over her chest, and when she moved, he pulled her in closer, nuzzling her neck with his whiskery face. She let out a satisfied purr, and his hands started roaming.

They spent far too long waking up, and Stella was rushed and running late when she finally got out of the shower. She tore through the apartment, putting her earrings in while she stepped into her heels.

"Slow down, Bear, you're making me dizzy."

"I'm going to be late! I can't be late!" She buttoned her shirt up and shoved her arms into her blazer—not a good idea. She stumbled when her heel caught on the edge of the rug with her arm stuck halfway in the jacket sleeve.

"Got ya." He gripped her around the waist and hauled her upright.

She took a deep breath and got her balance back before shouting, "I'm late! The last reporter in today has to cover the city commission meeting—so boring!" With a half-smile on her face, she pecked Lucky on the cheek and said, "I'm going to pitch to my boss this morning and we'll leave tonight. Don't leave the apartment!"

She barely saw him nod before she was in the hallway and running for the elevator. By the time she got to the sidewalk, a trickle of sweat ran down her back. The overcast sky was dark, clouds rolled in from the north, and the air felt oddly sticky for March. She was glad she'd grabbed her raincoat on the way out the door. She piled her hair on top of her head, secured it with a hair tie, and threw her bag into her car. The contents spilled everywhere, and she groaned first at the mess and then at what was missing: her wallet! It wasn't in the pile of junk now covering the floor boards—she must have left it upstairs. With another glance at her watch, she spun around toward the building and ran headlong into Lucky.

He grabbed her for a second time that morning to keep her upright.

She was out of breath and panted out, "I forgot my wallet," just as he said, "You forgot your wallet."

"What on Earth are you wearing?" she asked, stifling a laugh.

"This?" He tugged at the coat she'd found at the secondhand shop the night before. "Hey, you're the one who bought it." The jacket was clearly from the seventies and had a collar that would have made John Travolta in *Saturday Night Fever* jealous.

"It looked different on the hanger," she laughed. "Well, it's a good disguise, don't you think?"

He tightened his hold around her waist, and Stella felt an unexpected pull in her stomach at his touch. They locked eyes and her cheeks flushed as she thought about their night—and their morning.

She shrugged out of his hold. "I have to go and you have to get inside!" her eyes darted around the sidewalk. No one was close, but people were out and heading to work.

Lucky raised his hand and rested it against her cheek for a moment. He then nodded and pushed the wallet into her hands. His eyes never left her face, and she smiled. "See you tonight, Bear." He moved backward down the sidewalk, watching her until she drove away.

16

WORTH A THOUSAND WORDS

S he walked into the newsroom at ten minutes to nine and shook raindrops off her jacket. The clouds had opened up on her drive over, and the parking lot looked like a lake.

Joan rushed in five minutes later, and Stella stifled a celebratory yell over being saved from covering the city commission meeting! The day before, she'd set up a story with the Bristol Hunger Alliance. They were getting a huge shipment of food from a farm share that went out of business, and she was scheduled to get video of volunteers unloading the haul. She wanted to turn in one last good story before she and Lucky left for Alabama that night.

This was going to be a good day—she could feel it. The tides were turning.

She and Elbee were slated to work together, but not until later that afternoon. She had the morning free, so she decided to make some calls to the track in Talladega. She may have *said* "screw the plan" the day before, but the truth was that she really liked having a plan. A little reconnaissance before she and Lucky headed south couldn't hurt, after all.

While she was on hold with the track in Alabama, Keith

walked by the open newsroom door. "Stella, no glasses today?" he barked.

"Keith," she said, standing up, "it was a really unique idea, but I'm not going to wear them—it's too distracting. I'll keep working hard to get the best story out there for our viewers, though." She stared down at him—in her heels, she had a three-inch height advantage—and after a moment, he nodded and kept walking down the hall.

She smiled. Part one of her plan seemed to be working: be polite but firm and don't apologize. Check. Mistakes happened all the time on live TV; unless she blurted out a swear word, there was no reason for *her* to apologize.

A voice on the line interrupted her thoughts. "There's no update today, sorry."

"Is this Robbie Steemer?"

"Yes, and no update," he said.

"Well, I actually have a few questions for you?" She ducked her head. Why did she have to make everything sound like a question?

"Let's see..." Papers shuffled on the other end. "I've been dealing with Candice Cayne from your station. Are you taking over?"

Stella grimaced, hating to lie but feeling like she had no choice. "Um, I have an interview lined up with Jim Cruisner at the track this weekend and wanted to make sure I was up to speed on where the investigation stands."

"You have Jim Cruisner? How did you get *him*?" Robbie asked incredulously.

"Um, what do you mean?" she asked, trying to avoid his question.

"Well, it's just that we can't get ahold of him. He's been completely incommunicado since the crash. No one even knows where he is or how to reach him, but you got to him from Bristol?" She heard the doubt in his voice, and it made her feel prickly.

"Well, I have my sources, and they're good," she said smoothly.

"Wow. Well, it's not news that the investigation is stalling out. There's not a lot of information available. We'll be ready to release an official statement probably tomorrow. Come straight to my office when you get here this weekend, Stella, and I'll give you the latest."

She disconnected and then scanned the newsroom, looking for Marty.

He hung up the phone. "What is it Stella—want to switch stories with Joan?"

"Uh, no—no, I'm good, thanks. I wanted to talk to you about a story idea for this weekend."

"Sure. I can pass it on to the weekend crew."

"No, I mean a story for me to do this weekend."

"No can do, Stella. Keith has a hold on overtime for now." He tilted his head back so he could look through his reading glasses at the screen in front of him, and then he punched in a few more keystrokes.

"Well, I have a line on Jim Cruisner—an exclusive—but he'll only talk to me, and only in Alabama. I thought I'd drive there tonight after work, lay the groundwork, and then I was hoping you'd send out a photographer tomorrow."

Marty swiveled around in his chair to look at her. "You got Jim Cruisner?"

"Uh huh."

"In Alabama?"

"Yup."

Marty's eyes narrowed, but she didn't waver. He finally blew out a breath and said, "Let me talk to Keith. I'm not sure how we can pass this one up. I'll get back to you this afternoon."

~

AT THE FOOD PANTRY, she ran into Scott Lyon again. He seemed jumpy, but after a few minutes of chatting about Ohio State football, he warmed right up. The food storage room was small, and after Scott got video for his station, she walked outside with him so Elbee could move around the room more comfortably.

"Everything all right with you, Stella?" Scott asked when they were alone outside.

She looked at him sideways. She'd been sitting on the story that Lucky was alive for so long that, every once in a while, she thought she might burst. This was one of those times.

"Things have been a little crazy." He looked at her with a friendly smile and she balked. "I mean, you know, new jobs can be stressful."

"Oh yeah?" He fiddled with his camera, and it seemed like he was just being polite.

"Sometimes you run across a story that's bigger than you—do you know what I mean?—but then you're new to town and you don't even feel like you can trust your own bosses not to screw it up." He was still zoned out, not even paying attention, so she muttered, "Like, is an accident just an accident, or something darker—something criminal..."

Scott jerked to attention and grabbed his phone. "That's for me. Gotta roll. See ya, Stella."

He pressed the phone to his ear and headed to his car. It's funny—she hadn't even heard it ring, she'd been so caught up in her own thoughts. She blew out a breath, frustrated that she'd almost discussed her top secret exclusive with the competition. "Lock it down, girl," she said firmly.

When she and Elbee got back to the station, Stella didn't have time to wonder why it was so quiet. She walked straight into an editing suite to log her interviews, calling to Marty before she started.

"This is gonna be a good one. The farmers we interviewed were just amazing—"

Marty held up a hand. "Keith wants to see you. A picture's been making the rounds online, and it sure looks like it's you and Lucky Haskins."

17

ANCHORS AWAY

S tella's face scrunched up and the early flutters of panic gripped her stomach. "Huh?"

"Let's go. We'll talk about it in his office."

She left the editing bay and followed Marty down the hall. "Marty, what kind of—"

"I'm going to let Keith take this one, Stella."

She shrugged impatiently. There weren't any pictures of her and Lucky. What was Marty talking about?

"Stella," Keith called, and it looked like he'd been waiting for her. He was perched at the edge of his desk, his face calm but curious. His computer screen faced her as she walked through the door, and her eyes were immediately drawn to a picture of her and Lucky blown up full on his screen. She stared at herself with growing alarm.

HASKINS BACK FROM THE DEAD TO WOO UNKNOWN WOMAN! the headline announced in boldface caps. Her mind raced as she tried to come up with an explanation.

"Is this you?" Keith asked.

Her eyes locked on the picture again. It was from that very morning, out by her car. Her image was crisp, her auburn hair shining in the morning sunlight, and Lucky's hand cupped her cheek. With his hood up and the collar of his coat blocking his beard, it could have been taken anytime over the last two weeks.

"What is this?" she asked, buying time.

She had to pick her path in the next few seconds—the lid was about to blow off of this story, and she could be at the front and center or left behind. If they handled this right and sat on the news that Lucky was alive for another day or two, they'd have an even bigger exclusive. If Stella and Lucky could have a couple of days to work in Alabama, they just might solve a murder no one even knew about yet. So, the big question was did she trust her boss?

"It's the NAZZY website." At her blank stare, he elaborated, "The NASCAR gossip website. So, I want to know: is this you?" Keith had a devious gleam in his eye as he stared back at Stella.

She had her answer. "Yes, of course that's me," she said decisively.

"Who are you with?" Keith jumped off his desk; the illusion of calm was gone in an instant. "When was this taken?" He looked her up and down. She wished she wasn't wearing the exact same thing in his office as in the picture online.

"It must have been... hmm," she said as casually as she could muster. "I guess it was last week, when Lucky gave me the keys to my apartment. He's my landlord." Marty's eyes narrowed. "Was," she quickly corrected herself. "He *was* my landlord."

"You're wearing the same clothes, and the article says this picture was taken today," Keith said with confidence.

"I make twenty-thousand dollars a year, Keith; my work wardrobe is pretty limited." She looked at him steadily.

"Why didn't you tell anyone how well you knew Lucky when he died?" Keith said angrily. "We could have featured you on the news that night! It would have added a missing layer to our coverage of the explosion."

"Well, I mean... I didn't really know him that well. Big Bob probably knew him better."

He glared at her. "This is a small gossip website, but it might get picked up by the bigger players. This is something *Time* or *People* might jump on."

"Well, I'm so glad we got it figured out before anyone went crazy. Sorry for the confusion, Keith. There'll always be conspiracy theorists making claims, right? This is probably the first of hundreds. I mean, look at Elvis; people still say they see him all over the world." Stella looked at her watch. "Listen, I have a lot to get done for the five. Clock's ticking..."

Keith grunted, and she walked calmly out of his office, past Cam, and into the hallway.

She ducked into the restroom and sagged against the wall. Who took that picture? It wasn't taken with a cheap drugstore camera—it was a crisp, exact, bright photograph taken with a pricey, long-range lens. That moment between her and Lucky hadn't been caught by chance. Someone had specialized equipment ready and waiting. The thought was chilling.

She took a deep breath, pushed off the wall, and headed back into the hall. She really was on a tight deadline and didn't have time to spend on the mystery of the picture. She had two stories to write for the news before she could get home and discuss the situation with Lucky, so she picked up her pace, her footsteps striking the ground in time with her elevated heartbeat.

"Stella!" Marty called down the hallway.

She dropped her head in defeat. Maybe she hadn't been as convincing as she'd hoped. She turned to face the music when Marty surprised her again.

He walked close and leaned in. "You can trust me, Stella. If something's going on, I just want you to know I'm here to help." She stared back at him, not sure what to say. "Keith wants you to anchor the five o'clock news tonight," he said, turning away from her and strolling down the hallway.

She squinted at his retreating figure, immediately suspicious. When he didn't say anything else, she said, "Why would Keith have *me* anchor the five o'clock—"

"As soon as you finish your story, start reading over scripts," he called over his shoulder. Stella continued to stare after him, slack-jawed. After a few steps, he turned back around. "Oh, and the trip to Alabama is approved! We'll send Billy Joe up Saturday with the satellite truck to shoot video for the story. Elbee will follow Sunday for the live shot."

She nodded, still feeling slightly suspicious of Keith's offer but also overwhelmed with information. Anchoring, a special trip for an unknown-to-management murder investigation, and an exclusive interview with Jim Cruisner that she hadn't actually set up yet—there was quite a lot going on for week two on the job.

She walked slowly back into the tiny editing room and plopped down on the chair. Where was Alexa? Why would they have Stella fill in, instead of one of the more senior reporters? She caught a glimpse of herself in the black monitor in front of her and sucked in a sharp breath. Why did she look like crap?

It had rained all afternoon on her shoot with Elbee, and now her hair was a frizzy mess and her makeup was smudged and awful.

It was 3:32 in the afternoon. She'd already shot a story and staved off an inquiry into her personal life. With just under ninety minutes until the newscast started, she still had to write her story and get ready to anchor for the first time in her life. It was going to be a busy hour and a half.

Miraculously, the story practically wrote itself, and Stella found herself standing in the makeup room next to the studio with about twenty minutes until air—plenty of time to fix... everything.

The room was about fifteen square feet with long counters running the length of two of the walls and serving as a vanity tabletop. Bulb lights lining giant mirrors stretched the length of the room, and a wall plug was available every three feet. Stella waited for her flat iron to warm up when Alexa walked in.

"Are you back to anchor? To be honest, I'm kind of relieved." Stella smiled at the station's main anchor. They didn't know each other well, but she seemed friendly enough.

"No," Alexa said, "you're still doing the five. I needed some extra time for a story I'm working on, and Keith said you could fill in today." Her eyes met Stella's in the mirror, and Stella couldn't quite read the other woman's expression.

She shook off a feeling of unease. "Do you think he's going to insist on those glasses? Honestly, I'm going to throw them away and say I lost them..." her smile faded. "Are you okay?" she asked, picking up a makeup brush and dusting on some powder.

Alexa nodded through the mirror. "Here, let me help you with your hair. There will be lots of people watching tonight." Again, her words were normal, but her tone seemed forced. Stella's brow wrinkled as Alexa picked up the flat iron and got to work taming her tresses. Soon, her hair was glossy and smooth. Stella finished touching up her makeup, and before long, she felt ready to go.

"Well, you have fun out there. You're going to do great!"

Stella smiled. "Thanks, Alexa. Fingers crossed!"

She left Alexa alone in the makeup room and pushed open the studio doors, her stomach fluttering with nervous excitement. The studio was dimly lit, and as Stella walked in, the spotlights came up on the anchor desk and at the weather center.

She shuffled through the stack of papers at the desk, making some last-minute marks on the scripts to help her remember pacing when it was time to read them aloud.

A pedal on the floor alerted her to the fact that something was different about this studio than the one she'd most recently worked in, and she looked up and searched the room until she saw a man wearing a headset. "What is this?" she asked warily, pointing at the floor.

He walked over and looked down at her feet. "Oh, those are the teleprompter controls. You press down to make the prompter move forward. You and Larry both have one."

Stella's eyes widened at this late-breaking news. She'd be controlling her own teleprompter? It wasn't really a big deal, but at five minutes to air, she wished she'd had time to practice. She sighed. Ah, well, no better way to learn than on the job, right?

Soon, Larry walked in and gave her a broad smile. They hadn't really talked since the night of the explosion; Larry worked nightside and usually started his day when Stella was out on a live shot. She was gone by the time he broke for dinner.

"Stella Reynolds," he said, as if he was announcing her presence on screen, "welcome to the studio!"

Stella smiled, in spite of herself. "Thanks, Larry. What a surprise to be here!" She felt a flutter of nerves hit her again, and she gave herself a little pep talk. *Just like doing a live shot, only it lasts a little bit longer. No big deal.*

Her breathing picked up, though, and all of a sudden, she wished she had a sleeveless shirt on under her suit jacket. Was it hot in here? She glanced around the room and saw the floor director wrap his hands around a steaming hot mug of something. *Hmm. Must just be me.*

Samantha spoke into their earpieces and asked for mic checks. Stella took hers off a hook under the desk and clipped it onto her jacket. She and Larry then both spoke a few words so the director could adjust their audio levels.

"Standby, Stella, Larry. Show open in twenty seconds."

"Ready, kid? There'll be lots of people watching tonight. Let's hit this one out of the park!"

The studio was quiet with her beating heart the only sound. A red light illuminated on top of Stella's camera, and she started talking.

18

WHO'S THERE?

She wished she could say with certainty she did a great job, but she honestly couldn't remember much of what happened after the newscast started.

She didn't remember making any glaring mistakes, and she and Larry had some fun banter over a story about a lottery winner's plan to spend everything in one year. Beyond that, however, it was kind of a well-lit blur of pressing the teleprompter pedal and sitting through commercial breaks.

Alexa took her place during the final commercial. They had one minute and thirty seconds to switch seats and exchange microphones. "Great job tonight. Just your live shot for the six, and you can head home."

It was a funny thing to say, and Stella gave her an uncertain smile as she headed out of the studio and up to the newsroom. When she walked to her desk, she again felt an unusual quiet around her, but this time it was more pronounced. There had been a normal amount of noise right up until she stepped into the room and then people fell silent. When she looked around, she noticed everyone studiously ignoring her.

She sat down and worked on her script for a while, trying to ignore the odd silence around her. Finally, she picked up her phone. She hated to dial the numbers but knew she'd quickly get to the bottom of things.

"Cam, is there something I need to know?"

"Well, honey, everyone's talking about the picture. NAZZY updated their story. I could just tell you, but you'd better see for yourself."

Stella wrinkled her nose. An update? She dutifully punched in the address. After a minute delay while the pictures loaded, the website finally came up full. She stared at the screen in shock and finally muttered, "Good God."

The same picture graced the homepage, but the headline had changed. Now it read, **SMALL TOWN REPORTER STELLA REYNOLDS HARBORS HASKINS.** Her mouth hung open as she studied the pictures that went with the article. In clear, crisp color was her car's license plate and the sign to her building behind Lucky—basically, her whole life was on display for the world to see. That wasn't the worst part, though. Somehow, the website had gotten ahold of her press badge ID picture, and it was captivatingly terrible.

She scrolled down the page and read the article that accompanied the picture.

Sources have confirmed small town TV reporter Stella Reynolds is the woman pictured here with NASCAR legend Lucky Haskins outside her apartment at 3- - - State Street earlier this morning. That's right, race fans: contrary to popular belief, news reports, and your own eyes, Haskins was not killed during the explosion on the track last week. He is, in fact, holed up in a small apartment in Bristol, Tennessee, trying to woo a new woman. Those in the know say Haskins wanted some time off to foster his fledgling love with the NBC2 reporter without suffering in the points standings. Expect him to be back on the track by this time next week.

After the initial shock wore off, she barked out a laugh and then another. Soon, she was giggling uncontrollably in the middle of the newsroom with everyone staring silently at her. Lucky Haskins staged an explosion to woo her! It was too much. She knew she was only garnering more interested looks from her coworkers, but it still took her some minutes before she could compose herself.

"This is crazy," Stella finally said, gasping for air. She turned to address her colleagues, and the smile slid off her face as she took in their hostile looks. "Lucky's not going to start racing next week!" When she realized she'd been technically truthful about a picture featured on a website that was anything but, another giggle escaped. Soon, Candice relaxed and smiled, and even Billy Joe let out a weird kind of chuckle from across the newsroom. Only Joan's face scrunched up like she'd tasted something bitter. Eventually, the newsroom seemed to start moving again.

She sat back down at her desk and tried to ignore the sinking feeling in her stomach. The article was funny, but her name, address, and place of employment were all listed on a national website, along with some pretty crazy claims. Things were going to go south quickly here in Bristol, and she didn't think she could stop the slide.

Candice approached nonchalantly. Before she sat down at her desk, she said, "You're wearing the same outfit today. Isn't that an odd coincidence?"

Stella gulped loudly, but before she could come up with an excuse, the other reporter walked out of the newsroom. *Damn it!* Damn speedy technology that allowed someone to take a picture and post it online that very same day for the world to see! It all felt a little like *Back to the Future Part II.*

She dove into her bag and rooted around until she found her cell phone. There were three missed calls from her apartment, but Lucky would have to wait—she couldn't call him back with so many people around.

Barry walked by her desk with a cell phone pressed up against his ear, but he motioned to his watch and then pointed to the hallway. She needed to get into place in the studio for her six o'clock live shot. She groaned at the inconvenience of having to work during a life crisis but stood and gathered her IFB cord and script.

Now that the cat was out of the bag, the newsroom volume stayed normal, but Stella caught snippets of conversation around her.

"She must think she's pretty hot to trot. First Lucky and then anchoring..."

"That must be why Keith put her on the desk tonight. He knows everyone in the Tri-cities is talking about her..."

Stone-faced, she got into the elevator.

Now that she'd wrapped her mind around the picture, she came to an unwelcome realization: someone at the station had obviously called her identity in to the gossip website. How else would they have updated their headline and gotten her press badge photo? That brought up another question: who took the picture of her and Lucky? How did they happen to be close enough to get such a good shot? Too soon, the elevator doors opened and she walked woodenly into the studio.

Alexa shot her a look and opened her mouth, but before she could say anything, the floor director gave everyone the cue to standby. Stella was relieved for the excuse to stay quiet. If she could only get home, she'd have the weekend to figure things out.

"Show open in five... four..." Music filled the studio, and Stella watched the beginning of the newscast on the monitors nearby. Graphics swooped onto the screen, along with a voiceover Larry had recorded earlier in the day. "A convicted robber pleads for an early release in court today. We'll have his words of advice for others thinking about crime." A music pop and more swooping graphics set the scene for a different story, and Larry's voice continued, "One business has to close its doors, and employees make sure to help hundreds of families on their way out."

Stella breathed out a sigh. Even with everything else going on, she was happy to see they'd chosen to tease her story—it really was a good one that day.

Finally, the show open changed video again, and Larry's pre-recorded voiceover teased the final element for the six o'clock newscast. They usually saved the kicker for last, as a way to keep the audience engaged until the very end of the show. She knew from the morning meeting that the kicker that day was a story about elementary school kids getting to dump slime on their principal as a reward for reading some crazy number of books.

Instead of that video, however, the picture of her and Lucky flashed on screen. Larry's voice said, "And our own Channel 2 reporter is making headlines tonight. Find out why in just a bit."

Stella's mouth dropped open. She lost track of time as she thought about what Keith was trying to do on live TV. Cam had said on her very first day that ratings had never been better. She grimaced; ratings were easy to grow when you didn't mind selling out your own staff for an extra viewer. She went from shocked to steaming mad in about thirty seconds flat.

Unaware of what was happening in the studio, she ripped off her microphone and stormed off the set, prepared to go straight to Keith's office. As she marched out of the dark studio, however, she glanced up at the control room and saw him standing right there, looking down over his employees.

The sight was infuriating. Keith had put this strange, unbelievable picture on live TV without even a warning and now stood there, rubbing his hands together with glee. She stomped into the hallway and rounded the corner into the control room, shoving the door open with such force that it slammed back against the wall. The sound rocketed around the tiny room like gunfire.

"What are you doing, Keith? How could you put me on the spot like that—and without clearing it with me? Unbelievable!"

Six people were in the control room, and at least half had to have been in on the plan to put the picture on the news that evening. No one would make eye contact with her: Barry sat with his eyes glued to the screens in front of him, and the director, associate producer, and even Marty were all suddenly very interested in what was happening under their shoes.

Stella stood there, steaming, waiting for Keith to apologize. Instead, he grinned at her. "Stella Reynolds, we are a news organization. When presented with news, which we certainly were today, we put it on our air."

She opened her mouth to argue when he held up a hand. "Uh uh—please remember your employment contract not only makes you mine for two years but also has a very specific non-compete clause. If you quit, you can't work at any other station in the country for the duration of your contract, plus six months."

"You know what—"

"Oh, Stella, I'd hate to write you up for your behavior today. No one likes to hire employees with a history of problems in the workplace."

She was livid, but even in her anger, she noticed the director wasn't moving the show along. Alexa and Larry were stuck on a two-shot, forced to chat about who-knew-what for the last three minutes.

Stella turned on her heel and stomped out of the control room. Before the door swung shut, she heard Barry say, "Hey guys, sorry about that. We're going to have Brian tease weather now. Toss to him when you're ready..."

She had never been so angry in her life. She took the stairs two at a time and grabbed things off her desk in a huff. Her phone rang and she snarled, "Hello?"

"Whoa, Bear. Calm down."

"I'll be home in ten minutes," she growled, not caring who heard her.

"Stop—Stella, wait. If you can laugh this off on air, it will go away. If you can't, the paparazzi will be here in droves, like damn ants. This is your shot to shut it down."

She gripped the phone so tightly she thought she might crush it to pieces. "Now I have to play this off as some big joke?" she asked through gritted teeth. "This is so... I just can't..." she groaned at her inability to speak. "I am going to do this for you, Lucky, but then I'm out." She sat at her desk and blocked her mouth with her hand, speaking low and fast into the mouthpiece. "This is too much... *drama* for me! I don't want it, and frankly, Lucky, it's not mine! It wasn't fair of you to come to my apartment Monday night. It might not seem fair for me to say this now, but I'm saying it: *I'm out.*"

She threw her phone into her bag, and it banged straight to the bottom of her purse, which crashed to the tile floor. "Damn it!" she exclaimed.

She wanted to drive away from this place and never come back, but instead, she was walking right into the line of fire.

19

EXPLAIN THAT

Stella hunched over her desk and closed her eyes before she stood. This time, *she* refused to make eye contact with anyone. In a flash, she was back in the control room.

"What are you doing?" Barry asked, looking at her with a touch of fear in his face.

"You want to talk about the picture? I'll talk about the picture, but I'm going to sit at the desk with Larry and Alexa."

Keith actually *did* rub his hands together this time, delighted with this turn of events. "Yes—yes, at the desk. Right after weather, it'll close out the newscast."

As she walked out of the booth, Barry said, "Someone call Big Bob. Tell him we need to take sixty seconds from his sportscast for this."

She plastered a smile on her face and walked into the studio. Brian wrapped up the main weather forecast, and he, Alexa, and Larry calmly discussed the chance for a cool but nice weekend now that the storm front had moved past. She resisted the urge to laugh. Nice weekend? Not likely.

She barely heard Big Bob talk about high school basketball; all she could do was think snarky thoughts, like why did he have to be *Big* Bob? He couldn't have been more than 5'7" tall—it was a dumb nickname. Finally, they were in the last commercial break, and Stella sat down next to Larry.

"Stella, this is going to garner us a few extra ratings points tonight. I bet it even carries over for the rest of the week," Larry said with a smile.

Her lip curled. "Completely unprofessional, Larry. I won't forget this."

Larry frowned and jumped, and Alexa regarded Stella with interest as the floor director gave them a cue to standby.

Larry: Welcome back. We are joined now by our very own Stella Reynolds to explain this picture that's been making the rounds today.

Alexa was supposed to have the next line, but she missed it because she couldn't take her eyes off Stella. After a beat of silence, Larry continued without her.

It first showed up on a national gossip website but has certainly spread like wildfire ever since with multiple racing and sports websites picking up the picture, too. Stella, what can you tell us about the timeline of the picture? Surely Lucky Haskins wasn't standing outside your apartment this very morning?

She stared at Larry without blinking for a moment. "Larry, you just hate when people out there are determined to make money off a terrible situation, and I think we can all agree that the crash last week at Talladega qualifies. Lucky was my landlord and very briefly my friend, and any attempt to make money off the tragedy of the explosion is just so lowbrow—so very small and mean—that it's hard to even discuss it calmly.

"I have no idea when that picture was taken, but I know it's really struck a nerve for all of Lucky's many loyal fans who are still mourning his death. It's all so very sad."

Larry looked like he'd swallowed a rotten egg. He clearly had several questions cued up in his mind, but Stella's treatment of the picture made them impossible to ask. He squared his shoulders. "So true, Stella—just a tragedy all around. Thank you for explaining this picture for our viewers."

She exhaled silently and relaxed, but then Alexa unexpectedly directed a question at Stella.

"Just how well did you know Lucky?"

"Not well at all, I'm afraid."

"Well enough for him to be at your apartment with his hand on your face."

"Was that a question?" Stella snapped.

After another awkward silence, Larry closed out the newscast, and once the credits rolled, he hustled out of the studio without a backward glance. Alexa and Stella unclipped their microphones and walked off the set together.

"I don't know what's going on, but that picture was obviously taken today." Stella opened her mouth to object, but Alexa kept talking. "NAZZY will sell the image to the highest bidder, along with the information on you. It'll be all over the internet by this time tomorrow. Conspiracy theorists are curious, and now everyone knows who you are. They'll come to Bristol, even after you tried to deflect things tonight."

Stella frowned, knowing Alexa was right and realizing she'd have to thank Lucky for his good advice, despite the fact that she was still angry at him.

"They know where you live," Alexa spoke again, still staring at her. "I'd be surprised if they're not already there, waiting for you." Stella's eyes opened wide as she considered the news anchor's words. "I'll be there later tonight."

"What?" Stella asked, confused. She wasn't about to invite Alexa over for a nightcap after that newscast.

"It's a big story, Stella—there'll be a huge crowd. Stay inside if you don't want to be on camera."

"Is that a threat?" she asked incredulously.

Alexa didn't answer, and Stella watched her walk toward the elevator before she took the stairs up to the newsroom and packed up her desk for the weekend—heck, maybe for good, depending on how things went in Alabama. It looked like she was headed to Talladega, after all; she didn't have a choice.

The sound of a throat clearing drew her out of her own thoughts, and she swiveled around in her chair to find Candice, Kate, Jen, Amy, and even Joan standing in a loose half-circle behind her desk.

She opened her mouth but realized she didn't know what to say, so after a few seconds, she snapped it shut and stared at her coworkers through narrowed eyes. They hadn't exactly been comforting earlier when the shit was hitting the fan. What were they all doing here now?

Candice looked Stella in the eye and said in a low voice, "We wanted to let you know we're all on your side. It was completely inappropriate for Keith to put that picture on the news—dangerous, too, as he basically confirmed that ludicrous NAZZY article. Now everyone *knows* that's you in the picture, and they also know where you live!"

Amy stepped forward. "We sent an e-mail to corporate, letting them know we won't stand for that kind of treatment. We all signed it."

"What can we do to help right now?" Kate asked from the middle of the group.

Stella felt her heart soften. The show of support was overwhelming, and she didn't know how to respond. She didn't even know these women and they were going out on a limb for her. She took a shaky breath. "Thanks, guys. That means a lot, but it is what it is. Let's just hope it blows over soon."

Stella watched the women walked away, and her eyes lingered

on Alexa, Keith, and Stewart, a nightside reporter, huddled in the corner of the newsroom.

Keith looked at his watch. "Make it nine o'clock. You know where she lives?" Stella turned back to her desk just as they looked her way. Alexa was right: the station wasn't done with their coverage of the picture just yet.

She grabbed her bag and headed to the parking lot.

Lucky would be waiting on her back at her apartment. He was charming and funny but was also smart in business and certainly wasn't afraid to show his feelings. Would he be able to keep it together in Alabama, or would he let his emotions get the best of him when they started digging into his brother's death? She didn't know him well enough to have an answer, but one thing was certain: she'd find out over the next two days.

20

FINAL PREPARATIONS

The rumor about Lucky was out, and so were the crazies. She'd taken a few minutes to compose herself in the parking lot at work and then made a quick stop at the drug store on her way home. When she pulled up to her apartment just a few minutes later, several cars she'd never seen before were parked illegally in front of the building. A couple of the cars obviously belonged to big Lucky Haskins fans, as the vehicles were painted to look like exact replicas of Lucky's race car.

She parked in a lot adjacent to her building and pulled up the hood on her raincoat before getting out of the car. After sneaking in the back entrance, she ran into Mrs. Lanster in the stairwell.

"What a day, Stella. I've never seen so many people trying to get into the building! Thank goodness we have secure locks." Stella couldn't decide if her elderly neighbor was excited or worried. "You know, I saw one man try to climb over the garden wall on the lower level. He had no idea it was separated by an iron gate, and he got stuck between the two! You should have seen him splutter when old Mrs. Donovan had to call the police to get him out. Not a happy camper."

Stella nodded absently as they passed each other, more

focused on getting to her apartment that anything Mrs. Lanster was saying.

"You know, Star will be back, and my goodness is she going to be hot at you, dear. You're going to have to come up with quite a story to talk your way out of that picture mess."

Stella grimaced as the words floated up the stairwell after her. She couldn't decide if she was looking forward to seeing Lucky or dreading it. She had to both apologize and thank him, all because *he* had brought this crazy situation into *her* life.

She took out her keys at the top of the stairs, but the door opened just as she stepped in front of it. Lucky grabbed her hand and drew her quickly in before slamming the door shut and pulling her into a hug.

"I missed you," he murmured into her hair. She tried to pull away, but he tightened his hold and rubbed his whiskery face against the sensitive spot just below her ear. She squirmed, and he added some heavy breathing.

"Oh my God. Are you that bored?" she asked with a laugh.

"Not anymore," he said, his hands roaming over her coat.

She slapped them away and stepped back. "You're like a child, do you know that?"

He smiled and raised his eyebrows. "You're coming tonight, right? We'll leave for Alabama and you're still going to help me?"

She groaned. "Yes, I'll help you, but not because I want to. Thanks to that picture being published, I don't have any other choice!"

He ran a hand through his hair and it stood up on end; combined with his now-full beard, he looked like a lumberjack. "I know. I've been watching them come by all afternoon. It started out as just more traffic than usual—cars driving past the building really slowly." He glowered at the big windows facing the street. "But then they started parking and getting out and wandering and staring..." Lucky shook his head. "I'm sorry, Stella. I never imagined any of this when I came here Monday night."

She softened at his tone. "I know, Lucky. I'm sorry, too. I shouldn't have yelled at you earlier. I was pretty frustrated, but that's no excuse."

Her unanswered questions about the picture came roaring back to her now. Who took it? She froze in place as she thought about it, closing her eyes and picturing the angle of the shot. It must have been someone standing across the street, maybe one story up.

That couldn't have been by chance. Stella rubbed a hand across her face. She wanted to latch onto the mystery, just for the distraction, but she was too drained to focus. She walked over to the windows and pressed her forehead against the cool glass, closing her eyes again.

"Figure anything out while I was gone?"

Lucky took a beer out of the fridge, twisted off the cap, and took a swig before speaking. "Yes, ma'am. We'll go straight to Jim's hotel and get him to agree to your exclusive interview on Sunday. He's probably holed up in there, grieving. That'll give him a day to get it together, and it also gives us a day to look around the track, get the radio traffic from the race, and find surveillance video from the day of the accident to see who might have messed with my car."

Stella grimaced. There were so many problems with that plan, she couldn't even count them all, but she humored him. "Then what?"

"Then Jim—and a little legwork—can help us figure out what happened."

"Anything else?"

"We find the bastard who killed Hap and turn him into the police."

She sighed. It sounded like a terrible plan—one that would surely end with her fired, under arrest, or both. She leaned forward. "When do we leave?"

He strolled over to the windows. "Isn't that the million-dollar question?"

She peeked around the edge to the street down below and her eyes widened. "Oh my God. Ten minutes ago, there were four people out there. Now there must be—"

"Twenty." Lucky swore under his breath and drained the last of the beer in three gulps. "How the hell are we going to get out of here tonight?"

"I hoped they'd have heard me on the news and left us alone." She took a deep breath and wrinkled her nose. "I guess I need to thank you. You had good advice when the station put our picture on air, and I'm glad I didn't storm home from work without at least attempting to explain everything."

It was dark outside, but a yellow-orange light shined through the window from the street lamps outside, casting a warm glow on Lucky's face. "You were great tonight, Stella. I thought that Larry guy was going to melt off the screen—you managed to shame him into submission with just a few words. I had to go back and watch it again before I realized you didn't actually say the picture of us *wasn't* taken this morning. I could have sworn you did! That was good."

"Well, I couldn't lie. I mean, my job is to tell people what's going on. I know I didn't tell them everything, but it seemed like I shouldn't lie about anything, you know?" She hesitated. This was all so unusual; she didn't have time to think through it all. She hoped the viewers would forgive her in the end.

"Then that lady came out of left field with her questions! I wasn't expecting that."

"Alexa," Stella said with a frown. "Wait, Alexa. Hmm... that just might work." She narrowed her eyes at the rubberneckers outside. "We need a distraction, and I think I know the perfect thing." She took out her cell phone and checked the time: seven o'clock. Lucky stared at her, a question in his eyes.

"Don't ask," she said. "We'll leave in two hours." She dug into her bag for a notebook and started making bullet points. "We need a place to stay, directions to get there, money for gas, coffee —definitely coffee—let's see, snacks for the drive..." She looked up at Lucky's chuckle. "What? I need snacks for a road trip."

"Hap would have liked you," he said with a sad smile.

Stella put her notebook down and reached for his hand. "I'm sure I would have liked Hap."

"No," Lucky shook his head, "you wouldn't have. He could try the patience of a saint. He was unreliable. He could be mean..." He stared past Stella. "I hardly even liked him, but I can't believe how much I miss him. My heart hurts all the time."

She squeezed his hand. "We'll do our best down there, Lucky. Hopefully we can make a difference." She bustled around the apartment, packing; Lucky sat moodily on the couch for a few minutes but then seemed to rally. He organized the thrift store clothes Stella had bought for him that week and moved to the kitchen.

"'I need snacks for a road trip,'" he repeated with a grin, pulling down bags of candy and chips from the shelves. He started a pot of coffee and found the travel mugs, and they worked in tandem until Lucky moved back to the couch. He smiled and patted the seat next to him. "Come over here and sit down."

She looked at their open suitcase, the messy kitchen, and the pile of coats by the door, and then blew out a breath and sat.

He threw an arm across the back of the sofa and pulled her close. "How are you doing? I know I'm a lot to take on right now. I showed up out of the blue and kind of took over your life. I guess I just want to make sure you're all right."

Stella leaned her head against his arm. "This isn't exactly how I pictured my first two weeks on the job, but I don't think anything happened that wouldn't have happened eventually, to be honest." He looked at her, amused, and she stammered, "I didn't mean—not what happened between me and you. That was... totally unexpected." *And probably not real,* she didn't add out loud, but they both knew it. This relationship was the product of being squashed together in close quarters under stressful circumstances and wouldn't last. He tilted his head and looked ready to launch into something deep, but Stella saved him the effort. "But fun, right?" He nodded and she jumped up from the couch. "So, I'll pack the essentials and you finish the suitcase."

He blew out a sigh and nodded slowly. "Okay, Bear. You got it."

21

THE GETAWAY

S tella looked at her watch. "Any minute now. Are we ready?"

"Yes, Stella, for the hundredth time, we're ready. What are we ready *for*? That's the question."

"She'll be here any min—wait, that's her! Okay, let's go!"

They stood at the window wall inside Stella's apartment, looking down at the crowd below. At least fifty people milled around the sidewalk out front.

Lucky's signature blond locks were dyed dark brown from a box of temporary hair dye she'd picked up earlier that night. It changed his look dramatically—especially when paired with his full beard. The collar on the seventies-inspired (or maybe genuine seventies, judging by the musty smell) coat did a great job of hiding his face, and because it was at least two sizes too big, it swallowed his muscular frame.

He pulled at the collar. "This damn coat couldn't be any itchier." She could tell he hated looking so sloppy, but it made her smile. Finally, *he* was the grungy one—until he smiled back. His hundred-watt smile could identify him from a block away.

"Stop smiling. We should have blackened out a few of your

teeth or something." She hefted her backpack onto her shoulder and grabbed one of the rolling suitcases on her way out the door; she then reached back and pulled a bright orange knit hat down over his head. "Just play the part, Haskins, and maybe we can get out of here without attracting a crowd."

They rode down the elevator in silence. When the doors opened, Stella exhaled a sigh of relief that the lobby was empty. She crept to the front door and looked out the glass windows at Alexa and Stewart interviewing people on the sidewalk. The light from Stewart's camera shined toward the street, and the crowd was completely distracted by the arrival of the news crew.

She met Lucky at the opposite door, and they slowly pushed it open and looked warily around the back of the building to find it empty. They took a few tentative steps onto the pavement when a voice called out.

"Lucky?" Mrs. Lanster had materialized in the lobby, or maybe she'd been there all along. In her black pants, a black sweater, and even a black knit cap pulled low over her head, she blended into the dark room. "I've got your back, dear. Good luck!"

Lucky nodded and nudged Stella forward. "Let's keep moving, Bear." She threw a smile at her neighbor and started walking again.

After another few steps, they heard a different voice call out, "Someone's leaving out the back!" Before she could decide what to do, they heard two sets of pounding footsteps headed their way and then a commotion.

Mrs. Lanster yelled out, "Ow, my hip, my hip!" Stella chanced a look back and saw the older woman had somehow taken out both men; all three lay, groaning, on the ground. Mrs. Lanster winked at Stella. "Oh boys, you'll have to help me up. I think my hip might be broken."

The men jumped up and rushed to her side. There it was: southern manners wouldn't allow the men to move on with their plans until they'd helped an old lady up off the ground.

She and Lucky hustled to her car and hopped in, and as she pulled onto the main road, Stella saw the bright light of Stewart's camera pulling the crowd in like moths to the flame. Alexa didn't know it, but she'd given Stella the perfect escape route for Alabama.

"I think we made it." She turned away from the madness and pointed her car south. As she navigated her way through the busy downtown area, one stoplight at a time, she glanced at the empty seat next to her.

Her eyes flicked to the rearview mirror for the hundredth time when she heard Lucky groan, "Can't you go any faster?"

She tsked back at him and said under her breath, "It's not my fault we've hit every light since we left the apartment." Lucky complained again, and she added, "I'm not going to speed through a red light and risk getting pulled over."

He muttered something about folding his 6'2" body into a 5'5" space from where he lay in the footwell of the back seat of her Plymouth Reliant, covered with a blanket.

She smiled a big, phony smile at a little, old man in the car next to hers at their current red light. "We can't all drive a Camaro," she said through gritted teeth, feeling defensive about her ride. It was a good car that had been with her for years.

"I know," he sighed, and the car bounced as he changed positions yet again.

"Just a few more miles and we'll be out of town. Hang on." She drove faster than usual, and after three more red lights, they made it to the interstate.

Once they were out of town, Lucky climbed over the bench seat. "You couldn't have found some jeans?" He pulled at the pleated-front khakis she'd come home with.

"You're welcome, Lucky. I'm so happy you like them. Yes, it *was* nice of me to spend my time and energy finding you a disguise at a crowded secondhand shop."

His look softened and he said, "You're right. I'm sorry—and thank you."

As headlights flashed into the car, Stella felt like they were heading for a strange, unplanned vacation. "So, here we go."

"If anything goes wrong, I just want you to know right now that I'm so glad I came to your house after the race, Stella. I know I don't know you very well yet, but I knew I could count on you." She wrinkled her brow and looked at him sideways. He noticed her look and said, "I'm serious, Bear. I couldn't have gone anywhere else. It seems like fate that we met that day at the track."

She glanced at him thoughtfully. "It's funny how your own death really makes you rethink *life*, huh?"

His face grew somber, and Stella guessed her nonchalant comment had him thinking about his brother. "We'll figure this out, Lucky. He won't have died for nothing."

He nodded slowly, but they didn't talk for a while—just listened to the sounds of the highway as they drove across Tennessee.

Two hours later, she had the map out on the hood of the car while they both drank coffee from a Thermos. Lucky looked around the deserted rest area and scratched his head.

"What?" Stella asked, wondering what had put such a curious look on his face. "Do you think someone recognized you?" she asked, suddenly nervous.

"No, Bear, I'm just trying to picture little ole *you* driving across the country by yourself and stopping at dodgy places like this. I'll be honest, it kind of scares the hell out of me."

She scoffed. "Don't be ridiculous. I'm perfectly able to take care of myself." At his raised eyebrows, she elaborated, "I'd never stop at a rest area in the middle of the night by myself. Sheesh! Give me a little credit."

He laughed, and they gathered their things from the hood. It was just after eleven o'clock, and they still had four hours to go.

They would drive south diagonally through Tennessee, and then, after a quick jog into Georgia, they'd hit the Alabama border and continue straight to the track. If all went well, they would get there between two and three in the morning.

Stella yawned and Lucky said, "I'll drive, you sleep." She tossed him the keys and they piled back into the car. She settled into her seat sideways, leaning against the headrest and watching Lucky's profile as he drove. Occasionally, lights from passing cars flashed across his face.

He reached out and tucked a lock of hair behind her ear before running his fingers down her arm and grabbing her hand where it rested on her knee. She fell asleep with their fingers entwined, wondering what they were really heading for and how they'd ever escape unscathed.

22

OLD FRIENDS ARE THE BEST FRIENDS

"We're almost there." Lucky patted Stella on the knee. "What?" She felt the car slow as they approached an exit, and she stretched out her arms and yawned. "How are you doing?"

"I'm fine. I'm looking forward to seeing Jim. Another set of eyes on our problem can only be a good thing."

"I wonder if he'll still be at the hotel?"

"It's only been a week, Stella. According to the papers, he's not in touch with anyone in his family. Investigators probably still want to talk to him, so he's got no reason to go anywhere else."

Stella wished she shared his confidence. As he wove through the city, her heart rate accelerated. This is where Lucky's plan started getting sketchy, and she wasn't looking forward to phase one.

All too soon, they pulled into the packed parking lot of the Track Side Suites Inn. Lucky circled a few times before finding an open space toward the back corner of the lot, right under a lamppost.

He turned to Stella. "Go easy on him, okay?"

"Jim's not going to be happy when I wake him up at two in the morning, you know." She frowned and looked at the clock. "Jeez, how fast did you drive? I didn't think we'd get here until three!"

Lucky shrugged, a guilty smile on his face. "Did you know your car vibrates over seventy miles an hour? I'm talking serious shaking. I can't believe it didn't wake you up!"

Her stomach clenched. "What if he doesn't open the door?"

"Use your cell phone to call the room." He passed a slip of paper to her. "I wrote down his room number and Jim's cell phone, just in case. All you have to do is convince him to come down to the parking lot. I'll be waiting right here for you."

She nodded weakly and got out of the car; Lucky jogged around to her side and gave her a quick hug. He was hopped up with excited energy, ready for another friend to know he was alive.

No one waited at the valet stand, and she tried to look confident as she entered the front lobby and headed toward a bank of elevators past the front desk. The hotel was huge—more than 300 rooms—and the bar area opposite the front desk had dozens of tables, booths, and plush chairs arranged into comfy and private conversation areas. Smoke wafted out of the dark room.

She pushed the elevator call button, her heart pounding, and pressed the number five when she was in. After stepping off the elevator, Stella walked down the long hallway until she saw room 572. She raised her fist to the door and pounded three times for good measure.

She was so busy going over what she was going to say to Jim when he answered the door that it took her a minute or two to realize that wasn't going to happen. She didn't hear any sounds or see any light through the peephole. She knocked again and the sound echoed through the quiet corridor.

After another minute of silence, she looked at her watch. It was 2:17 a.m.; he was either asleep or not there. She took her cell phone out of her pocket and dialed the front desk from a hastily scrawled note in her pocket. The operator connected her to Jim's room, and the call rang a dozen times on her end, but she never heard a peep from inside the hotel room.

The second number on her paper was Jim's cell phone number. She dutifully punched in the number, expecting it to be disconnected. To her great surprise, however, the call rang through. She felt a kernel of excitement snake up her stomach. Could it be this easy?

After five rings, she got Jim's voicemail. Her shoulders drooped, but she left a message, asking him to call her as soon as possible.

She reversed her trip, and back in the lobby, a flash of light caught her eye and made her freeze. Star Coleman, wearing a glittery, sequined dress and holding a sloshing glass of wine in one hand, danced slowly by herself in the middle of the bar area. Her eyes were closed and she had a half-smile on her face.

What was Lucky's ex doing at *this* hotel? There had to be forty hotels to choose from in Talladega—what were the odds she was at the same hotel as Jim? Could she have been here with him? In Stella's head, dominoes fell with tiny clinks. Star had motive and Jim had access.

A throat cleared loudly near her and she jumped. An employee at the front desk said, "Can I help you?"

Stella smiled sheepishly. "Oh, uh, hi there. Any chance you have an open room tonight?"

The clerk shook his head. "Booked solid for the last three months. Sorry. The whole town is booked up, actually, and I heard you have to drive clear to Munford to find an open room. People flocked here because of the Haskins investigation."

As she headed out of the lobby, she took in as many details of Star as possible without slowing her stride.

～

"So, I didn't find Jim—no answer at his door or on his cell—but I did find someone else you know." At Lucky's look, she elaborated, "Star Coleman is in there, having a dance party for one."

"What do you mean?" he asked, eyebrows drawn together.

"Am I speaking in riddles? Star is in there, dancing alone." She didn't know why, but all of a sudden, she felt prickly toward Lucky. Why couldn't he see what was going on here?

His surprised face slid into a satisfied grin. "Bear, are you jealous of my ex-fiancée, who I caught cheating on me in my own house? Surely you can't think I have any feelings for her whatsoever."

Her anger flared. "I don't know anything about you and Star," she spat, "but don't you think it's odd she's staying at the same hotel as Jim? Wake up, Lucky. I think they were both involved in the crash."

"What do you mean?" he asked, matching her tone. "She came down after the explosion to get some of the spotlight back on her, playing the part of the grieving girlfriend—ex-girlfriend, of course," he corrected himself quickly at Stella's glare.

"Well, how did she get a room, then? The clerk just told me they've been booked solid for three months!"

They stared hotly at each other for twenty seconds before Lucky nodded sharply to himself. "Good question!" He reached for the door handle and shot out of the car.

"Dammit, Lucky, get back here—someone might recognize you!" she growled. She hesitated in the car for a fraction of a second, and that's all it took for him to gain serious ground. His stride was long and Stella had to run to catch up.

They stormed into the lobby, and in the second it took Lucky to orient himself to the layout, Stella was able to shove him over to the front desk area.

Star was just leaving the bar, heading toward the elevators, and Stella could now see she wasn't alone. She wasn't with Jim, however, as Stella had suspected. In an effort to hide, she wrapped her arms around Lucky's neck and pulled his head down to hers. "Shut up—don't say a word," she said in a low voice. She felt him relax slightly into her, but his eyes never left Star and her companion as they walked past.

"I don't know about that, Wex," they heard her say as she sauntered by. "If we're lucky, it'll only take a couple of days for them to wrap up the investigation and we can all go home."

Star and *Ryan Wexler* had arrived at the bank of elevators by then, too far away to hear any more of their conversation. Just before the doors opened, however, Ryan pulled Star in close, and they shared a passionate kiss that involved an obscene amount of groping.

When they were gone, Stella loosened her grip on Lucky's neck. He stared thoughtfully at the spot Ryan and Star had recently occupied.

"So, I guess we know how she got a room: she's staying with *Ryan*." That was a twist she hadn't expected. She wondered why the general manager of the Bristol track was still here in Alabama, anyway. She was just about to ask Lucky, but he spoke first.

"I just never—it never crossed my mind that this..." He was still staring at the closed elevator doors when he trailed off. His focus shifted to Stella. "Let's get a room. I need to just think on this tonight. I promise I'll explain everything in the morning, once I understand it all."

"There are no rooms, remember?" Lucky groaned and she added, "Back to the car, I guess."

"Maybe we can christen the Reliant?" he asked hopefully.

"Ugh, no! I'll take the front seat, you take the back."

Lucky started to object, but she cut him off at the pass. "You need to think, remember? I put some blankets in the trunk, and it's only three hours until sunrise. How bad could it be?"

It was bad. The old, worn bench seats were threadbare, and the springs underneath the fabric pushed up unevenly. Just when Stella got mildly comfortable, Lucky groaned.

Add to that the glare of the streetlamp directly overhead, and they spent a miserable hour trying to rest.

Finally, just before four in the morning, the light inside the car slowly faded to black, almost like someone had found a dimmer switch. Stella was startled out of her near sleep and watched a giant RV back into a tiny, open space next to them. By the time the huge vehicle came to a stop, Stella saw with exasperation that she couldn't open the driver's-side door. A scant two- or three inches separated her car from the luxury camper.

"Now was that necessary?" she grumbled, staring at the huge vehicle towering over them.

"It kind of blocks out the light," Lucky said. "I think it's an improvement."

She groaned but closed her eyes to test his theory. It was definitely darker. She scrunched up the blanket she was using as a pillow to make it more comfortable and settled in. Her eyes jerked open, though, when a squeal escaped the RV next door. The side started to expand out, making room inside the giant vehicle for a couch or a table.

"Uh oh." Lucky saw the problem a split second before Stella, but she was fastest getting out of the car.

"Stop!" she yelled, watching the RV's bump-out get ever closer to the windows of her car. "Hey—stop! You're going to hit my car!" she banged on the front of the RV and yelled again.

Finally, all movement stopped, and she breathed out a relieved sigh just as Lucky finally untangled his legs and climbed out the passenger side of the back seat.

"That was close," he calmly observed.

"Close? What kind of idiot doesn't look—doesn't even check —to see if there's room to do that?" She kicked the tire closest to her. "This isn't a campground, you know!" she called to the mystery driver.

The RV's door swung open with a metallic clang, and a woman's laugh, raspy from years of smoking, came drifting out of the vehicle. Stella took a step back and her eyes bulged—she'd recognize that laugh anywhere! She shook her head. *Surely not,* she thought. *Impossible.* The owner of that laugh should have been thousands of miles away. When a woman climbed down the steps to the ground, a huge smile lit up her face.

Stella felt her own grin widen with glee. "Janet? What are *you* doing here?"

23

JANET'S BACK

"Stella Reynolds, as I live and breathe!" Janet said in a huge, phony southern accent.

"Janet Black! Seriously, what are you *doing* here?" Stella repeated. Janet's brown hair was pulled back into a messy ponytail, and she wore grey sweats, a white T-shirt, and an unzipped grey hoodie. She clearly wasn't wearing a bra, and Stella's eyes flitted to Lucky to check his reaction. He studied the RV's wheels intently. Stella smirked; there were some things nobody wanted to see.

"Looking for a place to park this baby, obviously." Janet patted the RV. "All the campgrounds in the whole state are booked solid. We figured if we can't hook the lines up, we might as well get close to the action, ya know?"

Lucky shot her an amused look. Janet hadn't changed one speck since they'd met on her very first night at her first job in Montana. Their relationship had begun contentiously, but over Stella's six months there, they'd become friends.

Janet lit up a cigarette and inhaled deeply. With it dangling from her lip, she stuck a hand out. "I'm Janet, and you are *not*

John. Woot, woot, Stella. Playing the field—I like that." She wagged her eyebrows up and down.

"Janet, this is my friend L—"

"I'm Luke. It's nice to meet you, Janet," Lucky broke in. "What brought you to Talladega?"

"We drove all the way in from Bozeman, Montana, for the race last weekend. Our camping reservation just ran out, and we needed somewhere else to stay. We wanted to be here for the memorial service they're planning for Lucky Haskins—my man's a big fan." She looked from Lucky to Stella and back to Lucky again, and Stella panicked. Did she recognize him? He'd taken his hat off in the car and must have forgotten it when he jumped out.

"Are you two staying here?" Janet nodded toward the hotel. "Maybe we can use your shower, since there's no electric for us here..."

Stella and Lucky looked at each other, startled. "Not exactly," she finally said. "We're sleeping in my car for the night and hoping to get a room somewhere tomorrow."

"Mmm, a little pre-work quickie—I like that. Stella, you've really loosened up since we met!"

Stella ignored the comment. "Janet, whose RV is this—and who is your man?"

"This," she patted the hood with affection, "is mine, and uh... I'm sure you remember him, Stella."

As if on cue, the door flapped open again and a man stumbled down the stairs of the RV. Stella almost groaned out loud. Dereck was a loser Janet dated from time to time, and apparently this was one of those times. He had a habit of getting drunk and being loud, and it seemed things hadn't changed.

"Stella!" he shouted and then laughed at himself. "Where you been, girl?"

She wrinkled her nose. "Well, listen. It was super great to

catch up, but I think we're going to try to get some sleep." She motioned to her car and took a hopeful step away from Dereck.

"Sleep? We just got here! Let's at least have a drink to celebrate being reunited!"

Dereck stared at Lucky, a confused look on his face.

"Whoz tha?" he slurred. "Hucky Lazzins?" His eyes teared up and he searched in his pockets, finally pulling out a crumpled, dirty handkerchief.

Lucky looked at her triumphantly. "Handkerchief!" he mouthed.

Stella snickered, but Janet let out an irritated sigh. "Yes, Dereck," she annunciated each word, "Lucky Haskins is dead. We all know he was your favorite driver. Now let's go use the bathroom and then have a drink with Stella and her new friend, *Luke*." In a quieter voice, she said to Stella, "He's been driving me crazy for the last week. All he does is talk about how amazing Lucky damn Haskins was, like I give a rat's ass!"

Stella snorted, and she and Lucky watched the duo walk across the parking lot toward the hotel.

"I'm your *friend*, huh?" Lucky finally said, breaking the silence.

She looked at him out of the corner of her eye. Had she hurt his feelings? "Listen, the less Janet knows, the better."

He nodded, seeming to accept her answer, but there was an awkward silence that seemed to stretch on for minutes. Lucky recovered first. He grabbed her shoulders and started kneading them with his strong fingers. "Maybe we can sleep on their couch."

SLEEP JUST WASN'T MEANT to be, though. They found themselves sitting at the table inside a rather plain RV with Janet fifteen minutes later. She and Dereck had come back from the bathroom, and Dereck stumbled back to the bedroom and passed out.

Stella and Lucky declined an offer of beer from Janet but watched her shotgun a can of Budweiser outside. Stella checked her watch: it was nearly five in the morning. She was thinking about coffee, not alcohol.

Janet wiped her mouth on her sleeve as she walked back into the RV. "So, Stella, you gonna tell me why Lucky Haskins is sitting in my RV, alive as you and I?"

Her eyes opened wide and her mind went blank. "Uhhhhh..." was all that came out.

Lucky snorted. "I thought you were a fan. Is that a number thirteen tattoo I saw earlier?"

Janet proudly pulled the V-neck of her shirt down, revealing Lucky's car number and nearly her entire left breast.

"Wow!" Stella said in shock. "That probably wouldn't have stretched out like that if you'd wear a bra more often."

Janet cackled, "Ha! Stella, I forgot how funny you are!" She released the material. "I saw the picture yesterday online—it's all anyone at the campground could talk about. I recognized you in an instant, Stella. When I called your new station, they told me you were headed to Alabama. We've spent the last eight hours driving around, looking for you."

Stella's eyebrows shot up. "Why were you looking for *me*?"

"Well, it was obvious you got yourself caught up in some kind of *something*, and I figured you'd need help. I'd just about given up for the night and decided to find somewhere to park the RV. I couldn't believe it when I saw the Reliant next to the only open spot here. You still have your Montana plates! It's like it was meant to be, Stella!"

"Janet, I'm going to level with you." Lucky leaned across the table. "I think someone tried to kill me on the track, and the only reason I'm sitting here is because my brother was driving instead of me."

"Hap?" When Lucky nodded, Janet shook her head sadly. "That boy couldn't *buy* a break, could he? It was that way from day one. I'm really sorry, Lucky."

He crossed his arms and nodded slightly. "Sorry doesn't change that he's gone."

After a few minutes, Janet looked up. "I said to Dereck, 'Lucky Haskins would never let up on a turn like that,' but I just figured something went wrong with your car. You think someone *made sure* something went wrong with your car, eh?"

"Yes, and Stella and I are here to find out who and how. I can't have anyone know I'm alive until we've figured it all out, though."

Janet nodded sagely. "I'm like a lockbox, Lucky—I'll never tell. You let me know how I can help. Ask Stella; I'm good to have around when you're in a tight spot."

Stella nodded thoughtfully. That was true. Janet had helped her crack a murder investigation wide open in Montana; she had a knack for being in shady places at the perfect time to glean key information.

"Well, Janet, now that's a nice offer," Lucky said in a sugary voice. "I might could use your help real soon. My ex, Star, is staying in the hotel, and I want to know why. Maybe you can get friendly with her and find out."

Janet's eyes lit up. "Star Coleman is here? You know, the magazines said she was the jealous type, but she seems so sweet to me. I've always wanted to see her in person. I'll make it my mission, Lucky."

Stella gulped. Janet wasn't exactly stealthy, and she didn't think this was a good idea.

24

MISTAKEN IDENTITY

Two hours later, Janet moved through the buffet line inside the hotel.

"I'm a little worried about this," Stella said, blowing on her mug of steaming hot coffee.

"You said she saved you in Montana." Lucky's eyes searched hers.

"She did." Shortly after moving to Montana, Stella had gotten caught up in a murder investigation. She knew the sheriff had arrested the wrong person but couldn't figure out who the real murderer was, and Janet had played a key role in helping Stella when she finally identified the killer. "She did," Stella repeated more convincingly. "She'll be fine; you're right." Lucky fidgeted in his seat, too and Stella said, "Is that coat—"

"I've never been more uncomfortable!" He took his hat off and itched under his collar like a kid.

"Stop! Put your hat on!"

He shot her a dirty look and then stood. "I'll be in the bathroom."

She took a big swallow of her coffee when he left and ordered them both the Track Side Special for breakfast when the waiter came by.

Janet arrived at their table with her food, and soon all three were eating some combination of eggs, sausage and gravy, fruit, and coffee.

Ten minutes into their feast, Stella jumped when Janet dropped her fork and pushed her chair back. Before she could ask where she was going, she saw Star's reflection in the mirror over the bar. Lucky's ex poured coffee into a travel cup by the front desk.

The usually glamorous woman wasn't her perfectly put together self; with no makeup and dark circles under her eyes, she looked terrible. Stella was secretly relieved to see a night of drinking and late-night partying had taken a toll. Janet approached, and she tried to tamp down her feelings of glee as the women started talking.

The conversation was one-sided, and Star got increasingly irritated as Janet allowed for less and less room between them. She picked up Star's coffee, took a sip, and then added sugar and cream before handing the cup back. Star moved toward the door, but Janet was on her like checkers on a flag. Star left the building so fast that she walked right out of an expensive-looking sandal—and left it behind. She didn't even look back.

"Well?" Stella asked when Janet sat down. "What'd you find out?"

"She likes her coffee black—black, I tell you! Terrible."

Stella and Lucky looked at each other wordlessly before Stella said, "That's all?"

"That, and she doesn't mind being barefoot."

Stella shook her head in wonder.

"I really enjoyed watching that," Lucky said with a grin. "Star is usually so put together—hardly ever a hair out of place. She'd never come to breakfast without showering," he looked at Stella appreciatively. "It just wasn't normal."

She grimaced, not sure how she felt that her greasy hair and lack of makeup were what set her apart from Star in Lucky's mind.

After Janet made two more trips through the buffet line, all three walked back to the RV.

Dereck was still asleep in the back bedroom, and Janet put the food she'd swiped for him on the counter and looked longingly at the mini fridge in the kitchen area. "If we were camping, I'd have refrigeration, a cooktop, a bathroom..."

"It's been a tough week for everyone," Lucky deadpanned.

Stella studied the race car driver. "Let's discuss the fact that your 'Wes' is actually Ryan Wexler. How does that change your thoughts about the breakup with Star?

"What am I missing?" Janet asked, looking between the two.

Lucky rolled his head around to loosen the tension in his shoulders. "Ladies, let's sit."

They all crowded around the table as they had overnight, and Lucky looked out the window for a moment, collecting his thoughts. "Janet, Star and I broke up a couple of months ago, after I caught her screwing around on me at our house. I never saw the guy—just heard her call him Wes." He shook his head. "Last night, Stella and I heard Star call Ryan Wexler 'Wex.' I must have misheard her back at our house all those weeks ago. It was Ryan Wexler all along."

Janet's jaw almost hit the table in front of them. "What? *The* Ryan Wexler?"

Stella whisper-shouted, "SHHH!"

Janet bobbed her head down, and all three turned to look at the bedroom door behind them. When Dereck let out another snore, they turned back to each other.

"Star was having an affair with Ryan Wexler?" Janet said again.

Lucky looked at his hands folded in front of him. "*Is*, and yes."

"Doesn't that seem... like, well, I don't know, karma?" she asked slyly.

Stella looked back and forth between them, and then, stealing Janet's line, said, "What am I missing?"

Lucky stood abruptly and said, "I need some air."

Stella threw his dark sunglasses at his retreating figure. "Lucky, someone might recognize you!" He slapped on the frames and stalked out the door. "Janet?" she looked at her friend inquisitively.

"It's history time, Stella." She looked around the RV for something to occupy her hands, finally reaching into her bag and taking out a pack of cigarettes. At Stella's face, she said, "I won't smoke 'em; I just need to hold 'em. You already know Lucky rocketed to the top of the standings, like overnight, after he joined the circuit. Ryan Wexler, of course, had already made his millions. He developed and patented a system that creates huge, vinyl stickers for cars that look like custom paint jobs. It can be used in all kinds of ways—"

"I think we have them on the station cars and live trucks," Stella interrupted, remembering the creepy image of Larry Howard on all the station news cars and live trucks she'd noticed on her very first day on the job.

Janet nodded. "Well, it really caught on for race fans because tey could buy stickers to make their cars look like their favorite drivers' cars."

"People pay money for that?"

Janet pursed her lips and nodded. "Gladly. Ryan Wexler made a killing. He was on the governing board for NASCAR for years, and then he bought up some cheap farmland in the middle of Nowhereville, Tennessee, and used his contacts to build a speedway. The guy is a business genius."

"Okay, but what does this have to do with—"

"I'm getting there." Janet settled back into her seat, telling the story with relish. "Wexler had everything—money, fame, and a gorgeous wife—but then... he didn't. His wife left him and took up with a hot, new driver she'd met on the track..."

Stella's mouth dropped open. "No! Lucky?"

Janet nodded. "It might have taken a while, but it looks like Ryan finally got revenge."

"But murder? Why not just screw Lucky's fiancée and call it even? Why take it further?"

"Because, obviously, I wasn't nearly upset enough," Lucky said, walking back into the RV with a cup of coffee. "I've been going over it in my mind all night and it's the only thing that makes sense." He sat down. "Look, ten years ago, I was young— just twenty-three—"

"The same age our Stella is now," Janet said with a smile, enjoying this information session a bit too much for Stella's taste.

Lucky faltered, rubbing a hand over his face. "Yes, and Stella is much more mature than I was at that age. I had a fling with Kristy, but she was using me as a way to lash out at Ryan. Once that became clear, I ended things."

"Ryan was devastated," Janet said, putting a cigarette between her lips. "The gossip magazines all said he thought she'd come back to him after a little break—he never expected her to start screwing every driver in town. Plus, he had to split his fortune in half."

"So, taking Star from you just wasn't enough?" Stella asked, wanting to hear his theory.

"When I found Star with another man, it was almost a relief. I felt like I was at a point in my life where I should settle down, and Star was who I was with when I came to that conclusion. Things just moved forward, and it felt like a durn runaway train. I was just along for the ride but couldn't see a reason to change the course. Star was nice, you know, and loyal, I thought—until she wasn't. I was angry at first, of course, but within days, I saw the whole thing as a get-out-of-jail-free card."

"How would Ryan know that? You're not friends, obviously."

"He called me to the speedway in Bristol. That was the first time we met, Stella. He said someone was trying to blackmail Star. At the time, he told me she had called him for help—I didn't realize they were *together*. The story he told me was someone had a sex tape of Star and another man and it would be released to the tabloids unless I paid three million dollars. I told him I wouldn't get involved. God, that sounds cold now that I say it, but at the time, she wasn't my fiancée, anymore, and I was just done!"

"That's why you fought that day?"

"He started yelling at me, telling me I had to pay, and trying to get me all worked up, but I just didn't... *care* enough to get involved."

Janet whistled. "You know what they say: the opposite of love isn't hate, it's indifference."

"Yeah, but how does stealing someone's fiancée turn into killing Lucky Haskins?" Stella didn't think there were enough dots to connect just yet. "How would he know how to rig your car, anyway?"

Janet rolled her eyes. "You really don't know anything about NASCAR, do you? First of all, Ryan Wexler was a mechanic before he bought up a chain of mechanic shops and discovered the PMM system." At Stella's look she said, "Paint Magnet Magic, his patented—"

"Right, right, I got it!"

"Second," Janet continued, "he hated Lucky enough that he planned on wooing a woman away from him for ten years? Now that's the kind of devotion to a cause that borders on obsession, if you ask me."

Stella couldn't argue with that. Her cell phone rang, and she glanced at the screen before answering.

"Hey, Billy Joe. Where are you?"

"I'm still about four hours away, Stella. I should get into Talladega around three. Keith wants you to have the Cruisner interview live tomorrow night for the six. I'll be in today, so we can get video and interviews at the track about the accident. They're calling in Larry and Alexa to anchor the Sunday night news, and they're going to promote the heck out of your exclusive for the rest of the weekend."

"Whoa! You'd think someone would have called me!"

"I just did," Billy Joe said flatly.

Stella bit back a retort. "We'll be at the track, Billy Joe. Go straight there and we'll find you." She disconnected. "We need to get in touch with Jim. They're expecting a live interview with him tomorrow night, and we don't even know if he's here yet!"

Janet's eyes danced with excitement. "First, we need surveillance video from the track. Who was around Lucky's car who shouldn't have been? We need to see if Ryan was around the garages at any point in the hours leading up to the race."

"Are you..." Lucky watched Janet jump up from the table and load things into her purse. He scratched his head and then looked at Stella. "Is Janet coming with us?"

"Hell yes, I'm coming with you. Dereck won't be up for hours, and he won't be able to *get it up* for hours after that, so I'm all yours."

"Well," Stella said with a grimace, "how could we turn down an offer like that?"

25

ANOTHER MYSTERY

The Bristol Motor Speedway was known as the world's fastest half-mile. Short straightaways and steep banks allowed cars to keep their speed up as they flung around the corners. Talladega, by contrast, was long and lean with. Two-and-a-half miles around a narrow oval.

Stella flashed her press card and got through the outer gate with ease. They saw the spot inside the main fence where the national and local media set up for continuous live shots with new information on Lucky's death. Stella kept driving; Lucky needed to get inside the track to look around. She slowed her car as they neared the final barrier keeping them from the actual track. The man working the gate shook his head as soon as her car closed in.

She smiled her friendliest smile. "Hi there—"

"No, no, no. No press past these gates; orders from the top office. If you want in, someone has to come out and get you. Back up, back up, back up."

She backed her car up and parked near all the other press cars. "Guys, I think we should split up. We can cover more ground if we're apart." She looked at Janet and Lucky, and neither objected. "I'll go straight to the general manager's office and find out about getting a copy of the radio traffic from the day of the accident. Janet, you scope out where the security office is and who looks friendly there. I don't want you picking any locks, but just figure out where we want to be later today. Lucky, when exactly did your car get here?"

"They drove in from Knoxville on Thursday—started doing some work in the garage right away. We did some tweaking between practice laps and qualifying on Friday. I drove in the morning, we made some adjustments, and then Hap got behind the wheel. I was there, looked over the car, myself, and didn't see anything odd."

"So, if we're going to assume it wasn't Jim..." He nodded sharply and shot her an angry look. "Okay, then we'll need to watch surveillance video from Friday, just to see if we can find anything unusual happening around the track. Lucky," she warned, "you need to keep a low profile. I don't think you look like *you*, but Janet recognized you right away last night! You can't go parading around the track—at least not if you don't want anyone to know you're alive!"

He ducked his head. "Why don't I go with Janet? If there's a chance, I can peel off and do some looking on my own."

Janet and Lucky skulking around the track? More like marching through the infield like they owned the place! She bit the inside of her lip. "You think that's a good idea?"

"Bear, we'll be fine. You just try to get that radio traffic. Surely Hap knew something was wrong. I want to hear what he said."

The grandstands towered over the parking lot; the enormity of a track like this couldn't be overstated. Stella was used to basketball arenas or football stadiums where you could easily see the entire facility from every seat, but this was like being at the county fair.

She called up to the media relations office, and Robbie Steemer said he'd be right down. Her not-quite-official interview with Jim was really opening doors for them. As they approached the gate again, the same guard from before came out with a scowl on his face. This time, Stella beat him to the punch.

"Robbie Steemer told me to wait for him right here. I'm Stella Reynolds with NBC2 in Bristol, Virginia." She took out her press badge and passed it over to the guard.

He glanced at the picture and then did a double take. "Yikes! Who is this?"

"It's me!" she snapped, shoving the ID in her bag.

"Wow, all the way from Bristol, huh? Just when you think we're all full with reporters, more of you show up like dang cockroaches."

"Well..." she searched for a positive spin. "It sure is a big story, so I guess a lot of people want to know what's going on with the investigation."

The guard escorted them to the security shack and had Stella sign in. She scrawled three names, making sure they were illegible, and the guard went back to his magazine. Soon, a man inside the gate called over.

"Stella Reynolds?" Robbie Steemer was young—probably only five or six years older than Stella—and there was no noticeable twang in his voice. A two-way radio hung off a pocket of his khakis, and both his sandy blond hair and thick, coke bottle glasses, glinted in the sunlight.

She smiled and held out a hand. "Yes, hi. You must be Robbie —it's nice to meet you in person. Thanks for the info on the phone earlier this week."

"Well, the whole office is abuzz that you've got an interview lined up with Cruisner. No one can believe it."

Stella glanced at Lucky. "Yes, we're all set to interview him tomorrow," she lied, hoping they would be able to get in touch with him soon, now that Robbie's office and her own were expecting her to deliver.

"Well, we can't get him to return any of our calls. We need to interview him about the day of the race, but after the explosion Friday night, he disappeared. So, I want to know how you tracked him down and where is he now."

"Oh," Stella racked her brain, stopping to adjust her shoe while she thought about the best way to answer.

"Hey, Stella?" Janet asked loudly. "I'm going to meet up with you in a bit—have to find a bathroom."

"Oh, sure. Why don't you use the restrooms over there," Robbie pointed to an area under the grandstands off to the right. "Do you want us to wait for you?"

"Nah, you go ahead," Janet said seriously. "I might be a while. My system just ain't used to your Alabama biscuits and gravy, you know what I mean?"

Stella cringed, but Robbie took it all in stride. "It's not meant for everybody, that's for sure. Come on through the tunnel and across the track to our offices when you're ready, or we can meet you back here when we're done."

Realizing that couldn't have gone any better, Stella said, "Luke, why don't you stay down here until Janet's ready, just so she doesn't get lost?"

Lucky kept his head down and murmured, "Will do, boss."

They peeled off, and Robbie said, "So, you were about to tell me where you found Jim Cruisner."

"Right. Well, you know, I can't really give up my source, Robbie, but maybe we can work something out. My boss wants me to interview him live, and the speedway sure would make a nice backdrop for our live shot. Jim couldn't ignore you if you were next to him!"

Robbie nodded and led them into a tunnel under the grandstands that led to the inner circle of the track.

On race day, the speedway would swell to the size of a small town with seating for 147,000 people, along with garage bays, a media center, and suites up top for the best bird's-eye view of the action. The infield consisted of roads, campgrounds, trailer parking, and pit row.

The tunnel spit them out between rows of seats.

"Watch your step." Robbie flashed his credentials to a wary-looking track employee and then stepped onto the paved track. "Our offices are just on the other side of the road here."

They walked across the asphalt toward a glass-walled structure that sat in front of a huge bank of garage bays. The campgrounds off in the distance were packed full of campers and RVs, but no people were allowed in this part of the track.

"The kind of event cancelation we had last weekend after the explosion was unprecedented. We have tens of thousands of people stay on-track every year over race weekend, and even though the race was canceled after the explosion, the reservations weren't. Most are staying for the memorial we've got planned for Monday. It's honestly been a nightmare," he added under his breath. "Lots of people, lots of alcohol, and not much for them to do. The good news is they're not up and moving this morning—yet." He looked darkly toward the campgrounds and kept walking.

"How long have you worked here, Robbie?"

"I came here straight from college, so about six years now."

The media center structure had offices at each corner and four long rows of seats that ran in between. Waist-high countertops ran the length of the rows, as well, where reporters would work while they covered the race. Robbie took Stella back to his office. "So, what can I do for you, Stella?"

She decided to start big. "Any chance I can look through surveillance video from around Lucky's garage bay on Thursday and Friday?"

Robbie lurched forward in his seat and then tried to smooth over his reaction. "Oh, uh, afraid not, Stella. That's not something we can share with the media."

"Are you guys looking it over to see if there's anything suspicious?"

He looked at her with an odd expression. "No, we're not." She stared at him, willing him to give her more information. He sighed. "All signs in our investigation so far are pointing toward a terrible accident. The engine overheating combined with a faulty fuel line resulted in a deadly tragedy on our track. They're about to close the case on this one officially—I'd say probably after the weekend. Maybe Monday morning, so the memorial can proceed without anything hanging over our heads."

She leaned forward in her chair. "How about a copy of the radio traffic from qualifying last week?"

Robbie tapped a few keys on his computer and then put a thumb drive into the USB port. "You and every other media outlet in the state," he said with a small smile. After a minute, he handed it over. Anything else?"

Before she could line up her next question, his walkie-talkie came to life. "Uh, hey there, boss. I got a body in the east grandstands. Repeat, body in the east grandstands. Looks like some kind of news photographer. His camera's smashed all to hell next to him and the ID says it's Scott Lyon out of Kingsport, Tennessee. We need police, medics—no, you know what, scratch the medics. He's deader than a—" Robbie fumbled around with the radio, finally turning the right dial to silence the device.

"What?" Stella stood so quickly that her chair fell back against the floor with a bang. Scott was that friendly photographer she'd met one of her first nights in Bristol—the one from Ohio.

"Stay right there; don't move!" Robbie jumped up and hurried out of the office without a backward glance.

Stella stayed in the room for a beat and then hustled after him out the door. She spotted Lucky and Janet making their way out of the tunnel and waved them over. After quickly explaining what was happening, all three knew they were about to run out of time to sneak around the track undetected. Police would have everything roped off soon.

They separated again and agreed to meet back at the car. Lucky headed toward his trailer, the last one left in the infield after the canceled race, and Janet walked with purpose toward the main security office.

Stella surveyed the perimeter of the track. Her eyes zeroed in on a bevy of activity on one section of the grandstands and she started walking, her notebook and pen out and ready. She slowed as she got close to the crowd. The discovery was so new that security hadn't yet cordoned off the area.

Scott's body lay crumpled between a row of bleacher seats; his shoulders and head stuck out in the aisle. A trickle of blood crusted by his nose, and his face was swollen. His camera rested two rows away and had been smashed into hundreds of tiny pieces, black plastic scattered around like an impressionistic painting. Scott's open eyes stared blankly down the steps. Stella averted her eyes. She'd never even seen a dead body before, let alone a murder victim.

"Stella, I asked you to stay in the office!" Robbie called down the steps.

She took them two at a time and met Robbie halfway. "I know this man, Robbie. He's a photographer from ABC17 back in the Tri-cities. He's... he's from Ohio," she finished quietly, wondering how his family would find out about his death.

"Come with me."

Stella took one last look at the body and followed Robbie down the grandstand steps to the track below.

26

LOOK AT THAT

T hey hurried past the security guards now roping off a huge, circular space with yellow caution tape; sirens blared in the distance. She assumed she was being escorted out of the facility, so when the security office came into view, instead, she slowed down.

"Hey, listen, I didn't do anything wrong," she said, stopping outside the door. "I'll just leave—you don't have to write me up or anything, Robbie."

He used his credentials to swipe into the secure office and then looked back at Stella and motioned her in. She frowned but followed him through the doors. They walked into the reception area and stopped outside another locked door. Robbie held a hand out to an approaching guard, and the man in uniform backed away as Robbie turned a beady eye on Stella.

"What do you know?"

She was caught off guard by the question, and they eyed each other for a moment before Stella decided she had nothing to lose. "I know Lucky's car was tampered with," Robbie flinched, "and I have a source who was here that day and has some idea of who's responsible." She guessed Lucky counted as a source in his own death.

"Who are you looking for on the surveillance video?" he asked.

"I don't feel comfortable saying just yet... but I have an idea—someone with a motive and the means to make a murder look like an accident."

Again, Robbie stared at her for a long minute. "We could probably use your help. We've been looking over the video since the accident, but my guys don't see anything jumping out as strange. Maybe fresh eyes would help."

"I thought you said the investigation was about to wrap up—that it was mechanical failure?"

"That's what the track owner wants to happen, and with no other evidence, that's exactly what the general manager is going to announce Monday. So, we don't have a lot of time. I've never seen a car do that, though, and I don't think it was an accident. And now *another* body?"

They turned at a crack of noise at the door. The guard standing there was nearly bowled over by Janet. "Whoa, whoa, whoa!" He grabbed her by the arm. "You can't be in here, miss. This is a secure—"

"This is my... my associate producer, Janet Black. She's privy to my information on this case. It would probably help us go faster to have another set of eyes on the screen."

With a nod from Robbie, the guard released Janet's arm. "Thank you very much," she said with a raspy laugh. "I haven't been manhandled like that since last night."

The guard blushed, and Stella choked back a laugh. Robbie rubbed his chin and stepped back when Janet stalked into the room. "Are we this way?" She stopped at another keyless entry door.

Robbie shook himself and stepped in front of Janet. "Yes. Let me get in there and tell them what's going on. Where do you want to start?"

Stella looked back through her notes. "I guess Friday morning, when Lucky's mechanics started to work on his car before the first round of practice laps."

Robbie disappeared. In the silence, Stella realized she needed to start working on another story: Scott Lyon's murder. It would definitely be the lead on tonight's news, but she needed to see this surveillance video before she called the newsroom. This might have been her only chance to find Hap's killer.

"So many murderers, so little time."

Robbie opened the door. "Let's go. They're all cued up and ready for you."

She and Janet walked into a dimly lit room with a long, narrow table, six chairs, a slew of machines that resembled the video editors at her TV station, and two dozen monitors hanging in two rows across the wall. Robbie motioned to two empty seats on the far side of the room, away from the security guard keeping watch over the live cameras placed around the track.

"Go ahead. You can scroll through the tapes from Friday. Better move quickly, though—police will be here soon for the footage from overnight. They'll want to see what happened to that photographer."

Robbie left and Stella gave Janet a quick tutorial on how to use the toggle wheel on the playback machine while the security guard glared at them. "Turn it to the right to fast forward, left to rewind—it's pretty easy."

"Robbie said she was a producer, but she don't know how to use an edit machine?" the guard drawled.

Stella racked her brain for a reasonable explanation, when Janet snarled, "I'm new to the job, okay, asshole?"

The guy smirked, looking at Janet with new appreciation. "You ain't from around here, are you? Not many southern belles with a mouth like 'at."

Janet uncrossed her legs and ran her hands down her thighs. "Nope, I couldn't really pull off sexually reserved, you know what I mean?"

Stella stared unwaveringly at the screen in front of her, wishing she could unsee the last twenty seconds. "Uh, Janet, let's get to work. It sounds like we don't have a lot of time in here."

"I'm Nick." He looked appreciatively at Janet. "If you want to learn anything else today, just ask."

"Guys, no time!"

Janet flashed Nick one last smile as she ran a hand over her breast and said breathlessly to Stella, "Sorry, you're right. Let's get in there and take a long, hard look at the video."

Nick squirmed uncomfortably in his seat, but all three fell silent as the women started looking through video. They were hoping to spot Ryan Wexler near the garage bays in the hours leading up to the qualifying laps Friday afternoon; Stella had no idea how difficult it would be to find that needle in the haystack of people in and around the garages that day.

"Can just *anyone* walk around the drivers and their cars?" she asked a half hour later. She'd hoped to fast forward through the video until she saw something suspicious, but after watching dozens of people in frame every single minute, she soon realized she had to watch the video in real time. It was going to take forever.

"Not anyone," Nick looked up from his job, "but anyone who pays for an all-access pass—the golden ticket. Then, of course, you've got friends and family, guests of the drivers, the mechanics and crew.... There's a lot of action to see and lots of people want a front row seat."

After thirty more minutes of silence, a low buzzer sounded across the dark room.

Nick glanced at the door and then pressed a button under the desktop. A beam of light entered the room when the door behind them opened.

Robbie walked in with two officers from the Talladega City Police Department. "Nick, these gentlemen would like to see some video, starting with the area in the grandstands where the body was found this morning." He avoided looking at Stella and Janet completely, and she realized he was giving them the chance to be in the room when a murderer might be identified. She ignored the cops and was relieved to see Janet, for once, do the same without comment.

"Who are they?" The older officer gestured toward the women with his head but barely looked over.

"Just interns," Nick answered. "They're logging tape from Friday."

The officer nodded and spoke into the radio clipped to his shoulder before he leaned over the chair in front of him. "I want to see how the victim gets into the grandstands and who was with him when he died."

Nick rewound the tape until a man dressed in the standard track employee uniform poked at the body and then waved wildly with his two-way radio.

"That's one of our employees, discovering the body," Robbie said from the door.

The officer nodded. "Let's rewind."

Nick adjusted the toggle wheel in front of him, and the video went in reverse. "We have a total of 128 cameras placed around the track and garage areas, plus the parking lots and concessions booths, of course," he said, as if he were giving a tour and not helping with a murder investigation. "We're looking at video from a section called OV Hill North. As you can see, it's a pretty wide shot, but if we find something we want to investigate, we can match up the time code and access other cameras in the area."

Again came a nod from the cop, but he didn't lose focus on the video monitor. The body lay prone on screen now and the sunlight faded. As day returned to night, huge overhead lamps lit up the grandstands. The security cameras had night-vision capabilities, but even as the backdrop changed, Scott continued to lay dead or dying on the cold, metal steps. Stella had trouble pretending to watch her screen; Janet must have noticed, because she elbowed her in the side with gusto.

Stella grunted and everyone in the room turned. Janet smoothly continued looking at her monitor, but Stella smiled sheepishly. "Sorry," she said. "Allergies." She coughed for good measure and turned back to her monitor.

"Here we go—this looks interesting." The officer tapped Nick on the shoulder. "Here comes the killer."

27

THE SUSPECT

The room got even quieter, all eyes now glued to the same screen. The images were surreally captivating as a murder played out in reverse while Nick continued to rewind the tape. Scott's body rose off the grandstands at an inhuman angle. When he finally stood tall, a jerk rocked him forward, and then he gestured madly at his killer. Nick finally hit play when the screen was empty, and they all watched Scott walk into the frame in real time.

Scott Lyon, his camera slung over one shoulder by the strap, walked onscreen, followed closely by another person wearing dark clothes and a ball cap, which covered most of their face. Even on the black and white screen, however, Stella saw a glint of light at the killer's fingers. It was so fast, she wasn't sure anyone else noticed, but as soon as she recognized Ryan Wexler's big, obnoxious ring, she noticed other things that seemed to confirm his identity.

From afar, the killer walked with the same wide-legged swagger—the same confident strut. She even detected a kind of better-than-you attitude in the way he interacted with Scott.

The camera was located high on a light pole about half a

section away and showed the front side of Scott's head from above and his attacker's back. It would be impossible for anyone to identify the murderer, but Stella was certain it was Ryan.

The two were discussing something. Scott was angry, pointing accusingly at the other person, and then things escalated. Scott waved his arms wildly just seconds before the gunshot rocked him backward, and he fell to the ground. The killer moved in closer, fired a second shot, stomped on Scott's camera, and walked back the way he'd come, head down. There was never a clear shot of his face.

"Looks like he went down right around 4:32 a.m.," Nick said.

Stella looked over at Janet just in time. Her face was red from the exertion of keeping her mouth closed, and Stella barely had time to grab her arm in warning. She looked like she was seconds away from shouting out the name of the murderer, as if she were playing a game of charades.

Janet grunted in pain and shot Stella a pleading look. "I know who that is," she mouthed. "It's—"

"Let's try another angle," the officer barked at Nick. While the guard worked to cue up other cameras to the right time code, Stella stared blankly at the screen in front of her. Ryan Wexler killed Scott—she was certain of it—but was he also responsible for the explosion on the track? She zoned out, wondering about his motive in each case.

"There's Ryan Wexler," Janet said, and Stella groaned. She thought she knew to stay quiet! She turned to say as much to her friend when she realized Janet was pointing at *Stella's* screen, not the one police were watching.

She was right. Stella leaned in close, and there he was, wandering around Lucky's garage bay the day of the explosion. According to the time code on her monitor, it was just before four in the afternoon the day of Hap's murder. Ryan walked in front of the garage bays, pacing, and then Lucky entered the screen.

"Damn shame," the cop said from behind Stella. "He was a great driver."

Her shoulders tensed. As soon as Lucky walked out of his garage, Ryan pivoted and walked away. Stella's eyes narrowed.

"I didn't catch your names. You're with the speedway here?" The officer had his notebook out, and Stella reluctantly pressed pause, forcing her eyes away from the screen.

"Not exactly—just doing some contract work today. I'm Stella and this is Janet. You are?"

"Here we go," Nick interrupted, and the cop turned back to the main monitor in the room. "I found another camera—this one's by the concession stand." The angle was better, but it was so dark that you couldn't identify either person. "There are at least two more; give me a second to pull them up."

Stella anxiously turned back to her screen to see Lucky taking a cell phone out of his pocket and then shouted something back into the garage bay. Several other men walked out and closed and locked the garage door.

Janet leaned over, and in a low voice said, "Why is Ryan skulking around Lucky's garage?"

"Let's see if we find out," Stella whispered. Strangers walked in front of the bays, their expensive, all-access credentials swinging back and forth around their necks like trophies. Finally, after a few minutes, Ryan reappeared. He took something out of his pocket and approached the garage door; a moment later, the door rolled up and Ryan sauntered into Lucky's garage.

Stella sat bolt upright in her seat and stared wide-eyed at Janet. This was it: evidence that Ryan had been close enough to Lucky's car to do something to it minutes before the explosion. She couldn't believe it! She hadn't been able to get Star out of her mind—she seemed like the perfect suspect—but Star wasn't the one walking into Lucky's garage.

"Here we go, gentlemen. This is our last chance," Nick said as he pressed play once again on his control panel and video of another angle from overnight started to play.

Stella scribbled down the timecode when Ryan entered Lucky's garage in her notebook and shifted her eyes to the main screen. This time, Scott and the other person were far away, walking directly toward the camera in a well-lit area.

"This is the tunnel that leads from the parking lot to the inner track," Robbie said.

Everyone in the room seemed to be holding their breath. Just when Scott came into view, the other person on camera reached up and tugged his ball cap lower, obscuring his face at just the right time.

The officer groaned, but Janet jabbed Stella in the side with excitement.

"Goddamnit!" she exclaimed before she could stop herself— that one had hurt.

"I know, I thought we'd see him for sure that time." The officer sent a consoling smile Stella's way. She nodded back, relieved he'd misunderstood her sound, and then pummeled Janet in the side when he turned back to the screen.

Janet bit back a gasp, and Robbie glared at them both. "Ladies, why don't you take a break? You've been at it for hours," he said pointedly.

"Good idea, Robbie. Here's that information you were looking for." She handed him the page from her notebook with the time-code written down. "That should help wrap things up from Friday," she added, leading Janet out the door.

Once they were out on the pavement, Janet smacked her arm again. "Did you see that ring when the killer covered his face? That ring was from the 1979 NASCAR championship race—I could tell by the gemstone. That's the same race Ryan Wexler won in Daytona!"

"I know!" Stella said, grabbing Janet by the arm and propelling her toward the parking lot. "Well, I mean, I didn't know all of that, but I did recognize the ring as the same one Ryan wears. Are there any others like it?"

"No—there was only one winner that year, and 1979 is the only year they had a championship ring like that. In years before, they only had trophies, and in years after, they did a different color gemstone. The only year they did the ruby was 1979."

Stella's mind raced. "We saw Ryan in the lobby of the hotel when we first got to town—must have been quarter after two this morning. He could have taken Star up to their room and met Scott out at the track after she passed out. Remember how rough she looked this morning at breakfast? Maybe he got her drunk on purpose."

"We found evidence that he might have messed with Lucky's car, too. Stella, did we just solve two murders?" Janet looked dazed. "It still doesn't make sense why Ryan would kill *Scott*. What did Scott have to do with anything?"

"I think the question is what did Scott have video of that Ryan didn't want to get out? You don't smash a camera like that for no reason. Scott had something on somebody, and Ryan wanted to destroy the evidence, along with anyone who had any knowledge of it."

They walked in silence for a moment, Stella's mind spinning. "Scott told me the day of the crash that he did contract work for the speedway in Bristol, so he and Ryan definitely knew each other. What could Scott have possibly recorded to make Ryan want to kill him, though?" She was missing a connection but couldn't figure out what it was.

Janet shrugged and they walked in silence out of the dark tunnel and into the glaring light of the parking lot. As they passed the guard shack, Stella's cell phone rang. She looked at the screen but didn't recognize the number.

"Hello?" She took out her car key and slid it into the lock.

"Stella? It's Jim Cruisner. I understand you want to talk."

28

A SPARE PAIR

"Jim Cruisner?" Stella was so surprised she didn't know what else to say. She was frozen in place, the key shoved into the lock of her car, her mouth hanging slightly open. Finally, Janet smacked her arm. "Ow—I mean, wow, Jim. I'm so glad you called me back. How are you?" She shot a glare at her friend and rubbed her arm, leaving the key dangling out of the car door.

"I guess I'm surviving. You left a message that you wanted to talk to me?"

She motioned Janet over, and the two women put their heads together, the phone wedged between their ears so they could both hear the call.

"Yes, I want to interview you about Lucky's accident. We can come to you or you can come here—whatever works for you, Jim. I know this last week must have been difficult."

"You don't know anything," he muttered. They'd never spoken before, but something about him sounded off. He didn't sound like the grieving friend she expected. "Tomorrow. I'll be ready to talk tomorrow," he added.

"Well, we'd like to interview you for the news tomorrow night, right here at the track." She looked at Janet and saw her face reflected the same doubts about Jim.

"I guess that'd be fine. It's been a rough couple of days, and Lucky spoke so highly of you. I just thought, if I was going to talk about the kind of man Lucky was, it should be to you."

Stella nodded slowly. It made sense, but for some reason, her inner alarm bells clanged. "Yes, I want to talk about your memories of Lucky and what you think happened before the explosion. Everyone has been waiting to hear from you since the accident. It'd be live, of course."

"Yes. I really do want to tell everyone about Lucky."

"Well, I really appreciate that. Do you want to meet me by the NBC2 satellite truck tomorrow at four? That'll give us enough time to run mic checks and get the shot set up. I have a feeling I'm not the only one who'll want to talk to you. People here at the track want an interview, too. Does that sound all right with you?"

He mumbled noncommittally and disconnected the call.

She closed her phone and turned to Janet. "That was weird, wasn't it?"

"Super weird, like finding-sprinkles-on-your-hotdog weird. Sprinkles are good and hotdogs are good, but sprinkles on your hotdog is just weird."

Stella snorted. "Seriously?"

Janet smiled. "Or like waking-up-to-a-strange-man-in-bed-with-you weird. Strange is good and a man in bed with you is good, but having a strange man in your bed is weird, right?"

"Oh, shut up, Janet."

"All I heard is 'a strange man in bed with you,' and my ears perked right up." Lucky came from the other side of the car with a smile. He wore fresh clothes that fit and had a normal-looking hat pulled low over his floppy locks, which were already fading back to blond from the box of brown hair dye they'd used Friday night.

"What have *you* been doing?" Stella asked accusingly. "You

said you'd keep a low profile, but it looks like you hit a spa and a department store! Just how big is that infield, anyway?"

"I broke into my trailer—didn't even break in, really, it was unlocked. Some damn race fan, no doubt, ransacked the place, and it was tossed to pieces, but it still had running water, and that's all I needed. I had to wash my hair again—the smell of that dye job has been driving me crazy."

"Lucky!" Stella exclaimed. "They have security cameras everywhere! What if someone saw you?"

He threw an arm over her shoulders and pulled her close. "But nobody did, so we're fine."

"Well, you just missed Jim," she said, holding up her phone.

"You should be glad you did," Janet added, and they quickly explained his odd call.

"Well, it sounds to me like he's just taking this whole thing really hard!" Lucky said with a sigh. "Did you tell him I'm alive?"

Stella wrinkled her nose. "No. I thought you definitely needed to be here for that bit of news. Speaking of news..." She dialed the station back in Bristol. The weekend producer answered, and she filled her in on Scott's murder. "We can go live for your newscast tonight, but you'd better call Marty. This is huge—he'll want to know about it."

When she disconnected, a rumbling engine motored close. Billy Joe nodded from the driver's seat of the satellite truck and turned into an empty spot nearby.

"We're going to have to let Billy Joe know what's going on." Stella watched him inch the truck forward into the space. When Lucky started to object she said, "He's part of the team, Lucky, and we're going to need to be on the same page if we're going to pull any of this off."

"You're right. We'll tell him everything."

The diesel engine cut off and Billy Joe climbed down from the driver's seat. Bigger than a live truck, it was square and boxy, like an armored truck. Instead of a mast rising up from the middle, a huge dish laid flat against the roof, ready to swivel up and beam their signal to a satellite in the sky.

Billy Joe stretched out, arching his back with a grimace as he worked out the kinks from driving all day. His light brown hair waved in the breeze, and he smashed a ball cap down over his head, muttering something about the sun being "too goddamn bright" as he moved around the truck, checking tire pressure, opening the door to the editing area, and taking out his cooler.

"Hey, Billy Joe. How was the drive?" Stella called.

"Too goddamn long. Any changes in the plan?"

"Well..." She trailed off, trying to decide where to start.

The silence stretched so long that Billy Joe finally stopped messing with his cooler and looked over. First, his eyes landed on Janet leaning over Stella's car. She guessed the pose wasn't by chance, as her boobs were smashed together and nearly falling out of her V-neck top. As soon as Billy Joe's eyes traveled up Janet's body and landed on her face, she purred, "Hi there, handsome." She had been worried about Billy Joe immediately recognizing Lucky, but it was clear that wouldn't be a problem. He finally tore his eyes away from Janet, and she snickered, "Still got it."

Stella cleared her throat and said, "There's been a murder at the track, and I'm sure they'll want us live tonight." Before Billy Joe could react to that news, his eyes landed on Lucky, and he stepped back, his gaze focused but unseeing. She walked between the two men. "Billy Joe, you remember Lucky? He'll be staying with us while we, uh... while we figure out a few things."

"Wha... huh..." Billy Joe took off his cap and scratched his head, his eyes never leaving Lucky's face.

"It's been a long few days, friend. We'll explain everything in the truck." Lucky held his hand out, and Billy Joe shook it quickly before dropping it and wiping his hand off on his jeans.

"He's not a ghost, Billy Joe—you can't catch anything from him! He wasn't driving the car on Friday." At his blank stare, she motioned toward the back of the satellite truck. A group of campers was heading their way and Stella felt exposed out on the blacktop. "Get in and we'll explain everything."

∼

"WELL, I'LL BE GODDAMNED."

Billy Joe sat back in his chair, and his weight made him slowly roll downhill, toward the front of the truck. Stella, Janet, and Lucky had all contributed parts of the story, and even Lucky looked interested at the end as she and Janet explained recognizing Ryan Wexler as Scott's killer.

"He was in my garage just before the explosion?" Lucky asked doubtfully. "I think we'd know if someone broke into the garage."

"Lucky, he had a key! He opened the door like he owned the place!"

Lucky ripped his hat off and ran a hand over his head. He fussed with the hat for a minute and then finally looked up and said, "Okay, so he definitely had access, and we know why he had it in for *me*. Why would he kill this photographer guy, though?"

"That's the part that doesn't make any sense," Stella agreed with a nod, "and there's something else I've been thinking about. I think Star is the one who tossed your trailer, not a random race fan. She's been looking for that prenup since you died—maybe she thought it would be in there!"

"She's honestly not that smart."

"But she's obviously that motivated!" Stella exclaimed.

Billy Joe sat forward. "Uh, excuse me, but none of this makes sense." He rolled his shoulders and then folded his arms across his chest. "You're saying Ryan Wexler had it out for you," he pointed at Lucky, "because you screwed his wife all those years ago—"

"Soon-to-be ex-wife!" Lucky corrected. "I think they were officially separated, just not actually divorced..." Stella glared at him and he mumbled, "Yes, that's about right."

Billy Joe picked up as if he hadn't been interrupted. "And y'all think he did something to your car that made it explode, but Hap was driving." There were nods all around. "Now Scott Lyon is dead, and you two think you recognized Ryan Wexler on surveillance video pulling the trigger." There was more nodding.

"Scott did freelance work for Ryan at the Bristol Motor Speedway all the time," Billy Joe offered. "You said the killer smashed Scott's camera after he shot him—maybe he had something on tape Ryan didn't want to get out."

"Yeah," Stella said, wrinkling her nose, "but smashing a camera doesn't necessarily ruin the tape. Doesn't everyone know that?"

"Well, Ryan is old—maybe he doesn't understand the technology," Janet said decidedly, as if her two-minute lesson on using a toggle wheel on the security office editing machine made her an expert.

"I don't know," Stella said, unconvinced. "He runs the Bristol Motor Speedway. You'd think he would know how a camera works." She rubbed her forehead, thinking, and the ringing of her cell phone interrupted the quiet inside the truck.

"Stella, we need you live at the top of the six, but I don't know how we're going to do it," Marty said. "Billy Joe has to run the satellite truck, so we need a second photographer to operate the camera. Any ideas?"

Billy Joe watched Janet with hungry eyes, and Stella had an idea. "We ran into an old friend out here, Marty, and I think Billy Joe would be more than happy to train her to run the camera for tonight."

"Has she done any shoots before?"

"She's definitely done a lot of shots," Stella answered with a smirk.

"Great. We'll start with information on the murder, but as of now, we're not releasing the victim's name—they can't find his mother to notify her. We'll have a straight live shot on that and then toss to a preview of your interview with Jim to tease tomorrow's exclusive."

She looked at her watch and saw they had about an hour to get ready. "I'll let Billy Joe know."

"Oh, and Stella?"

"Yes?"

"Keith wants you to uh... wear those glasses."

She shook her head incredulously. "I didn't bring the glasses, Marty, and I wouldn't wear them, anyway!"

To her right, Billy Joe patted his front shirt pocket and then pulled out the offensive frames and offered them to Stella. "It's a spare pair."

"Marty, what the f—" but she stopped. He'd already hung up. "Coward," she muttered.

"You wear glasses?" Lucky asked innocently.

"Oh, shut up!"

29

HOTEL CAMPING

"Standby, Stella. The show open starts in twenty seconds."

Janet's chest thrust out, her words stern yet slightly uncertain. She wore the headset Billy Joe had given her back at the truck, but the band kept sliding down, so the earphones hung lower than her actual ears.

Stella tamped down the urge to smile, but she knew, without her help, there would be no live shot. Federal safety rules around using a satellite truck couldn't be overlooked, even in a breaking news situation like they had that night.

Janet put her face up to the viewfinder to check the shot and accidentally bumped the tripod. The camera tipped dangerously to one side, and Janet's face became the picture of horror as she stood frozen, watching it reach the point of no return. The camera swayed at the top, balancing on only two legs, before it stopped for an agonizingly long second and changed direction, crashing back to all three legs.

Billy Joe's voice snapped into their earpieces. "Don't touch the camera, Janet—just leave it alone! All you have to do is stand there next to it, okay?"

Stella looked down at her notes to hide her grin, but the smile faded when the cheap, plastic glasses slipped down her nose.

Her image was being beamed back to the station in Bristol, and she decided to take the opportunity to make a change. She made a show of looking back down at her notes again, and the thick, black frames slid off her face and fell to the ground below. She pretended to stumble and smashed the frames with her heel —which was off camera—and gasped dramatically, "Oh, no!" She picked up the broken, crushed frames and held them up to the camera so anyone back in the control room in Bristol who might be watching could see. "What a shame!"

Samantha came into her ear. "You show 'em, girl."

Stella fidgeted with her earpiece in the glare of the spotlight. The heavy IFB box cut into her waist uncomfortably, but she kept the grimace off her face as the music that signaled the start of the newscast trumpeted.

Alexa: Good evening, everyone. I'm Alexa Robinson.

Larry: And I'm Larry Howard. Thanks for joining our special weekend edition of NBC2 news. We begin with more shocking news out of Talladega. Even as the investigation into Lucky Haskins's death continues, track officials are now dealing with a murder.

Alexa: Our own Stella Reynolds is live at the Talladega Superspeedway tonight with the latest on the new investigations. Stella, this time, the victim is from our area?

Stella glanced down at her notes one final time while Alexa was talking. She held the microphone up and nodded. "That's right, Alexa. We're withholding his name until police can notify his next of kin, but we know he was shot twice and died alone on the cold, metal floor of the grandstands."

She looked down at her notes and blinked. That's not what she had intended to say, but as soon as she started talking about Scott's death, a wave of emotion crashed over her. That poor man had been killed in cold blood!

She cleared her throat. "Track officials certainly didn't want another tragedy so soon here at Talladega, but that's just what they're dealing with tonight after an employee found a body in the grandstands this morning.

"Police from Talladega are investigating; we hope to have more on that tomorrow. Meanwhile, track officials are close to wrapping up their investigation into the explosive crash Friday that took the life of Lucky Haskins." She saw on the monitor that they'd taken video from Friday's crash. "Take a look at the wreck that stunned the racing world. Haskins' pit crew chief, Jim Cruisner, the one man no one has been able to talk to since the accident, will break his silence right here in an exclusive interview with me tomorrow night at five."

Back on camera, she bounced forward on the balls of her feet. "We will have a lot of new information tomorrow—information you'll see only on NBC2. Again, that exclusive interview with Jim Cruisner starts at five o'clock. Reporting live, I'm Stella Reynolds, back to you."

Janet whistled low. "When did you get so good, Stella? You sounded like network right there."

Billy Joe came out of the satellite truck. "Tomorrow's going to be crazy," she said, looking at the photographer. "Is there anything we can do to get ready tonight?"

He scratched his head. "Naw—not that I can think of. I think it's just gonna be a lot of action right before the live shot."

"I was afraid you'd say that. I guess we'll make some calls to the press office tomorrow, but otherwise it's all going to hinge on whether Jim shows for the live interview."

Soon, all four were in Stella's car, ready to leave the speedway for the night. She cranked the engine. "Where is the station putting us up?" she asked Billy Joe through the rearview mirror.

He was too busy looking down Janet's blouse to hear her, though. She cleared her throat and Janet smirked. When he looked away, she adjusted her boobs and tugged her shirt down a smidge lower. Stella decided to keep her eyes on the road.

"Billy Joe, where are we staying?" she repeated.

"Oh, I don't know. Marty said you had a place and we would just stay there."

"He thinks we're going to share a room? That's ridiculous!" Lucky coughed.

"I don't even have a room!" she exclaimed. "We didn't sleep last night!"

"Ha!" Janet cackled. "Looks like we're all sleeping in the RV!"

Stella groaned. "All of us *and* Dereck?"

"Nah, he's gone—he texted me earlier today and is headed for more action. He got tired of the parking lot."

Stella glanced back at her friend, wondering if she was upset by this turn of events. One look into the backseat had her remembering her earlier vow to not look again, however, as Janet had obviously set her sights on her next mark. Billy Joe was only too delighted to have been gotten.

"Whoa," Stella said as they turned into the hotel parking lot. Janet's RV had clearly inspired others in the same situation, and now at least a dozen campers lined the back corner of the lot, like a mini-camping area without power or water.

She squeezed into the only empty spot in the lot, right next to Janet's RV, and all four climbed out of the passenger side doors.

"What's that?" Janet pointed to a web of extension cords running through the lot.

"Looks like the hotel is letting the campers plug in," Lucky said. "Let's go ask about getting hooked up."

As he and Billy Joe headed for the hotel, Stella couldn't believe how little Lucky resembled himself. His beard was full and bushy, and at her insistence, he'd put the awful coat back on, so he was once again wearing ill-fitting and unstylish clothes. He might as well have been an out-of-work truck driver.

She climbed into the RV after Janet and froze by the kitchen —the place reeked of Dereck. Janet opened the windows and sprayed some Febreze.

"Now it smells like flowery Dereck." Janet ignored her and took the spray to the bedroom area. "I'm going to make some calls," Stella said, escaping to the fresh air outside. She tapped in the station's number, and Barry picked up on the third ring. Stella sighed; he was not the person she wanted to deal with just then. "Hey, Barry, I just wanted to touch base about tomorrow."

"Stella, glad you called. We're running promos all night and tomorrow about your exclusive with Jim. Elbee will join you all tomorrow morning to run the camera during the live shots. Hang on." He spoke to someone else in the newsroom, and when he came back on the line, he said, "Sorry, Larry's here next to me, and he wants to make sure I get this right. He wants you to have Ryan Wexler on for a live interview at five, too. I guess Larry will set it up," There was more muffled conversation, and he finally said, "He apparently has it set up, already. Wexler will join you live at five there in Talladega."

Stella's brow wrinkled. "Ryan and Jim together at five?" That could be interesting.

"Yes," Barry said airily. "Larry thinks the people in Bristol would like to hear from *our* head of racing about Lucky's death." There was more mumbling away from the phone, and then Barry said, "See you tomorrow, man." After a minute of silence, he said, "God am I tired of him ordering me around."

Stella was so surprised to hear a breaking in the ranks that she stayed quiet. "Just because Larry is friends with Wexler, we have to have him on the news all the damn time. If I have to hear another story about how Larry knows everyone in NASCAR, I'll..." His anger robbed him of words. He finally snapped, "It's a done deal, Stella. Ryan Wexler will join you all for the five and get his minute of free press for the day." He slammed down his phone.

Stella pulled her cell phone away from her ear with the ghost of a smile on her lips. Although Barry was annoyed, this was a lucky break for her. Now she'd have the one person she thought was responsible for two deaths trapped in a live interview the next night. Her smile broadened. She was going to nail him on live TV.

"We're in!" Lucky called from a few rows away. He was carrying a coil of bright orange extension cord in one hand and a six-pack of beer in the other. She looked from him to Billy Joe, who was holding two bags of food, and stifled a groan. It was going to be another long night.

30

HAP'S HISTORY

They spent the next hour brainstorming. After the food was finished and the beer was drunk, all four leaned back into the cushioned bench seats at the tiny table in the RV. They had a plan to get Ryan to confess. It was dicey and had plenty of room for error, but they'd come up with something they thought might work.

Stella yawned. "So, we all agree we'll get Jim out of the way first—give him time to be sad about Lucky's death, tell us what he'll miss most, and then talk to us about any suspicions he might have about Lucky's car."

"Then we move right on to *Wex*." Lucky set his bottle down with a clank.

"Oh, boy." She rubbed her forehead, "And you're going to come out during the interview, Jerry Springer-style, the big reveal on live TV?"

"It seems like the best way to get an honest reaction out of that slimeball, don't you think?"

"I do. God help me, I do." This was why she had come to Talladega: to conquer the live interview, and it looked like she was going to do it with flair. *This* live interview would go national, with every network around replaying for weeks—years, maybe— the clip of Lucky coming back from the dead, and she would be a part of it—hopefully in a good way.

She folded herself in half to retie her shoelace and felt something jab her in the hipbone. When she leaned back, Stella fished the hard, plastic strip out of her pocket. "Oh my gosh! With the murder this morning, I completely forgot about it. Lucky, I got a copy of the radio traffic from last Friday." She held the thumb drive out to Billy Joe. "Can we listen to this through your camera?"

"Nope."

"Then in the truck?"

"Maybe."

She saw Lucky's disappointment and glared at Billy Joe. "Care to expand on that, Chatty Cathy?"

He rubbed Janet's shoulder with one hand and stopped to glare back at Stella. "Fine. That's not a usual format for us, but I think the equipment we need to listen to it is in the satellite truck, which is parked back out at the track. Tomorrow, when we're back out at the track, we can listen to it." He turned his attention back to Janet.

Stella's shoulders stiffened at his tone. "You know what—"

Lucky grabbed her hand and said softly, "It'll keep for one more night."

Billy Joe and Janet stood up in a coordinated move. "We're going to call it a night," Janet said, pulling him toward the bedroom at the far end of the RV. "You know what they say: if this camper's rocking—"

"Don't come a-knocking," Billy Joe finished with a grin. They disappeared behind the door.

"I can't help but think about the state of the sheets in there. They weren't even washed in between..." Stella shuddered and stared at the door.

Lucky leaned over and gave her arm a squeeze. "Let's call it a night, too, Stella. I know you've got to be exhausted; we didn't get any sleep last night and had a full day today, and we have another full day coming at us tomorrow."

They stood up and she assessed the table. "So, what? We each take one side of the bench to sleep on?" Honestly, it looked less comfortable than the Reliant.

Lucky crouched by the seats and pulled a lever; the table lowered on a hinge and locked into place about four inches below the bench seats. He pressed a button and the benches folded flat before sliding together over the tabletop, creating a double bed.

"Well, aren't you full of surprises?" She stood back and looked appreciatively at Lucky's handiwork. "Sorry I forgot about the tape. I know you're anxious to hear what Hap said."

"You know what, it's probably for the best we didn't hear it today. I'd never get any sleep, and I'd rather have one more night with you without anything else on my mind."

"Things are going to get crazy tomorrow, huh?" Stella rummaged through the cabinets nearby, finally locating a neatly folded set of sheets. She worked the fitted sheet away from the pack and tossed it to Lucky, and he wrangled it around the bed.

"I suspect this will be our last normal night for a long while, yes, but it'll all be worth it. Hopefully we'll get a killer to confess on TV."

Stella flicked out the top sheet and they watched it sail down to the mattress. She followed up with a blanket and then tossed Lucky his pillow. "Well." She looked around the tiny space and turned off the overhead light. When they were both standing in the dark, she heard Lucky unzip his pants. After a moment of uncertainty, she stepped out of her jeans, slipped her bra from under her T-shirt, and climbed into bed.

Lucky pulled her close, and they lay together in silence. Just as she started feeling that familiar charge in the air, the sound of

Janet and Billy Joe's passion blew Stella's out like a match in a storm.

"Ew. I can't listen to that all night." She rolled into Lucky and buried her face in his chest. "Tell me a story. I need to focus on something else."

A crash issued from the back bedroom, and Janet cackled and said, "You like that, eh? Get over here to Mama, so I can—"

Thankfully, Lucky's slow chuckle filled Stella's ears, and she couldn't hear her friend's plan for Billy Joe. He ran his hand down Stella's arm. "Can I tell you about Hap?"

Stella nodded in the dark. "I'd love to know about him, Lucky."

His eyes shined, and he took a moment to gather his thoughts. "Hap was six years younger than me. I was just old enough when he was born that I could really help with him, you know? I gave him bottles and could get him to calm down, sometimes when even my mom couldn't." His eyes took on a faraway quality, and she was certain he didn't really see her, anymore.

"He looked up to me. Man, I knew it, and I tried to watch out for him even when I was young. He was always picking fights on the playground, and I made sure everyone fought fair. After a few too many fights, though, you realize something's just not right. Hap would find a reason to fight when there were ten reasons not to. Even then, he needed the adrenaline rush."

Lucky looked down at Stella with sad eyes. "Do you have any brothers or sisters, Stella?"

"Sure: two sisters and a brother. They're all a lot older, though, so I don't know them well." She said it matter-of-factly, because that's the way it had always been, but Lucky's expression made her a little sad for the first time that she wasn't closer with any of them.

"I didn't know that. Hmm. How did I not know that?" he asked, distracted from his tale.

Stella half-laughed. "We don't know each other very well,

Lucky. When we first met, I had a boyfriend and you were just out of a serious relationship. Now I'm single and you're dead. It's been a busy couple of weeks."

His quiet laughter shook the mattress, revealing a squeaky spot.

"Stella!" Janet shouted with glee through the door. "That's my girl out there, making the mattress bounce! You go!"

Lucky continued to laugh and Stella joined in, the mattress squeaking rhythmically until they both calmed down.

"So, when did you know?" Stella asked, bringing them back to the story at hand.

"When did I know Hap was a total screw-up?"

"Well, I was going to say when did you know Hap was going to have trouble in this life?"

"I guess when my dad died. I was sixteen and Hap was only ten. He just couldn't make the transition. Mom was a wreck and I was a punk kid, ready for the next adventure—Hap had too much time on his own and no one there to drop the hammer when he got out of line."

Stella shifted on the bed and laid her head on Lucky's arm. "You and Hap didn't see each other much?"

"We went in phases. Sometimes he was always around, sometimes he'd be away a lot. Something changed maybe five or six years ago—I remember because it was the first time Jim and I had trouble on the track, and Hap up and left, too. Gone—didn't even hear from him for six months. I wasn't sure what happened to him. He finally called and said he needed a break from my life. I couldn't disagree—he needed to spread his wings. I didn't see him for a couple years, and we'd been in and out of touch ever since. He'd come by when he needed something or when there was something he needed to avoid."

Stella yawned and snuggled closer, exhaustion finally getting the best of her. "So, which was it this time?"

Lucky laid his head on the pillow but didn't answer. She was drifting off to sleep when she thought she heard him finally mutter, "I don't know. Which *was* it?"

31

RADIO SILENCE

T he next morning dawned bright and warm, and Stella and Lucky woke up early and snuck into the hotel. Stella knew, and could feel it in Lucky, too, that it was going to be a long, emotional, and stressful day. The door to the hotel gym was propped open, and the room was empty, so Lucky locked the door behind them before leading the way into the roomy bathroom and cranking the water to hot. Soon the air was steamy.

"Oh, so today the shower's a good spot?" Stella asked innocently.

"Yup. Handles."

"Huh?"

"This shower has handles to grip. Handles help with traction." He smiled wolfishly and then helped Stella peel off her clothes.

They enjoyed a long, lazy shower together in the deserted bathroom. She ended up with every square inch of herself lathered, rinsed, and dirtied all over again.

They met Janet and Billy Joe in the hotel restaurant, and all four cruised through the buffet line. Lucky kept his hat pulled down low and his sunglasses on, but as Stella walked toward him with her plate piled high, she realized his two-hundred-dollar sunglasses were a bit out of place.

"You look like a celebrity trying to hide out—which you are, but... hmm. Switch sunglasses with Billy Joe. At least you won't look like a millionaire if you're wearing knock-off Ray-Bans."

Billy Joe twitched. "Those are genuine. They were two for twenty-two dollars—best price of the year."

Janet took a huge bite of her Belgian waffle. "It's not gen-u-wine if it's less than a hundred dollars, BJ."

Stella looked at her coworker with raised eyebrows. BJ? He sneered back, daring her to say something.

Lucky handed over his sunglasses and put on the other pair. It did the trick; the extra-large lenses made him look like he was recovering from eye surgery. Stella grinned.

"First stop, the satellite truck. After we listen to the radio traffic from last Friday, we'll get any updates from the track on Scott's murder, and then we can get ready for the show."

"Keith hates it when anyone calls it a show. It's a *newscast*." Billy Joe folded a piece of bacon into his mouth.

Stella made a face. "I can see his point, but tonight, we'll definitely be putting on a show."

An hour later, they climbed into the satellite truck. The parking lot at the Superspeedway was already crawling with activity, and all the networks and local stations were counting on big updates in both the crash and the murder investigations.

After connecting some cords to one of the playback decks in the truck, Billy Joe connected the thumb drive to a machine. Pops and a buzzing sound broke the silence in the truck, and Billy Joe rotated the toggle wheel to the right and pressed play again. After a moment, some excited radio chatter broke out.

Billy Joe said, "Sounds like Jenkins Jones was just starting to give him the business there."

Stella thought back to the moments before the explosion. She remembered Hap and Jenkins Jones had been vying for the top spot when Hap let up.

Hap's voice crackled over airwaves again. "Too hot. Advise."

Stella's face wrinkled in concentration. She leaned forward, trying to make out the words.

"Thirteen to chief, repeat, running hot. Advise."

Hap's question was met by radio silence—the term finally made sense to Stella.

He tried one more time. "I'm coming in. Something's wrong!" After a few more seconds, Hap's gritty voice said, "Shit, this is bad! I just can't control—" There was a scream, more screaming, and then... nothing.

The silence stretched for minutes; Lucky's face was blank of emotion.

Billy Joe cleared his throat. "We'll give you a minute. Come on out when you're ready." He herded the others out of the truck, leaving Lucky by himself with Hap's final words still hanging heavily in the air.

"What—" Stella started when they were outside, but Billy Joe cut her off.

"Not a word from Jim as his driver is in crisis? That's unusual —he should have been getting advice from Jim after his first radio call. Something's not right there."

Her cell phone rang before she could fully comprehend how Jim had let Lucky—and Hap—down, and what it might mean.

"Hello?"

"It's Marty. I want to make sure we're all on the same page. We pulled in the A-team at the station for your big interview tonight. Larry says you'll have Jim Cruisner and Ryan Wexler. We also want you to update the Scott Lyons murder and maybe do a memorial piece on Lucky. Sound good?"

"We'll be ready, Marty. When will Elbee get here?"

"Should be by lunchtime."

"We can use the extra hands. Hey, we just heard the radio traffic from Friday. Have you had a chance to listen to it yet?"

"No," he barked, irritated to still be on the line. "The track said they're not releasing it until the investigation is complete. Wait—do you have it?"

"Umm, what?" She panicked. At the track yesterday, Robbie made it seem like no big deal to give her a copy.

"Do you have Lucky's radio traffic?" Marty demanded. Stella cringed. If he knew they had the audio, there was no way he'd let her sit on it—her station would be teasing the new exclusive all day, and that could ruin her chance at getting a real reaction out of the suspect during her live shot.

"No, I was saying we *want* to listen to it. Hopefully they'll release it today."

Marty banged the phone down, and Stella stared at her cell phone, lost in thought. For some reason, Robbie was committed to helping Stella investigate the crash and the murder, but why? They didn't know each other at all until yesterday. She was missing something, but she just couldn't put her finger on it.

The door opened behind her and Lucky walked heavily down the steps. His eyes were dull, his face an emotionless mask. "I don't know who I want you to grill harder tonight," he said, "Jim or Ryan."

Stella opened her mouth to reply when she saw Robbie headed their way from the track. "Billy Joe, let's have the camera ready."

He walked around to the back of the truck and dug out the equipment.

"Stella Reynolds, do you know I had at least ten people tell me they swore they saw Lucky Haskins not only alive but also walking around the track yesterday?"

Stella forced a surprised expression onto her face. "Oh my, that would be a shock, wouldn't it?" Lucky turned away from them and buried his face behind his cell phone.

"Well, you know people: they'll see what they want to see, regardless of how impossible it is, and that's true whether it's seeing a murder as an equipment malfunction on the track or seeing Lucky Haskins when we all know he's dead." Robbie shook his head, an innocent smile on his lips. "Are you ready for your big live shot?"

Stella shifted her weight. He knew a lot, and she wondered if he was going to let her carry on with her plan. "Yes, we'll be live off the top of the show right at five. Is that still a go?"

Robbie nodded, "Yes, we are ready for you. I can't wait to see what you dig up—or who you dig up." He winked and turned to walk back to the track. Stella jogged after him, leaving the rest of her motley crew behind.

"Hey," she said, "what's your deal? Why are you being so helpful? I mean," she grinned when he lifted an eyebrow, "I'm glad you are, but I'm just curious. Why?"

He stopped walking and turned toward her. "You're the only reporter who seems to have a clue as to what's going on. Everyone else bought the 'terrible accident' story from that very first presser just two hours after the explosion. Anything suspicious I've brought to my boss gets buried, because he wants this whole thing to go away, but I want to make sure it's done right. You seem ready to do that, so I want to help."

"So... you're just fighting for truth, justice, and all that jazz?"

He smiled. "I guess. Help me get it, okay?"

"Already in the works, Robbie. Did you check out that video from Friday—the one at the timecode I gave you?"

Robbie smirked. "Yes, and while interesting—my chief security officer, Nick, probably won't stop talking about it for a month —it unfortunately doesn't really prove anything."

Stella squinted at Robbie. "Interesting? You saw Ryan walk into Lucky's garage?"

Robbie nodded, a slight smile on his face. "That sly dog."

She wrinkled her nose. "What are you talking about?"

He squinted back. "What are *you* talking about? That time-code you wrote down showed Ryan Wexler walking into Lucky's garage, followed just a minute later by Star Coleman wearing heels and a trench coat. They were in there for about five minutes, and both came out buttoning up, zipping up, and grinning from ear to ear." At Stella's incredulous look, he shrugged. "Yup: you found video of a love connection."

"Are you sure? Maybe she hid something under her coat—"

"I'll say," Robbie snorted.

"That doesn't make any sense!" she exclaimed. "If Ryan didn't mess with Lucky's car, who did?"

Robbie shrugged again and they parted ways.

"Where's Janet?" she asked back at the truck, but neither Billy Joe or Lucky answered. She threw her hands up, exasperated. "Questions, questions, and more questions. Will anyone ever have any answers?"

32

FAMILY TIES

I t was one of those days without any normal constraints of time. Some stretches felt like they'd never pass while others flew by without any consideration for Stella's deadline.

She and Billy Joe covered a press conference with the track general manager, Kevin Nalor, and more than a dozen reporters crowded around, all vying for the best camera angle. It was a bunch of non-updates, with Kevin saying the investigation continued and they hoped to have more information available by that evening.

Just before lunch, Stella sat on the back bumper of the truck, working on her questions for the live interview.

"Are you... Stella Reynolds?"

She looked up from her notebook and squinted into the sunlight toward the voice. She couldn't make out who was there but said, "Yes?"

Lucky and Billy Joe were in the truck, watching race highlights from past weekends on the Race network. She heard a curse word come out of the open door, and then Billy Joe said, "Excuse my language, but that was a bullshit caution flag and everyone knows it."

Lucky chuckled and they both fell quiet.

A woman walked over and Stella, smiling at the banter, repeated, "Yes, hi. I'm Stella Reynolds. Can I help you?"

The woman was short and curvy, with blond hair and pale, smooth skin. She was pretty, but exhaustion had worn her down and dark circles ringed her blue eyes. "Hi. I'm Chloe Cruisner, Jim's daughter. He said to meet him here today for a live interview?"

Stella stood quickly and slid over to the open satellite truck door. "Jim's daughter?" she said into the cabin of the truck before pushing the door closed and turning to face Chloe again. "I didn't know he—I didn't know you were going to be here." She eyed the truck, hoping Lucky and Billy Joe heard her warning and would stay put. "Did you know Lucky well?"

Chloe nodded. "I practically grew up with the Haskins family but lost touch with Lucky about six years ago."

"Well, I'm so sorry for your loss," she said truthfully. Chloe looked pretty upset. Stella looked down at her notebook again before setting it down on the bumper. "Jim told you to come here for the interview tonight?" He hadn't mentioned that to Stella the day before, but then again, their phone call had been brief.

"Yes. He's taking this all really hard, and I think he just wanted a supportive face in the crowd, you know? He's not big on being in the spotlight, and he's so torn up about Lucky's death. It's just been a terrible week for all of us." Chloe looked down at her shoes and said, "My dad said Lucky was really taken with you. He'd never seen him so over the moon for anyone—even that one supermodel he dated a few years ago." Stella blushed. She thought that was a bit of an exaggeration, but it was nice to hear. "You must be feeling just devastated."

Stella jumped. "It just doesn't seem real, I guess."

"I don't suppose anyone's heard from Hap?" Chloe asked. "He's as unreliable as they come. I just wonder if he even knows his brother is dead?"

Stella smiled sadly. "I don't know, Chloe, I'm sorry. I really didn't know Lucky all that well before the crash and didn't even know he had a brother until this weekend. Have you tried his cell phone?"

She shook her head. "He gets in touch with you, not the other way around."

"Well, listen, we're not expecting your dad to get here until around four. Maybe you can come back then?"

"Sure. That works out well, anyway—we drove in from up north last night, and my son is at a friend's house taking a nap. I'll bring him back with me then."

Stella squinted. "How old is your son?"

Chloe's eyes lit up, even through her exhaustion and sadness. "Taylor's five. He hasn't napped in years, actually, but the drive in wore him out. He's what gets me through tough times like this, you know?"

Stella nodded. She imagined being responsible for a little one would change your attitude about a lot of things.

Chloe got into an old, brown Toyota Corolla parked nearby and backed out of her spot. Stella stared after the vehicle long after it was out of sight, her mind working slowly to connect what now appeared to be some very obvious dots. Chloe hadn't seen Lucky in six years, and she had a five-year-old boy. Lucky told her that *six years ago*, he and Jim had gotten into a fight over a woman.

She closed her eyes and shook her head. "No, no, no. It just can't be." A dull ache formed behind her right eye. She'd assumed Lucky meant he and Jim had been after the same woman, but apparently the problem was that one didn't like the other screwing his daughter! She looked accusingly at the door to the satellite truck just as it opened and Lucky walked down the steps.

"You are unbelievable," she snapped.

His eyes opened wide. "What? What are you talking about?"

"When is the last time you saw Chloe Cruisner?"

Lucky stared at Stella for a moment before answering. "I guess it was about six years ago. Jim didn't want her around the track, anymore. She was just eighteen and he wanted her to have a chance at college and everything else—lots of unsavory people hang around the track."

"And you might be one of them!" At his offended look, she continued, "Did you know she has a five-year-old son?" His mouth hung loose for a moment while he processed that information. "You told me you and Jim fought over a woman six years ago." She looked at him accusingly. "Was that woman Chloe? Now I understand why he was angry: he thought you knocked up his daughter! Is that why you fought?" She couldn't get enough air and clawed at the neck of her shirt.

Lucky ran a hand down his face and grimaced. "Okay, yes, Jim and I fought about Chloe years ago. He thought—wrongly—that I was fooling around with her. I told him then, just like I'm telling you now, that I had nothing to do with her! She was eighteen and I was twenty-seven—she might as well have been a child to me!"

"Oh, come on. You were a famous driver and she was eighteen: old enough to feel like your equal and young enough to think she was an adult."

He sat down on the steps hard. "He never mentioned a baby, but it explains why we never saw her again. She used to come to all the races and practice sessions—she was everywhere—and then we stopped seeing her. Jim never mentioned anything about a grandson. I asked about him about Chloe a few times, but it only made him upset, so eventually I stopped asking."

Stella wasn't convinced, but she didn't have time to dwell on it any longer. Her cell phone rang. "Hey, Elbee. What's up?"

"Ooh-wee, Stella. I'm about ten minutes away and thought I'd pick up lunch for everyone on my way in. What do you and Billy Joe want?"

After a quick discussion with Billy Joe, she relayed their orders and snapped her phone shut. "Elbee's close. You need to make yourself scarce until just before the live shot. I brought the razor and your bag of regular clothes—they're in the passenger seat of the truck." For their big reveal to have maximum impact, Lucky needed to look like himself, not a grizzled hunter. She looked at Billy Joe. "Are you set?"

He nodded. "Yes. I'll operate the sat truck for the live shot and have Elbee work with you. That way, Lucky can come back and watch everything from inside the truck until it's time."

Stella rubbed her face with both hands. "Okay, this could work. This could also implode into a flaming ball of—"

"It's going to be fine," Lucky interjected. "It's going to work out." He walked down the steps and grabbed Stella's hands, entwining their fingers. "Stella, look at me." She raised her eyes until they locked with his. "I swear to you, I was not involved with Chloe *at all*."

"You do realize Chloe's one year *older* than me, right? She's twenty-four—I'm twenty-three." All of a sudden, it seemed like they faced insurmountable obstacles. Age was probably the least of them, but it was still an issue.

He tilted his head sideways. "There's a big difference between eighteen, which she was then, and twenty-three, which you are now." He shuddered. "She was a child back then. You are a woman," he lifted her hand and kissed her knuckles, "and I'm so glad." He grinned endearingly and planted a kiss on her lips. "I'll see you on the news, Bear. Go get 'em."

He walked away with a bounce in his step. Billy Joe cleared his throat, and she looked over. "Do you think he slept with her?" she asked.

"Probably," he said, nodding, a thoughtful look on his face. "He probably has a son he's never met named Taylor, too."

She sat back down on the bumper and picked up her notebook. Their live shot was only four-and-a-half hours away. Lucky looked like an absentee father, Ryan might have been innocent in Hap's death, and despite being certain of a suspect twelve hours ago, she now had no idea who'd rigged Lucky's car. Even worse, she was running out of time to find out.

33

THE CALM

S tella had to shelve her worries about Lucky and Chloe because, once Elbee arrived, they had a ton of work to do. She had to write and edit a package on Scott's murder that would air during the five o'clock news after the live interviews and also write a memorial piece on Lucky that would probably never see the light of day. The script had to be approved by the producer back at the station, however, so she had to go through the motions.

They got sound from campers and updated information from track officials. While Elbee worked on editing one story, Stella wrote the next, and it wasn't until four that they finished their work and started switching gears for the live shot.

Billy Joe and Stella surrounded Elbee in the truck. "Bob," Billy Joe said, putting a hand on the other photographer's shoulder, "something strange is going to happen tonight during the live shot, but we just need you to roll with it, okay?"

Elbee's nose wrinkled, and Stella's did, too. "Bob?" she asked, "Who is Bob? This is Elbee, Billy Joe. Are you feeling all right?" She resisted the urge to put her hand on his forehead to check for fever. Both men chuckled. "What's so funny?"

"Stella, I'd like to introduce you to Bob, otherwise known as Little Bob or, as we like to call him at the station, LB, for short," Billy Joe said with a grin.

She blinked in the silence that followed. "What? Are you telling me I've been calling you *Elbee*," she spelled it out for good measure, "for the last however many weeks, and your name is really *Little Bob*?"

Elbee shrugged, a smile on his face. "Elbee and LB—sounds the same to me, Stella."

"Why can't the station just have two Bobs?"

"Well, when Bob Buchanan started in the sports department a couple of years ago, it just got confusing—too many Bobs running around, shooting video. He became Big Bob, and I became Little Bob, but *Little Bob* doesn't really roll off the tongue, so everyone started calling me LB."

"That is so... wow. I'm speechless. LB, it's so nice to officially meet you." She shook her head at the misunderstanding and then got back to business. "So, like Billy Joe said, things are going to get crazy tonight. Just keep rolling, no matter what happens."

"Sure thing, Stella. Sure thing. Ooh-wee, sounds exciting! I can't wait to see what y'all have up your sleeves! I bet Keith will be sorry to miss it all. He's on leave back at the station—have you heard? Bigwigs came in from corporate Saturday morning and put him on notice. They got lots of complaints from the ladies about how he put you on the spot Friday night, and I guess it was the last straw. HR flew in yesterday to make changes. They're not too happy with Larry, either, truth be told. I was puttering around the newsroom last night and overheard some fancy lady telling him that, if he calls a reporter by anything other than their given name again, he'll be sitting at home, watching the news, instead of anchoring it. I wish you'd seen his face, Stella! Having that lady give him orders... God bless—it was too much for the heart."

Billy Joe whistled low. "Usually they leave us alone when the ratings are so high." A knock sounded on the satellite truck door. "Show time," he said under his breath as Stella opened it.

Chloe Cruisner stood at the bottom of the steps, her arm resting comfortably over her son's shoulder. Stella felt like she was looking at a pint-sized Lucky—the resemblance was uncanny.

"Hey, Stella, we're back," Chloe said with an easy smile. "I haven't seen my dad yet. Have you?"

"No, not yet," Stella said, her voice strained. She couldn't take her eyes off the five-year-old. After a minute, she realized the silence had grown awkward, and she racked her brain for something to say. "Well, let's get the shot set up. LB, do you have a spot picked out already?"

"Ooh-wee, I sure do, Stella. Look at how the grandstands just tip the horizon if you look over that way, toward the sunset. Now usually I wouldn't set up with the sun behind us, but I think..."

Stella tuned out LB's idle chatter about how to best frame the shot and thought instead about Taylor. Did Jim know Lucky was the father? Is that why they'd fought six years ago? If that were true, why did Jim continue as Lucky's pit crew chief?

She didn't have to check with *her* dad to know he'd be ready to kill anyone who didn't do the right thing by her. Was that motive enough for murder? If so, why now—why not six years ago? She was so engrossed in her thoughts about Chloe's kid that she almost bumped into Ryan Wexler.

"Stella, nice to see you again. This is bad business here." He shook his head, his expression dark. "It's a blow for so many racing fans, but especially you. I bet you'll be glad to get back to Bristol tomorrow—and all of your... friends there."

She had to work to keep her face neutral. Was he talking about Lucky? What did he know? She was saved from answering by LB.

The photographer stopped and set his gear down. "This is the spot, all right. Y'all stay here and I'll pull cables."

"I didn't know Lucky well, Stella, but you know what they say: rumors are based in truth. The tabloids can't be wrong all the time."

She felt a tinge of unease and glanced up at him. Tabloids? Was that a reference to the picture of her and Lucky? He was nonchalantly looking at his watch, however, when he said, "I'm afraid Lucky was a womanizer, plain and simple."

Before she could say anything, Chloe cleared her throat angrily.

"Lucky Haskins was a true southern gentleman. I knew Lucky my whole life, and he was always honest about his feelings, spoke the truth, and looked out for his family. That's more than most men can say these days." Her nostrils flared and her breath chopped out.

Stella gulped. Chloe obviously still had feelings for Lucky— and why wouldn't she? He was the father of her child!

Ryan looked at Chloe through new eyes. "You knew him well?"

"Yes, I did—grew up with him on the track, actually. I'm Chloe Cruisner."

"Ah, Ms. Cruisner, I'm sorry I offended you. I agree, Lucky had his charms. He's leaving a hole that will be difficult to fill in the racing world, that's for sure."

"Dad!" Chloe exclaimed. They hugged, and Jim crouched to wrap Taylor in an embrace. "How ya doing, champ?"

Taylor grinned impishly and said, "Go long!"

Jim stood quickly and jogged back a few steps. Taylor produced a football from somewhere and threw it toward his grandfather; Jim caught it easily and launched it back to Taylor.

Stella smiled at the pair. Chloe did, too. "Did Lucky and Taylor get along?" she asked Chloe innocently. She knew they'd never met, but she hoped it would prompt the other woman to open up.

"Oh, uh... no, they didn't." Stella stared at her, willing her to say more. Jim and Taylor were off and running through the crowd, and Ryan had moved off to the side and was on his cell phone. Chloe finally sighed and ran a hand through her hair. "They actually never met. Lucky didn't know anything about Taylor."

Stella feigned surprise. "Oh, I'm sorry—I just assumed. It seemed like your families were close."

"They were. I... we grew apart about six years ago. My pregnancy came as a shock. I wasn't prepared to tell anyone who the father was, and my dad just couldn't handle the shame of an out-of-wedlock baby."

"Really? In this day and age?"

"You're in the south, Stella. We have different rules," Chloe said ruefully.

"Can I ask you something personal?"

Chloe looked away from her family and tilted her head to the side. "Sure. I'm apparently ready to spill my guts to you, a perfect stranger."

Stella smiled. She had that effect on people; it was one of the reasons she decided to become a reporter. "Does Jim know who Taylor's father is?"

Chloe looked at her sharply. "No. I refused to tell Dad—or anyone." She looked defiantly at Stella. "It was a mistake all those years ago, and h—" she took a deep breath and continued, "he just wasn't in a place to take on any responsibility. Dad was furious that I wouldn't tell him and flat out refused to talk to me because of the pregnancy. I moved in with a friend, and he missed the first five years of Taylor's life. We only made amends a couple of months ago, after I read Dad had a health scare—some kind of heart condition. I sent him Taylor's school picture, just to see if we could reconnect, and it did the trick. Who could be mad at that face?" she asked, looking over at her son.

That explained why Jim quit as Lucky's pit crew chief at the beginning of the season: he must have taken one look at Taylor and known Lucky was a deadbeat dad. Why, then, had he changed his mind and stayed on the team?

"What about your mom?"

"She died about ten years ago."

"You were eighteen, pregnant, and alone?" Stella was floored. "Your dad just... abandoned you? What about L—" she stopped herself, unable to even say Lucky's name. "What about the father? He wasn't involved?"

"I never even told him. He was a mess back then—in and out of relationships—so I thought it was best to go it alone. I did it," she finished proudly.

Stella didn't blame her. What an amazing feat to be a single parent; she couldn't think of anything harder. It was weird, however, that in one breath, Chloe defended Lucky as amazing and good, and with the next, called him irresponsible and unreliable.

"Excuse me," she said to Chloe when her phone rang. She looked at the screen. "Janet, where are you?"

"You're not going to believe what I found out."

Stella looked at Chloe, now staring lovingly at her family again, and shook her head. "It can't possibly be more interesting than the last five minutes here, but go ahead, shoot."

34

DOMINOES

"Wait, what do you mean?" Janet asked, distracted.

"Well, unless your news has to do with Lucky fathering a love child with Jim Cruisner's daughter," she glanced furtively at Chloe and stepped farther away, "then I'm not interested."

"Whoa," Janet breathed into the phone. "That's huge."

"Yeah, it is. We're about thirty minutes away from the live shot. Meet me at the satellite truck and tell me your news then. This will all be over soon."

They hung up, and Stella felt deflated. She'd really started to like Lucky, but this... this was more than she was ready for. Back from the dead and a kid with another woman? She rubbed a hand over her face. "LB, can you get everyone miked up and do some audio checks? I'm going to head to the truck. I'll be just a minute."

Not only was she trying to digest all the information from Chloe, but she also had to figure out how it all affected her live interviews. She had less than thirty minutes, and it felt like the game plan they'd worked out last night was shot.

"Bear, you ready for this?" Lucky was back, ready to watch the interviews from the truck.

She looked up at him with tired eyes. "Billy Joe, can you ask LB to get a shot of the kid?"

Billy Joe murmured some words into his headset, and the video feed from LB's camera panned the crowd.

When it landed on Taylor, Lucky's eyes narrowed. Recognition dawned and he gasped. "What am I looking at? Who is that?" he asked.

"That, Lucky, is your son." Stella watched him watch the screen. Despite her jumbled emotions about everything, she felt herself tearing up at Lucky's expression, which morphed from shock to love, just like that.

He stared at the screen in wonder and then took a shaky breath and said, "That's not *my* son."

"Lucky, I tried to give you the benefit of the doubt, but Taylor looks just like—"

"Hap. It's amazing. That is my nephew—that's Hap's son! I had no idea; it just never crossed my mind. Hap hardly stayed anywhere long enough to drink two beers, let alone... well. I don't even remember him crossing paths with Chloe, but this boy could be Hap's twin at that age!

"This changes everything, Stella. We can't go out there on live TV and surprise everyone that I'm alive—it will kill Chloe. She thinks Hap is off on a bender somewhere. She has no idea the father of her child is dead!"

Stella stopped short. If Lucky was right, the news would be devastating. She sat heavily in an open chair and raked her hands through her hair. "What are we going to do?"

"No time like the present," Billy Joe said with a frown. "Everyone's going to find out tonight—might as well give her a head start." He muttered some words into the headset again, and a few minutes later, there was a knock at the door.

Stella ushered Chloe into the tiny space and sat her down in a chair. Lucky stepped forward. She looked up at him politely and then turned questioningly back to Stella. Within seconds, though, her eyes were back on the man in front of her.

"Who—how—" she stuttered and was then struck silent, her gaze locked on the race car driver.

"Hey, Chloe. Been a long time."

"Lucky? Is it... can it be you? You don't look like you, but... but... you died, Lucky! I watched the crash." She stared at him for another minute, and her eyes glazed over from the effort of not blinking. A single tear slid slowly down her cheek, then, like it was made of something thicker than water. "If you're here, does that mean Ha... Hap was driving? Did you let him drive like he told me you used to? Lucky?" By now, the tears were falling fast and her face crumpled in despair.

Lucky dropped his gaze to the floor and nodded once slowly. "I'm sorry, Chloe. I'm so sorry."

Stella and Billy Joe slipped out of the truck, leaving the others to their grief.

After a few minutes, he tapped Stella on the shoulder. "I don't mean to be insensitive, but we're about out of time. You've got a big interview in twenty minutes. What are we going to do?"

"What are we going to do?" Janet said, walking up to the truck. "We're going to nail that sonovabitch to the wall for killing Hap, and we're going to do it with Scott Lyon's help." She held up a videotape triumphantly.

"What's that?" Stella asked.

"It's what I called you about a few minutes ago! It's a copy of the video from Scott's camera the day he was murdered. I saw Robbie Steemer about ten minutes ago, and he gave it to me, your trusted associate producer." She laughed at her own joke.

"Did he say what's on it?"

Janet shook her head. "Nope, he just said we'd want to watch it before the live shot, not after."

"How did he get a copy of this? Didn't police confiscate it at the scene?"

"I guess they needed the track's video editing system to dub the video over, and Robbie made sure to sneak a second copy. He says we owe him one."

"I'll say!" Stella exclaimed, grabbing the tape. She took two steps toward the satellite truck before she remembered who was inside and froze. She didn't want to kick Chloe out, but at the same time, they were working against a pretty hard deadline.

"I got this," Janet said after Billy Joe quickly explained what was going on. She walked into the truck and was back out two minutes later with Chloe and Lucky in tow. All three headed toward the grandstands.

Stella stared after them for a moment and then jumped when Billy Joe said, "Girl, let's go!"

Inside the truck, he punched a half-dozen buttons to get the right playback machine cued up. Scrawled on the tape label were the words NOT FOR USE ON-AIR. As Stella inserted the tape and pressed play, the anticipation was sickening. What did the killer not want anyone to see?

Black and white snow came up on screen, and she pressed the fast forward button on the deck. Soon, the screen turned to black, and then Stella saw... herself.

She must have made a sound, because Billy Joe said, "What is this?"

There she was, walking to her apartment in Bristol. The camera stayed on her until she walked through the front door, and then it jumped to another day, when she was jogging outside. Another cut, and she was at that fire, where her live shot had gone so disastrously. Finally, there was a shot of Stella running late for work, dropping her bag, and Lucky coming out to deliver her wallet.

"What the hell is this?" she asked, so shocked that her mind was unable to make sense of what she was seeing.

Billy Joe whistled low. "This is from Scott Lyon's camera? Stella, why would he have this video of you, and who would care enough about it to kill him?"

She continued to stare at the TV screen, watching herself walk around town, cover stories, and head into her apartment. She remembered having an unsettled feeling last week, but how could she have been so unaware that she was being recorded? She'd even chatted with Scott just two days ago on a story and never would have guessed he was the one who'd taken the picture of her and Lucky. Why had Scott, her fellow Ohioan, spent so much time filming her? There were only more questions the longer she looked at herself on screen.

She vaguely heard Billy Joe on his headset. "LB, we're about five away, but standby. Things have taken a strange turn." He squeezed her shoulder. "Stella, should I cancel this? It seems like we've got too much on our plate right now. If you want, the live interviews can wait."

"No," she said, resolve filling her stomach like acid and more clinks sounding in her brain as facts started falling into place. "I'm ready—let's do this. I want Lucky watching from the truck, and make sure Chloe gets Taylor out of here. Things are going to get ugly, and I don't want them caught in the middle." He nodded and walked out. When he was gone, she picked up her phone and dialed the station. "Cam? I have to ask you something."

They only talked for a minute, but when Stella hung up, she felt secure in her understanding of what happened. She didn't know *why* everything had happened, but she had a good idea of who'd done what over the last week.

She stood, feeling ready for whatever might happen next.

35

THE BEGINNING

S tella took a deep breath and tried to clear her mind. A lot of people would be tuning in for this, and she didn't want to screw it up.

She walked over to her mark. "Gentlemen, I had LB set you both up with earpieces tonight. It's a long live shot, and I didn't want you to miss anything important. Everything sound okay?" Ryan nodded and looked impatiently at his watch. "Jim, just answer my questions honestly and from your heart. People want to hear about Lucky, and you're their rock in a time like this."

Jim nodded solemnly. "Did you see where Chloe and Taylor went?"

"I think I saw them heading toward the bathrooms." Stella motioned vaguely toward the grandstands behind them, and Jim nodded again.

LB had roped off an area for their live shot, and a crowd was already gathered, waiting for the action. Just at the edge of the madness, Stella caught the unwelcome sight of Star walking toward them with purpose. Nothing good could come from this last-minute visit. Before she could figure out what to do, Janet sidled over from the other side of the crowd and cruised stealthily closer—out of Star's sight—until she popped up directly in front of Lucky's ex.

Star stopped short, a look of revulsion on her face. Janet's mouth started moving, and after a few short seconds, Lucky's ex pivoted and left the area. Janet turned toward her with a smile and two thumbs-up.

Nerves kept her from smiling, but her heartrate slowed.

A friendly voice came into her ear. "Stella, this is Samantha, your favorite five o'clock producer. Can I have a mic check, please?"

"Mic check one, two. Mic check one, two."

"Sounds great. I have you down for four minutes total. I'm picturing two with Jim, about a minute on the murder update, and then about a minute with Ryan. Uh oh. You've got a lurker—twelve o'clock, right behind you."

Stella turned and saw a man in his thirties waving goofily at the camera. He had a cell phone pressed to his ear, and she could read his lips as he said happily into his phone, "Can you see me? I'm right behind the reporter lady." He then started doing the Roger Rabbit, followed by the Sprinkler and what Stella could only guess was a dance called the Bathroom Break by its vulgar motions.

"Oh my!" Stella said before she could stop herself. The dancer grinned and gyrated faster.

Samantha groaned. "Just tell LB to keep the shot tight. Standby. Show open in thirty seconds."

Stella's heartrate accelerated. So many things could go wrong in the next few minutes. This live shot could ruin her career or make it. Even if things only went as planned, she might not survive to tell the tale.

She heard the tinny music that started off the newscast in her ear and said, "Standby, gentlemen. We're live in twenty seconds."

Alexa: Good evening, everyone. Welcome to another

special weekend edition of NBC2 News. I'm Alexa
Robinson.

Larry: And I'm Larry Howard. We begin this evening in
Talladega with an exclusive interview with Lucky Haskins'
pit crew chief, Jim Cruisner.

Alexa: Stella Reynolds has been at the track all weekend.
She joins us live with the latest on the investigation into
Haskins' death, and the first words from Cruisner since
the explosion. Stella?

"That's right, Alexa, what an emotional time at the track—not
just for people here in Talladega, but also for race fans all over
the world. Losing Lucky Haskins was something nobody was
prepared for, especially his pit crew chief, Jim Cruisner. Jim,
thanks for joining us."

"Stella, there's nowhere I'd rather be."

Her throat felt pinched, but she plowed forward—she had no
choice. "Jim, it's been over a week now since that terrible explosion on the track. You disappeared after the race, and everyone
wants to know: how are you doing?"

"It's—it's been a tough week," Jim allowed, shifting his
weight.

"Where have you been?"

He was fidgeting with his hands while Stella spoke, first
putting them behind his back, next in his front pockets, and
finally letting them hang loosely at his sides. "I, uh—I needed to
be alone and process what happened on my own. It's been... it's
been devastating."

"Jim, you'd been with Lucky since he started on the track thirteen years ago. What can you tell me about those last laps? What
do you think went wrong?"

"I wish I could say, Stella. I didn't know anything was wrong until the car spun out. There just wasn't anything we could do."

She pounced. "That can't be true. I heard the radio traffic from the last lap just this morning, Jim, and you can hear your driver ask for help three times."

"I don't know what—"

"Let's go ahead and roll that audio, please."

"What are you talking about?" Samantha hissed in her ear. The producer and director would usually be in charge of rolling tapes back at the station, but Billy Joe had assured her he could do it from the truck. Before she could feel bad about not clueing Samantha in on everything, Hap's terrified voice filled the airwaves.

"Too hot. Advise." The cackle of the radio sounded deafening. "Thirteen to chief, repeat, running hot. Advise." Jim's eyes closed and his head dropped to his chest for Hap's final words. "I'm coming in. Something's wrong! This is bad! I just can't control—"

The crowd around them remained silent—only those wearing an IFB, and of course everyone watching from home, could hear Hap's scream of terror right before the audio cut off.

"Well?" Stella prompted. "Is there a reason you didn't answer him? Would you say you let your driver down last week?"

Jim's shoulders shook, but his lips remained sealed.

The lurker danced his heart out behind them.

"Stella, if I may?" Ryan's smooth voice came from her right. She hated to take the camera off Jim, expecting a full confession at any moment, but she also didn't want dead air filling the live shot. She turned to Ryan and saw LB pan the camera over, too. "Not everything makes sense in the racing world. Things happen at breakneck speeds—the crowd is loud, the laps are fast, and sometimes things don't go as planned. I think we're seeing a case of that right here."

Stella worked hard to keep her face from breaking out into a full-fledged grimace. Of course Ryan would come to Jim's defense

—he and Jim had planned Lucky's murder together! She just had to prove it. Before she could force her mind to switch gears, however, Ryan spoke again.

"I spent many years on the track, won many races, and lost a few, too. I know how draining it can be to work for NASCAR—especially for someone like Jim, who has spent decades on the track." Ryan held up his hand, and his ruby-red ring glinted brilliantly under the spotlights. "I won this championship ring in 1979—it's the only one like it and I wear it all the time. It reminds me what's at stake for all of our drivers: the glory and the risk. I think Lucky's tragic demise is just one of the terrible *risks* of being a NASCAR driver."

Stella bit back a smile. She knew his ego would be her saving grace tonight. "You knew Lucky almost as long as Jim, here, but there was a much more checkered history between the two of you. How are *you* feeling today?"

Ryan was caught off guard by her question. He looked off to the side, but the bright bulbs LB had set up to light the live shot made it impossible to see anything beyond their small circle. He opened his mouth and shut it again.

Stella pressed on, "I understand that Lucky and your ex-wife had a fling many years ago, and then, more recently, Lucky caught you having an affair with his fiancée—ex-fiancée, now. That couldn't have been a coincidence?"

A swell of noise rose up from the crowd. No one knew about the breakup, and Stella's declaration had caught their attention. She held the microphone out to Ryan, but he couldn't seem to make words come out of his mouth.

"Stella, what the hell are you doing?" Samantha growled through the IFB.

She couldn't take the distraction, and ripped the earpiece out. "When I first met you back in Bristol, you were in the middle of a heated argument with Lucky Haskins. What were you fighting about?" Ryan's eyes shot daggers at Stella, but his lips were now sealed, too. She turned to include Jim in the interview again. "What happened last week, Jim? Why were you so angry at Lucky?"

Jim wrung his hands, his face white. "I-I don't know what— this isn't why I'm here..."

"I spoke to your daughter, Chloe, today. She introduced me to your grandson. He sure looks a lot like Lucky, doesn't he? Jim, did you think Lucky was the boy's father—that Lucky left your daughter with a child to raise on her own?"

Stella glanced back when a shocked muttering rose from the rapidly expanding crowd surrounding them. The lurker appeared to be cradling an invisible baby in his arms now as he danced, his shock of red hair flopping distractingly back and forth as he bumped and bounced to his own beat. She shook herself and turned back to Jim. He didn't say a word, but his face was quickly turning the shade of a ripe red apple.

"Your grandson was born five years ago, so what got you so angry *last week*?" She looked at Jim, honestly curious. She'd figured out much of what happened, but that was the one link she couldn't connect to anything else.

Jim threw his hands up in the air and growled, "I was angry because of *you*, Stella Reynolds." He said her name like a swear word, his eyes cold and angry as he glared at her from inches away. "I've never seen Lucky act about any woman the way he was acting about you, and it's not fair. He's been a womanizer from the minute I met him—even his fiancée didn't really seem to captivate him—so I didn't care that he wasn't with my Chloe. You came into the picture, though, and he changed. You were all he could talk about! He should have changed for my Chloe, but he never did—he just knocked her up and left her to raise his son. So, yes, I was angry with Lucky, and I was angry at him because of you."

Stella's mouth hung open, and she didn't even realize silence filled the airwaves until she saw LB move around the camera. She hastily shoved her IFB back into her ear and caught Samantha mid-sentence.

"... cleared the entire show. Take as long as you need. I hope you have a plan to wrap this up, otherwise you're going to get all of us sued."

She looked around her, quickly taking in the two angry men facing her, steam coming out of their ears. The crowd pressed in on them. Even LB gave her a wide-eyed stare that made her feel utterly alone.

Finally, she saw a chocolate brown, messy head of hair pushing through the crowd. She squared her shoulders to the camera. Her station had no idea what was about to hit the airwaves from Talladega, but Stella knew they would have all the answers out in the open in the next two minutes.

36

FIREWORKS

She threw her notebook aside—it was out of date now and wouldn't help her for the rest of the night. "If everyone watching at home can stay with me, I think there's someone here who will really help us figure things out." Before she could say Lucky's name, however, Jim exploded out of his stony silence.

"You know what, I'm not sorry he's dead! There, I said it! Lucky Haskins was a womanizer—the worst kind of man," he glared at Ryan, "and I didn't need someone *else* telling me what had to be done. I already knew what a father would—what a father should..." He pressed his fist to his mouth and stared silently into the crowd. "What a..." He reached a shaky hand out toward Lucky. "I killed... I killed... who did I kill?"

He staggered back and lost his balance. His knees hit the ground, his eyes rolled up toward his forehead, and he crashed into a heap on the ground. The crowd gasped, although whether from the sound of Jim's head cracking on the asphalt, his admission that he planned a murder, or because they finally recognized Lucky Haskins standing in front of them, Stella didn't know.

Janet flew into the circle and put her fingers to Jim's throat. "He's breathing—I think he just passed out from shock!"

Stella's hand fluttered to her chest, relieved there wasn't yet another death at the track.

"Network is going to take our feed," Samantha hissed into the earpiece. Stella ignored it—she had to focus.

Lucky walked into the center of the live shot circle and came to a stop by her. Even with his shaggy hair more brown than blond and the dark circles under his eyes, he stood among them like a star. His face looked more angular now that the beard was gone, hastily hacked off in the satellite truck with supplies Stella brought from home. Some wisps were still visible along his jaw, which was currently clenched tight. He had just stared his brother's killer in the eye and it had shaken him to the core. She willed his eyes to meet hers. They finally did, and his breathing slowed under her steady gaze.

"Lucky Haskins, we just heard Jim Cruisner admit to killing you—but you're not dead! A lot of people are adjusting their TV screens right now, wondering how they're seeing you alive." Another murmur went up from the crowd, but Stella kept talking. "Can you explain what happened?"

"Stella, I'll be honest; I wish I wasn't standing here with you today, because that would mean my brother, Hap, was still alive."

"A lot of people don't know this, but you sometimes let him drive your car, even when it was a violation of the rules, and that's what happened during Friday's qualifying laps?"

"Yes, that's right," he nodded, needing her to lead him along for this part of the night.

"It wasn't you behind the wheel last Friday, it was Hap. Hap was the one who died in the crash."

"Yes," Lucky said, his voice breaking.

"Why not come forward right away, Lucky? Why let everyone think you were the one who died?"

"I was worried about Hap. He was the only one left in my

family. I wanted to make sure someone paid for his death, and I worried it wouldn't be investigated. I knew I needed to figure out who killed him before I could let everyone know I was alive—I *am* alive."

"We just heard your longtime teammate and friend, Jim Cruisner, admit that he tried to kill you. Now we know your brother was the victim, instead. How will you move on?"

"I don't know, Stella. I just don't know what went wrong between us. A big misunderstanding got out of hand because silence, anger, and pain were left untreated. I hope Jim's family and I can mend fences and work through this devastation."

"Lucky, just one more thing. Are you the father of Chloe Cruisner's son?"

"No, I am not, but I am his uncle and will do everything I can to support Chloe and my nephew as they go forward in life. Hap had a big heart, and I want his son to know that."

A cackle of laugher split the otherwise touching scene in half. Ryan Wexler couldn't hide his glee. "So, you're telling me Jim tried to kill you for being the boy's deadbeat dad but killed Hap, instead, who ended up *being* the deadbeat dad? Oh, that's just perfect."

Stella turned to face her other opponent of the night—the only person in the crowd not shocked by Lucky's appearance. "Hap wasn't the only one killed on the track in the last week, Ryan. What can you tell me about the other victim at Talladega, Scott Lyon?"

Ryan shook his head. "No, no, we're done here, Stella. I'm done. I am officially ending this interview, and my lawyer will be in touch. This is slanderous behavior. I am not involved in anything illegal. I'm done."

"That's not what our video says." She looked pointedly into the camera. "Billy Joe, can you roll the footage from the morning of Scott's murder?"

There was a lag of about ten seconds while Billy Joe cued up the video from the satellite truck. Stella was worried Ryan might walk away from their interview, but his feet were glued to the ground, his eyes hungry for the information he hoped Stella didn't have.

Earlier that day, Stella and LB had spliced a few scenes from the track surveillance cameras together in slow motion, so each of the three shots of Ryan's ring were shown slowly gliding across the screen. The video stopped just short of showing Scott's murder.

With the first shot of the killer, Ryan's body grew more tense. While everyone at home watched the exclusive video, Stella couldn't take her eyes off Ryan's face. He tore his gaze from the screen and twisted his ring around his finger, his expression confusing her.

When the video ended, he seemed to steel himself. A look of superiority returned to his face and he said, "What I see is a killer operating under the cover of darkness. I don't think anyone can claim to see their face."

"But Ryan, the killer is wearing your championship ring, and you have the only one. That reminds me what's at stake for everyone: the glory and the risk." She didn't know why Ryan would kill Scott, but she wasn't a prosecutor and didn't have to present a motive. Her job tonight was to uncover the facts before they could be buried forever.

He stilled, but he wasn't angry, anymore. She tried to name the emotion flitting across his face. Disappointment? Resignation? Her study was interrupted as Jim moaned before he sat up and rubbed his head. She turned back to Ryan.

"Where were you the morning Scott Lyon was killed? Is that your ring we can see on the surveillance video?"

Her gaze didn't waver, but neither did Ryan's. He crossed his arms over his chest and it became apparent he wasn't going to say another word. The crowd around them had grown silent—even the lurker stood still, his mouth hanging open. Stella blew out a breath, almost surprised to find they were still on camera.

She turned away from Ryan, ready to send the live shot back to her anchors, but before she could get a word out, something flashed in the corner of her eye. Jim was up off the ground, still off balance, and his recently pale face had flushed red again. He headed toward Lucky with a gleam of hatred on his face and let out an almighty cry of pain that seemed to come from deep within his soul. He'd missed the explanation about Hap not only being his grandson's father but also being dead—he still saw Lucky as the one who'd let his daughter down.

"Jim, wait!" she cried. She understood what was going to happen a split second before it did, but her reflexes weren't fast enough to move out of the way. Jim's fist, drawn back in anger, launched toward Lucky's head just as she stepped between them, her hand outstretched. The punch landed with a crack against her jaw, and she staggered back, her body stiffening for the inevitable contact with the ground. Instead, she landed against Lucky; he'd caught her on the way down.

In the haze of Stella's cloudy vision, she saw Janet fly through the crowd and jump onto Jim's back. She put the larger, heavier man into a straight-jacket hold from behind, and he was stuck.

Stella knew she was about to lose this live shot, but she wanted to end it professionally after everything that had happened. She pushed away from Lucky, her legs wobbly, and raised the microphone to her lips.

"Tho many thocking revelationth—" Her rapidly swelling lip made the letter "S" impossible to pronounce. She tried again, hoping for the best. "Thith ith Thtella Reynoldth... oh, Jethuth Chrith, back to you."

37

THE LAST PIECE

After other breaking news situations, Stella had always celebrated with coworkers. This was different. There was something unsettling about the way the live shot ended. She'd hoped both men would confess—two murders solved in less than four minutes—but that hadn't happened, and it rankled her that Ryan might have gotten away with such deadly serious crimes.

Talladega police waited at the edge of the crowd, no doubt talking to supervisors through their radios. There wasn't any protocol for what to do with people who confessed—or came close to confessing—on live TV. Before officers moved in, Ryan stepped close to Stella.

"I do wear this ring all the time—I guess you got *that* right tonight, Stella," he twisted the gleaming, red ring, "but Friday night, Star asked if she could take it. She said she wanted to get it professionally cleaned, and then she gave it back to me Saturday afternoon, after Scott's body was found. *I* wasn't wearing this ring, but somebody was." A patrol officer approached and led Ryan away.

Stella stared after him. Was that true, or was it just another lie in an already twisted tale of murder and betrayal?

A medic pressed an icepack into her hands, and she winced when it touched her face. Police took Jim into custody, too, and LB moved around her to get video of both arrests.

"Interns, huh?" The officer who'd been in the security office with her and Janet raised his eyebrows.

"You're welcome?" She touched her lip with her tongue; it pulsed with her heartbeat.

"Keep the ice pack there and take four Tylenol. That's going to hurt for a few days. Don't go far—I have a lot of questions for you."

"Did you see her jump up, though?" Stella heard the second cop say as they headed back to their cruisers. "Like she was a daggum professional boxer. She's tough, that one..."

Fans surrounded Lucky. She knew she'd never reach him, so she left LB to shoot video of Lucky's return and wound her way back to the truck.

Janet hugged her. "How did you figure it all out, Stella? I thought we were sunk, but something clicked for you somewhere along the way. What was it?"

She set the icepack down and leaned into the truck to grab her coat. Her hand shook as she tried to do up the buttons, and she finally gave up, merely pulling the coat closed tight. "You know how one revelation can help you see something else with new eyes?"

Billy Joe walked over, holding onto his camera. He'd finished shooting video and was ready to tear down the live shot, but he stopped and stood next to Janet. Stella looked at him and said, "I'd been hearing LB as Elbee all these weeks. It's the same thing, but also totally different.

"When I saw Scott's video, that misunderstanding was still in the back of my mind, and it shook something loose. I realized it didn't have to be Jim *or* Ryan—it could be both. Why *wouldn't* it be Jim *and* Ryan?" She frowned and tried to shake off her feelings of unease; she *knew* Ryan had convinced Jim to rig Lucky's car. Even if Ryan hadn't pulled the trigger on Scott, he had played a part in Hap's death—of that she was certain.

"What was their connection?" Janet asked, squinting with concentration. "How did Jim and Ryan even know each other?"

Stella shrugged and rested her cheek against the cool window of the satellite truck. Ryan and Jim had a connection all right, but she wasn't ready to reveal it just yet. She was planning on leveraging the information soon.

A throat cleared behind her and she turned to find Star. "Your pitbull told me we could talk privately after your live shot." Lucky's ex shot a dirty look at Janet. Before Stella's most trusted advisor could open her mouth, Stella shooed her friend and Billy Joe away.

"What do you want?"

Star exhaled heavily and pushed her hair away from her eyes. "I just wanted to talk, off the record. I know Lucky probably won't talk to me now, but maybe... maybe you can explain..." Stella crossed her arms. "*I* asked Ryan to have you followed." She pawed at the ground with her foot. "After I saw Lucky's hat in your apartment, I knew something was going on—he *always* wore that hat—but I had no idea, no idea at all...

"I uh... I think you're right about Ryan killing Scott. He didn't tell me as much, but I know. He was gone when I woke up Saturday morning, and he threw all of his clothes away when he got back. He told me he was out watching a BMX race and got dirty, but I checked and there weren't any races."

Stella pursed her lips. Ryan had said he wasn't wearing his ring at the time Scott was killed. She'd seen his face when he watched the video of Scott's killer during her live shot, and she believed him, not Star.

"Are you going to tell that to police?" Star stared silently at the ground and Stella sighed. "Why do you think he did it?"

Star wrung her hands and didn't say anything for a few moments. Finally, she cried, "Scott called me Friday. He was worried about you. He didn't like spying on you and said he was done. He said he'd turn the tape over to police if anything happened to you."

"Let me guess, you told Ryan, and he got angry and killed Scott?" Stella had to hand it to her: it was a good way to explain why Scott had called her the night of his murder. If investigators hadn't dug that information up yet, they would soon. Was Lucky's ex trying out her alibi?

A small smile passed over Star's lips. It lasted only as long as a bolt of lightning, but it was just as illuminating. Stella's stomach dropped, and she realized with a shudder that Star was the one she should have been grilling on live TV that night. Lucky's ex just might have orchestrated the whole thing—from luring Ryan into her bed all the way to pulling the trigger on Scott. She thought back to how rough Star had looked Saturday morning at the hotel. She'd chalked it up to being hungover, but she supposed killing a man hours before would do it, too.

"Why?" Stella asked, and the other woman seemed to know she wasn't asking about Ryan's motive.

Star's face hardened, her mouth disappearing into a thin line. "I don't get *left*, okay? That's not what happens to *me*. I knew Lucky was going to break up with me, so I made sure to end things on my terms, with another man. When Lucky blew himself up on the track, things started looking up: he was dead, no one knew we broke up, and there was a prenup that left everything to me." She leaned in close, her eyes narrowed to slits as she spat her words at Stella.

"But then I couldn't find the paperwork, and you were in the way. I wanted Scott to follow you to see what was going on. I'd heard your name before when you called Lucky at his house—I was there and answered the phone. When I saw his hat in your apartment, though, I got worried. Had you been dating? If you knew Lucky and I weren't together, anymore, when he died... well, I couldn't have that. Call the legality of the prenup into question? No, no, no. I told Scott to follow your every move and wanted him to find out if you were going to go public with what you knew. Instead, Scott found out Lucky was still alive.

"The idiot got nervous—said things looked suspicious and that I looked guilty. I couldn't have him telling anyone that, now could I?"

"So you killed him?"

"I just wanted the tape destroyed. He got in the way of that."

"And Ryan?" Stella asked.

"Ryan," she flicked her hand, "might have called Jim on my suggestion. Poor thing, caught in the middle of all of this... drama," she tutted, another small smile on her lips.

The two women stared at each other for a full-minute before Star turned and walked slowly into the crowd.

The relief Stella had felt after the live shot was gone; instead, weight pressed down on her shoulders that Atlas himself couldn't carry. She felt like an idiot. How could she have missed Star's involvement? A lot of people were guilty here, and now she wasn't sure any of them would be held accountable in Scott's murder.

"What did that crazy lady want?" Janet asked. She and Billy Joe had obviously visited the concession stand: she gnawed off a bite from a giant Bavarian pretzel as Billy Joe slurped his Coke.

Stella rubbed her forehead where the pounding felt the worst. It now seemed clear that Ryan wasn't the one who'd planned revenge—Star had. She'd wanted revenge on Lucky for not loving her. Stella looked over at Janet, feeling too drained to explain.

"To confess," Stella answered honestly. "She wanted to confess."

Janet took another bite of pretzel and salt sprinkled down her chest. "Goddamn."

"Yup. Goddamn."

Her live shot was over, but the night had just begun. Stella spent hours talking to police, packing the truck, and wishing, yet again, that she had a hotel room.

They hadn't seen Lucky in hours, and Stella was worried about him. What an overwhelming way to reenter the world of the living—with a surprise live reveal surrounded by adoring fans. She was leaning against the truck, thinking about him, when Robbie walked over.

"Quite a night, Stella."

"Robbie! Thank you so much for getting Janet a copy of that video. I never would have been able to link everything without it."

He took his thick glasses off and rubbed the lenses clean with his shirttail. He squinted at Stella before slapping them back on his face. "Are you okay?"

She ran her fingers lightly over her face. "My jaw hurts, but it definitely feels like the swelling is already down."

"No, I mean, are you *okay*? It sounds like you've had a lot of drama in your life this past week because of Lucky."

She chuckled. "Thanks for asking, Robbie, but I'm fine. I mean, I'll be fine—as soon as I can sleep in a normal bed, anyway," she looked darkly at her beloved car. It was a great vehicle, but not where she wanted to spend the night again anytime soon. She'd been watching Janet and Billy Joe flirt all night and couldn't stomach the thought of sleeping in the RV again.

"What do you mean?" Robbie asked. She told him about their sleeping arrangements over the last couple of nights, and he laughed and said, "Stella, I think you've earned a good night's sleep. We have some rooms on hold at a hotel near here. I'd love to arrange for you to have one tonight, on the speedway."

"Really? Oh, Robbie, that would be amazing! Thank you."

"I'll call over and set it up." He took a business card out of his back pocket and scribbled the name of the hotel on the back.

"Good to meet you, Stella. If you ever move over to sports, I'll be happy to work with you again."

They shook hands, and he walked back toward the track.

She touched her jaw gingerly, glad the swelling had gone down, but her lip was still sore from where Jim's fist had made contact. She felt a tap on her shoulder and turned to find Lucky standing behind her.

"Hey." She reached out to touch his arm, but he stiffened at the contact, and she dropped her hand. "How are you doing, Lucky?"

"I'm all right. I just wanted to make sure you had somewhere to stay tonight. I don't want you driving back to Bristol this late."

Her brow wrinkled, and she stared at him for a moment before answering. "Um, yeah. I'm fine. I got a room at a hotel nearby, so I'll be fine. What about you—do you have somewhere to stay?"

The question hung in the air awkwardly for a moment while Lucky stared, unseeing, to the right of Stella. "I'm just going to stay in my trailer tonight. It's been a stressful few days, you know? I just need some alone time. You're okay?"

As he stared straight ahead, she felt a flutter of unease. "Sure, Lucky. I'll be fine."

He bobbed his head and then walked away without another word. She watched a police escort meet him a dozen yards away to bring him safely back inside the track.

Janet nudged her on the shoulder. "That was brutal."

"Right? I thought it was weird, too."

A strange expression crossed Janet's face. "Stella, can I say something?" Stella nodded and she continued, "Jim essentially said he tampered with Lucky's car because of *you,* so right now, Lucky's thinking Hap is dead *because of you.* That's going to take a while to come to terms with."

"But I didn't—"

"I know that—hell, he knows that—but knowing it and *knowing it* are two different things, you know?"

Exhaustion weighed Stella down like a layer of cement. "I'm glad you're here, Janet. I'm going to call it a night. Billy Joe?" He poked his head out from behind the satellite truck. "You all set here?"

"Yup. I'm going to crash with Janet and then head back in the morning. LB's driving back tonight. Great job tonight, Stella. You okay?"

"I'm fine," she said tiredly, and then muttered to herself as she walked to her car, "I'll be fine."

AN HOUR LATER, she was in her hotel room, lying fully clothed on the bed. She was exhausted but also oddly wired, like she'd just run a marathon and drank a pot of coffee. She still had one thing to do and decided she'd better just get it over with. She called the station, and Samantha picked up on the second ring.

"Stella, I've been going back and forth all night as to whether I'm pissed *at* you or amazed *with* you."

"What have you landed on?"

"Amazed—but Stella, next time, keep me in the loop. We're a team here, and I want to *help* you with these situations—and maybe keep them from getting so out of control."

"I'm sorry. I hope there won't be a next time like this, but I'll let you know what I know from now on, all right?"

"Deal."

"Is Larry around?" Stella asked, trying to keep her voice light.

"Sure, hold on." Samantha put her on hold and Stella used the few minutes of elevator music to psych herself up for what was about to happen.

"News," a gruff voice barked over the line.

"I know you set everything in motion, Larry. You were on the

NASCAR governing board with Ryan and you grew up with Jim —you helped unite them in their anger against Lucky, and I'll tell everyone unless you do exactly what I tell you to do."

Stella had known about the connection but wasn't certain Larry was involved. Just before her epic live shot, she had called Cam from the track to ask whom she'd been talking to in the hallway on Stella's very first day in Bristol. She only realized then, sitting in the satellite truck minutes before going on air, that she'd heard someone help plan Hap's murder weeks ago. *She* had never seen who was talking on his cell phone in the hallway outside Keith's office, but Cam had.

After the admin confirmed her suspicions, Stella knew Larry was involved—no matter what Star's role was, Larry had definitely played a part. He had known Jim was mad enough to do something, and he'd told Ryan how to leverage it to his advantage.

Larry spluttered, instantly enraged. "I'm not going to listen to—"

"I heard you in the hallway, Larry. You were talking to Ryan on your cell phone, right outside Keith's office. You told him to get in touch with Jim—that Jim might be angry enough with Lucky to do something. You were the connection that set Hap's murder —and in a way, Scott's—in motion."

"That's just—I can't..."

"Why, Larry? What did you have against Lucky?" There was silence. "You want to know what I think?" He was quiet, but she was on a roll. "I think your ego just couldn't take the fact that Lucky forced you off the NASCAR board. But murder, Larry over a board position?"

"It wasn't just the board!" he snapped. "It was my very way of life! I am a NASCAR expert, and I shouldn't have to listen to some young idiot tell me otherwise, just like I'm not going to listen to *you* tell me what to do next! You have no proof that I'm involved in anything."

"Oh, Larry, Ryan and Jim will turn on you in an instant. Is that how you want to be remembered—as the news anchor who helped plan a murder?"

She didn't know whether any of her information would stand up in court, but she knew it would stand up to Larry's scrutiny. She'd attacked his legacy and knew *that* would get to him faster than anything else. His silence let her know she had him.

"Here's what you're going to do..."

38

IT'S A WRAP

I t had been two months since the big interview, and the dust had finally settled at the station. Stella and Lucky hadn't talked much, as he was busy with national interviews, making the rounds on talk shows, sports shows, radio shows—it was mind-boggling. After the first few days, she'd stopped waiting for him to call. He needed space and she was ready to find some normalcy in her life again.

She'd been the object of many unflattering stories on national gossip websites since Lucky came back from the dead—most of them claiming she was pregnant with Hap's love child. It was some small consolation to know the gossip pages were back to complete fiction. The station still occasionally got requests for an interview with Stella, but she was, thankfully, not allowed to talk to other media outlets. The terms were very clear in her employment contract, and for once, she was so glad to have signed it back in Montana.

The day she'd gotten back to the station, Larry Howard announced his retirement—to everyone else's shock and surprise. Samantha had been named news director a week later. While Keith was on leave from the station—under investigation for sexual harassment, improper hiring procedures, and various other HR violations—he'd gotten an offer to run the Bristol Motor Speedway in Ryan's absence. He'd jumped at the chance to leave NBC2 before the formal investigation began, and Stella suspected corporate was delighted to be rid of him, too. Every once in a while, she got the giggles thinking about Keith surrounded by *men* all day at the track.

Ryan Wexler put up bail money and was waiting for the trial of the century to start on charges that included conspiracy to murder Hap Haskins and first-degree murder in the death of Scott Lyon. He and Star were still together, and Stella wondered why he would take the fall for Scott's murder.

Star wasn't facing any charges—yet. The prosecutor in the case threw around terms like "accessory to murder," and "blocking the investigation," but hadn't made it official. Stella was now almost certain Star had been behind the entire plan from the beginning.

Jim Cruisner was behind bars, unable to make bail on his murder charges in the death of Hap Haskins. Prosecutors admitted they didn't have any hard, physical evidence, but Jim had confessed in court, in addition to his live TV confession, and his sentencing was scheduled for the following week. Stella was off both cases due to her personal connection to so many people involved and had to watch it all unfold on the news as Candice and Kate took over as the main reporters on the stories.

It was after the news one Friday night that she found herself on her couch, watching TV and eating dinner, when a commotion in the hallway interrupted her show. When it became clear the clomping footsteps and banging sounds weren't going to stop anytime soon, she opened her door to investigate. Her eyes locked with Mrs. Lanster across the hall.

"Well, I guess Lucky's done renovating the apartment on the end," she said, looking thoughtfully at a burly, handsome young man in coveralls as he walked down the hall carrying a stack of boxes like they were filled with feathers.

"Huh?" Stella asked, not sure she'd heard the older woman correctly.

"Lucky owns the unit on the end, didn't you know? I figured he's your landlord—he would have mentioned he'll be living next door." She took one last look at the mover before clucking her teeth and closing her door.

Stella did the same and stared after the mover for a long minute, wondering if Mrs. Lanster was right.

"Stella?"

She jumped and turned toward the elevator, where Lucky leaned against the wall about a foot away. She hadn't heard him walk up. "Are you moving in?" she asked.

"Yes. I uh... I feel bad for not getting in touch sooner." He looked down at the floor, his arms crossed loosely over his chest.

She stared at him, not sure what to say.

Lucky looked up and smiled sadly. "I had a lot of anger inside after listening to Jim and Ryan that night. It took me a while to work through it all and come to peace with what's happened."

"So... have you made peace with it all, Lucky?"

"I still can't believe Hap is gone, but I've reconnected with Chloe, and my nephew, Taylor, is amazing. I started a trust fund for him, and I'm making sure Chloe is taken care of. She's really struggling with what her dad did—it's going to take them a long time to heal, too." She nodded. "I was hoping we could reconnect, too, Stella. I—I miss you. I got closer to you that week I was dead than I think I've ever been to anyone in my life. I know I screwed things up, but it seemed safest for me to walk away so I didn't completely ruin everything while I was still so angry. Does that make any sense?"

She looked at Lucky, so honest with his heart on his sleeve. "Lucky, I—" She had to clear her throat. "That was an intense week that we were together, and I'm not sure anything was really *real*, you know? The stakes were so high and the stress was unbelievable. And you—you're famous, and jet-setting, and never home." She laughed, wondering how he could have a relationship with anyone. "I guess I'm saying I hope we can be friends."

He searched her eyes, looking for something; she reached out and squeezed his arm. She meant it as a friendly way to show her support, but that damn bicep was surprisingly hard under his long-sleeved, blue polo shirt, and she gulped and licked her lips.

His face broke out into a sunny grin. "Sure, Stella. Friends sounds like a great start to me." His eyes raked her over from head to toe. "You free for dinner tonight?"

"No."

"Tomorrow night?"

"Friends, Lucky. I'm serious!"

"Friends need to eat, Stella. Let me take you out tomorrow night."

"No!" she shouted, but she laughed, too, so the word was lost on Lucky.

"I like having friends, Stella. Friends are my favorite."

She groaned and went back inside her apartment, slowly closing the door. Why did she have a feeling things were going to get complicated again with Lucky living right next door? She grinned to herself, then; she wouldn't have it any other way.

Turn the page to check out *The Big Overnight*, Book 3 in the *Stella Reynolds Mystery Series*.

ABOUT THE AUTHOR

Libby Kirsch is an Emmy award winning journalist with over ten years of experience working in television newsrooms of all sizes. She draws on her rich history of making embarrassing mistakes on live TV, and is happy to finally indulge her creative writing side, instead of always having to stick to the facts.
Libby lives in Ann Arbor, Michigan with her husband, three children, and Sam the dog.

Turn the page for a preview of the next book in the series, *The Big Overnight.*

Connect with Libby
www.LibbyKirschBooks.com
Libby@LibbyKirschBooks.com

f facebook.com/LibbyKirschBooks

y twitter.com/LibbyKirsch

a amazon.com/author/libbykirsch

BB bookbub.com/authors/libby-kirsch

g goodreads.com/libbykirsch

BOOK 3 IN THE *Stella Reynolds* MYSTERY SERIES

LIBBY KIRSCH

The Big Overnight

A "uniquely riveting tale"
—BookLife Prize in Fiction

THE BIG OVERNIGHT

SPECIAL PREVIEW

The news van screeched into an open spot in the parking lot behind the police department, and Stella was out on the pavement before her photographer had even cut off the engine.

"They're walking!" she called back, craning her neck to see over cars in the packed lot. "They're already walking!"

"Take the mic, Reynolds. I'll be right behind you," came Bob's gruff response as he climbed stiffly out of the driver's side of the live truck.

Bob was older and he moved slower, but nothing seemed to faze him and he hadn't missed a shot in the nearly two years she'd worked with him. Stella grabbed the stick microphone and took off across the parking lot, flipping the switch at the bottom of the mic to the "on" position as she walked.

The blondish-gray, day-old stubble on the homicide detective's face glinted in the late afternoon sunlight as he strode across the blacktop, as did the handcuffs clamped around the wrists of the man walking in front of him. The prisoner, pushing six feet tall, was long and lanky, and his baggy jeans and T-shirt left skin exposed to the harsh winter air. Detective Brian Murphy slowed he saw Stella hurrying over and she shot him a grateful look.

"Cas Rockman," she said, extending the microphone toward the pair. "Did you shoot Oliver Bennet?"

Rockman's eyes raked over Stella from head to toe and he smiled a slow, deliberate smirk before answering.

"Yeah, Red," he bobbed his head twice, "I shot him."

"You did?" She was so surprised by the admission that she stopped walking, and Bob swore under his breath as he crashed into her from behind. She winced and started moving again, first catching Murphy's victorious look and then noticing that Rockman's smile was gone.

She had to scramble to come up with another question. She'd never had anyone confess on camera before—usually they didn't say anything at all.

She stole another look at Bob and was surprised to see him staring back at her, eyebrows raised. The interest on his face was almost enough to shake her brain loose.

"You know you're admitting to shooting someone right now," she said, only realizing when she heard Bob groan that she hadn't actually asked a question.

As they neared the side door to the county jail, Rockman slowed to a stop. Seconds later, the lock clunked over and the door swung toward them. Stella peered inside. Even with the door wide open, the winter sunshine couldn't penetrate the gloom within.

"Why?" Stella finally asked, as Detective Murphy's pen scratched out his signature on a form.

Rockman stared straight ahead, all emotion wiped from his face. Murphy pushed him inside the secure facility, and they disappeared into the darkness without another word. Moments later, the heavy, metal door swung closed with a clank. The lock flipped over soon after, and Stella found herself staring at Bob.

"Why did he shoot him, or why did he just confess?" Bob asked, taking the camera off his shoulder.

"Both," she answered, somehow dissatisfied, even though they got their exclusive. Her hair blew wildly around her face with a sudden gust of wind, and she hastily smoothed it with her free hand. "Call it in. We'll need to wait here for sound with Murph, but we can be live at five with the story." She flipped open her notebook and started outlining her live shot. She'd been working here for almost two years and still couldn't believe her luck at landing the job. Stella had done her time in tiny TV markets and felt like a seasoned pro with nearly four years as a reporter under her belt.

While they waited for the detective, she looked around downtown Knoxville, realizing she felt more at home in the concrete and asphalt surroundings than she did in her own apartment.

Her roommate, Janet, was an old friend who was full of surprises. They shared an apartment in an up-and-coming neighborhood in town, and her two former flames lived just miles away in what was an oddly cordial friendship triangle that she had to spend a lot of time telling herself not to overthink.

It was times like this, however, when she had nothing to do but wait in a live truck with a crotchety old photographer, that she found it difficult to keep her mind off the men in her life. Despite the fact that one had a girlfriend and the other was too busy to date, she spent a lot of time thinking about them both.

"THANKS FOR THE CALL, MURPH," she said, after the detective walked out of jail twenty minutes later.

"No problem. Glad you made it," he added with a sly smile.

"You said you were going to walk him at three thirty! We pulled up at 3:28 and you were already halfway across the parking lot!"

"Oh, stop your bitching. You got your perp walk—and a confession. I'd say you owe me."

She nodded grudgingly. "Yeah, yeah. How's Annie?" she asked, changing the subject. Murphy's wife had been Stella's soccer teammate in Ohio when both women were in high school. Annie had seen her on the news right after Stella had taken the job in Knoxville, they'd reconnected, and now, thanks to Annie's husband, Stella had one of the best sources at the station.

"She's good," he answered. "She says you girls need to get together for coffee soon."

"I'll call her this week."

A throat cleared behind Stella and she ducked her head. "Sorry, Bob. You ready?"

"Been ready for half an hour, Stella. Let's go."

She winked at the detective and started the interview. Murphy didn't give out much information about the arrest, refusing to divulge a motive, what led them to Rockman as the suspect, or anything about the victim beyond his name and age of forty-six, so the interview didn't last long. Before they wrapped up, though, Stella felt another set of eyes boring into her from behind. She looked back and saw a stranger staring at her, his eyebrows drawn together. His expression wasn't angry, exactly, but it wasn't far off.

While Stella waited for Bob to get the live truck up and running, she walked over to the stranger, who was now sitting on a bench and staring at the cement under his feet.

"Check your sources," he said, looking up. The glare was back, and she stopped short, not wanting to get too close.

"Excuse me?"

He blew warm air into his cupped hands and then dug a pair of winter gloves out of his coat pocket. A black skull cap followed, and after he'd adjusted it over his shaved head, he glared up at Stella.

"I said, check your sources. My son did not shoot that man

any more than you did." He had a funny way of speaking; it was very proper, which was unexpected, given his distinctly rough appearance.

"Well, uh, my source is the suspect, himself. He just told me he shot him." She shifted on her feet and added, "I'm sorry that, umm," but clamped her mouth shut, unsure of how to phrase why she felt bad. She shook her head and fell silent, instead.

He brushed her words off and stood. She was five-foot-nine and wearing heels, but he still towered over her. The sound of popping joints and cartilage made Stella wince, but she sensed an opportunity.

"Did you want to—"

An annoyed wave of his hand cut her off mid-sentence and revealed a sleeve of tattoos up his arm. "No, I do not want to talk, but I do want you to do your job and find out who the shooter was. That guy is not the guy."

He walked away, weaving through cars in the packed municipal parking lot, and disappeared into a throng of people crossing a busy street. She stared after him thoughtfully. Why would Rockman lie about shooting someone, and why should she believe Cas's father over his own admission? She blew out a breath, preparing to forget the entire exchange when Bob whistled for her attention.

"Hey, Red!" he shouted. "What did Harrison Keys want?"

"Who?" she asked, looking behind her and catching a glimpse of her hair, which wasn't red, for heaven's sake, but definitely auburn.

Bob took a pack of cigarettes out of his back pocket and tapped the bottom until one slipped forward. He carefully plucked it out and took his time lighting it. He blew a giant puff of smoke toward Stella before answering, "I guess it was before your time, but I figured you'd have heard of him by now. That man you were just talking to served twenty years in prison on murder charges."

She spun back around to look at the intersection Harrison had melted into. Like father, like son, or was Harrison onto something and his son actually was innocent? She felt her heartbeat surge and fingertips tingle. This could be the beginning of something big—only time would tell.

Her cell phone rang, interrupting her mounting feelings of intrigue. It was Lucky, but before she could answer, a second call beeped in from John.

Oh, boy, she thought, tossing the phone back into her shoulder bag without answering either call. Suspense and intrigue seemed to be building on so many levels these days.

Usually an on-camera confession was the end of the story, so why did Stella have a sneaking suspicion that today's confession was only the beginning?

To keep reading, get THE BIG OVERNIGHT, Book 3 in the *Stella Reynolds Mystery Series* today!

ALSO BY LIBBY KIRSCH

The Stella Reynolds Mystery Series

The Big Lead

The Big Interview

The Big Overnight

The Big Weekend

The Big Job

The Janet Black Mystery Series

(Coming Soon)

Last Call

Last Minute

For updates on new releases or to connect with the author, go to
www.LibbyKirschBooks.com

Made in the USA
San Bernardino, CA
22 December 2018